I0656754

Albert Mitchell

To the end of time a prophetic work

Albert Mitchell

To the end of time a prophetic work

ISBN/EAN: 9783741189760

Manufactured in Europe, USA, Canada, Australia, Japa

Cover: Foto ©Andreas Hilbeck / pixelio.de

Manufactured and distributed by brebook publishing software
(www.brebook.com)

Albert Mitchell

To the end of time a prophetic work

DEDICATION.

———

<small>THIS THEOLOGICAL WORK IS INSCRIBED TO THE
VICTORIOUS MONARCH OF THE NORTH, AND TO THE
PRIME MINISTER OF ENGLAND, AT THE PERIOD AND
DATE OF 1927 A.D.</small>

Oh! mighty Tsar, ordained and bless'd,
To o'erthrow the callous *moham'* pest,
By dealing the *"sixth-head" his deadly wound,
That the satanic-erring sway, might be entomb'd :
Be not wary, 'tis JEHOVAH's chart,
But valiant, for nations play their part
Courageously, when 'tis God's predict :
Mercy to Jews, Go brave Monarch ! inflict.
Britain ! thy vast lands, now dome the earth :
Spare to this nation—another of God's birth—
This rod-in-hand task, a dower from *"on high,"*
For all nations must grow, till they wane and die !
Therefore, Christian nation, in love, submit,
To the acts of an inevitable edict.

With exceeding-humbleness,

Albert Mitchell

---

*Revelation xiii.3.

Minds unoccupied, give the tempter an invite !
Who, then besets a five-sense weakness,—
Giving bent of heart to that which o'errules right,
Which closes the soul's vision from interest.
Desire prophecy, 'tis a high gift of God! (i Cor. xiv.)
To read interpreted predicts, diverts the mind—
Leaves no room for thrusts of Satan's subtle-sword,
And the soul gleams of unseen things destined.

A.M.

PREFACE

Every writer who undertakes the task of unfolding the symbolically-written Scriptures, touches, more or less, upon that deep, and momentous question, THE PURPOSE OF GOD. And this, more than any other subject, produces diversity of opinion, not at all to be wondered at : because, the very best literary power of a finite mind, no matter how well cultured, has absolutely no knowledge, and cannot produce anything of a spiritual character, except, indeed, it is specially given by God. To accomplish anything in this direc-tion, the expositor must have *the lamp* which not only shines at his feet, but also reaches the *invisible man* and illuminates the soul. This being so, errors of misinterpretation must be expected ; because, the desires of men to please their five senses is sure to lead some into the path of self, which, by growing into the motive power of wealth, or exaltation of person by fame, will fasten itself upon the mind, and men will write expositions regardless of Divine inspiration. These errors, it will be found, are invariably so entwined with literary skill, that the arguments put forth are reflected in the mirror of feasibility, and the reader is led to accept these commentaries as being true.

There are some expositors, however, who do not err in this direction; but who err, nevertheless, by trusting to their own knowledge, and reason, for things of the Spirit, which, I need hardly say, is of no avail in their endeavours to open the obscure things which it has pleased God to set before men. It is like trusting to the natural sight, for the knowledge of the subject of each of the pictures which are hanging upon the walls of a darkened room.

The Scriptures are wonderfully compiled: no finite mind is able to ascertain the hidden things which it has pleased God to seal up until the time appointed for their disclosure, which, *if knowledge is to be increased, and the spiritually-wise, are to understand,*—and we have the angel's testimony to this effect (Danl. xii. 4, 10.)—men may rest assured, will be unsealed according to what was ordained to be accomplished. "For there is nothing hid, save that it should be manifested; neither was anything made secret, but that it should come to light (Mark. iv. 22. R. V)—nothing covered up, that shall not be revealed: and hid, that shall not be known" (Luke. xii. ii. R. v). But who was to be the instrument in revealing these things?—must

it not be some human creature—some one "called,"
and taught for the purpose (John.vi.45)? and then be
able to bring forth from the Scriptures, "THINGS NEW
AND OLD" (Matt.xiii.52.); for "MY DOCTRINE," saith
the Lord," SHALL *DROP AS THE RAIN "(Deut.xxxii.2).
To be taught, is the flashing of light upon Scripture,
and whilst the spiritual perception of the "called
one," glean, the Spirit of God speaks as a whispering
"small voice" in the mind of the re-born; therefore, as men of olden times were moved by the Holy
Spirit to write prophetic Scripture (ii Peter.i.21.), so
must the interpretation thereof, come from the same
whispering source; for He who compiled the mysterious book, is the only One that can supply the means
of its being understood; and until then, the prophetic-
Scriptures are," *as the words of a book that is sealed,
which men deliver to one that is learned saying, read
this I pray thee; and he saith, I cannot for it is sealed"*
(Isa.xxix.11.).

At no other date than the set time appointed is it
possible to break these seals of obscurity; and then,
at these times, "*shall the deaf hear the words of the
book, and the eyes of the blind shall see out of obscurity
and out of darkness" (Isa.xxix.18.)*; hence the words
of Christ, "I have yet many things to say unto you,
BUT YE CANNOT BEAR THEM NOW" (John.xvi.12.).

---

*Rain falls, drop after drop, and shower after shower; therefore God
inferred by the rain-drops, that the true doctrine would come through
"called"men, by instalments—little by little, down to the consummation.

I am aware of the given-command to search the
Scriptures: but to do so, necessitates a Spirit-born
mind, because, God's word, which consists of three
languages, figure, literal, and spiritual, must be read
and understood spiritually; and this is impossible for
a natural mind, which can neither see, nor understand spiritual things.—"*The natural man receiveth
not (possess not) the things of the Spirit of God: for they
are foolishness unto him: neither can he know them, because they are (or must be) spiritually discerned"(i Cor.
ii.14*).   Therefore, he that unseals prophetic Scripture,
must needs be a "called" and "chosen" vessel in God's
hands.

And then again, it is absolutely impossible for a
"chosen" man to be ignorant of the fact: once he has
complied with the "call" by entering upon its purpose,
he is sure to become so entangled in matters which
are opposd to self-interest, and humiliating, that the
very fact of his submission to these things,—he having
the earthly power to alter them—is more than sufficient to settle the question: but God does, in many
other ways, even more convincing than this, show
to the man who has been "called," that he is "chosen"
for some special work, although the nature of that
work may not dawn upon his mind until the Holy
Spirit has led him well into the subject.   Had I not
been "called" to write this book, my presumption in
doing so, would have been as a scarlet robe!

Moreover, Scripture has opened a way of test

which is within the reach of every man : it states,
"When *(or if)* the word of the prophet SHALL COME
TO PASS, then shall the prophet be known, that the
Lord hath truly sent (or "called") him" (Jere.xxviii.9.).
It means, that if a man predict a thing in the name
of the Lord, and it takes place, he is to be believed
as to his further statements and prophesying.   Now
God has got his earthly servants at this period, as well
as in all other ages, as the following Scripture verify :
" To one is given by the Spirit the words of wisdom ;
to another the word of knowledge...; TO ANOTHER
PROPHECY..."(i Cor.xii.8,10).   " Having then, gifts
differing according to the grace that is given to us,
whether prophecy, LET US PROPHESY according to
the proportion of our faith" (Rom.xii.6).   And this
question of prophesying, did not exclusively refer to the
disciples of early date : if it had been so, to whom was
St. Paul speaking when he said, " Follow after charity,
and desire spiritual gifts, BUT RATHER THAT YE
MAY PROPHESY "(i Cor.xiv.1) ?—Did he not refer
to men of the subsequent generations ?—yea to every
man, down to the consummation !

Well then, if any man get hold of my biography,
he will see, by authentically-proved information therein, that I have not only been " called," but that, also,
in me the above conditions of prophet-testing has
taken place : and I say this, not boastingly, but rather,
that the words of this book might be believed ; for it
is the only explanation of prophecy that truth can

supply. It may be improved in language; it may be so written that the explanation of the different subjects will be better understood: but the explained-truth itself cannot be improved, to attempt to do so, would be to produce a garnished misrepresentation of the truth, and the world would be the loser of the knowledge of some of its future events.—" No prophecy of the Scripture is of any private interpretation."

The solution of prophecy, and especially that of the symbolic "ten-horned beast," was made known to me, as it has ever been the wont of God to enlighten His servants (ii Peter.i.21; Ephe.iii.3-5.), for probably, two reasons: that of the fulfilment of the Scripture which says, "*nothing is covered, that shall not be revealed; neither hid, that shall not be known;*" and that of acquainting Russia, who is immediately concerned in the things which have been revealed unto me by the prompting whisper of the Spirit, with these things, which are of momentous character, and are herein described. The latter of the aforesaid reasons, that of pointing out certain facts, has its precedent type :—At the time of the Jewish captivity, Daniel pointed out to Cyrus, king of Persia, the drawing near of the end of the seventy years which it was ordained the Hebrews should undergo; and acquainting the king with the Scriptures which predicted their liberation by him, whose name had been divulged over a century previous (Isa.xlv.1—13.). In conclusion of this article, I ask my readers to be indulgent and not too critical, seeing that I am but an instrument in God's hands.

Come hither poor soul, lay hold of my *treasure!
Wilt thou give up self, that I may use thee in light?
Go tell of hidden things, men's perception to measure,-
Secrets, which 'ill warm kings hearts, and brighten man's sight.
                                                        A.M.

The Apocalypse, or Revelation by St. John, consists of seven written, but sealed events, and which
are within the power and prerogative of Our Lord
Jesus Christ for their fulfilment (Revl.v,vi.), He at
that time descending to the earth. The first six of
these events are to take place as single incident's, but
the seventh (Revl.viii.1.), which is divided into seven
woe-visitations, is invested for its fulfilment, in seven
Angels who sound a signal-trumpet previous to the
taking place of each woe. This goes on until the
seventh trumpet-sound, when there is to be a further
production by subdivision unto seven other Angels,
each of which, figuratively hold a vial containing the
wrath of God; these are to be poured out upon
the mohammedan, and idolatrous community of the
Asiatic races. This figurative portrayal of twenty-
one events, are the extraordinary things of the first
part of the Christian era, or period between the first
and second Advents.

The principal events of prophecy are: the overthrow of Muhammedism in two stages; restoration

*St. Matthew xiii.52.

of the Hebrews also in two stages, partly at first, then
finally; Our Lord's second and third Advent; the
Millennial age; the Judgment; and the production of
the Lake of Fire. Three other nations from this
date, will, in succession, supersede the present dominant nation; the last of the three being ruled by the
"ten-horned beast." If the reader will keep a Bible
handy, and refer to the various passages treated, especially those which are taken verse by verse, it
will facilitate their perception of this work, and add
to the conviction of its truth. The manner in which
I have separated the thirty-first verse of Daniel xi.,
however, may not seem consistent with feasibility:
but it has been distinctly shown to me that this verse
had, bound up within itself, the prediction of two
events, but only seen in spiritual discernment; for
feasibility being the door of facts to the finite mind,
and God's word being full of spiritual language, reasoning in this case is quite out of place.—If God tells
a servant that a certain passage of Scripture, although
obscure, is set forth to represent certain facts, it not
only seals it as truth, but also seals the servant with
a decision that is unalterable.

This maxim ought never to be forgotten:—If the
true interpretation of prophecy is desired, think not
to find it in the production of a great scholar's pen!
because the mind of the man to whom God intends
to prompt with the words of truth, to enable him to

write a certain Scriptural work, must be free from self-knowledge, and finite-perception eagerness, to enable him to have the patience to listen for the still voice of inspiration—the man that has no knowledge is only too willing to listen to another for information, and especially if the other be the Spirit of the living God ! JEHOVAH takes the least of men to perform the greatest tasks ! David the sheep-minder, bears me out in this : also the poor Jewish fishermen of no learning : all these have become the leaders of men, by their listening to the voice which overuled their pen.

> Without Thee 'tis a wastepaper theme !
> Like opaque glass, makes vision no plainer !
> But glittering gems, if Thou shed the gleam !
> And the world then becomes the gainer. A.M.

It is impossible to misunderstand the Scripture, as to the events connected with the "ten-horned beast" being yet of the future : for Danl.vii.7., and Revl.xiii.1., being a figurative portrayal of the same monarch, and by the voice of heaven which said, (in reference to the "ten-horned beast" and other events of the apocalypse) "I WILL SHOW THEE THE THINGS WHICH MUST COME TO PASS *HEREAFTER " (Revl.iv.1. R.V.), settles the question of this event not having taken place during that period between the time of the life of Daniel

---

*In Revelation i.1., it says, "must shortly come to pass :"—Now, a thousand years with God being as a day, the word "shortly," is truly applicable to represent two or three thousand years ; especially when we consider what a few thousand years re compared with eternity.

and of St. John, the writers of these two accounts ; and
we know by history, that the event in question has
not taken place since St. John's time : therefore it is
proved without a doubt, that the "ten-horned-beast"
event, is yet of the future.

The prophecy of Daniel xii. 11, 12., in which two
periods of time are given, both of which indicate the
taking place of a great event at the end of their respective terms, required a KEY to unlock the EPOCH, from
which these two terms of year-days were to start to
count. This EPOCH that was indicated, was to be a
SET-UP-ABOMINATION in Jerusalem, but the nature and
date of the event was kept secret ; but Jesus spoke of
it as an event of the greatest importance (Matt. xxiv.
15; Mark. xiii. 14). The nature and date of this EPOCH-
abomination, will be divulged to the reader in due
course. The most astounding part of this matter is,
that the KEY, which consisted in the knowledge of
both nature and date of the abomination-setting-up,
in order to enable the unlocking of the door of the
epoch-secret and allow the travelling on of these two
periods, HAS BEEN HELD OUT TO THE WORLD for the
last twenty-four centuries, and yet no one seems to
have been able to lay hold of it !—All that was needed
to be done was simply to lay the 1,290 years, and the
1,335 years, alongside of the abomination-date ; but
the finite-mind has failed in this ! the Lord, however,
having broken the Seal, has now revealed this EPOCH.

Those who are eagerly looking out for Our Lord's coming should bear in mind, that prior to this great event, two witnesses must appear (Revl. xi. 3—6.); that these are the forerunners of the "ten-horned-beast's" kingdom (Revl. xi. 7.); and that it is after these events, and prior to the Millennium, that Our Immortal King is to gladden the earth with His presence. Also the SEVEN SEALS must be fulfilled before this event can take place, and the SEVENTH one is a long way off yet; for it has been shown me that the events subsequent to the date of 1895, at the time of the Armenian massacres, and when the mohammedan retributive-famine and bubonic-plague of India which immediately followed these Turkish atrocities, WAS THE OPENING OF THE "FOURTH SEAL" ONLY (Revl. vi. 7,8).

In perusing the account which I have given of Esau being the aboriginal of the black race, I trust there will be no flying off at a tangent, accompanied by the exclamation, how can he know this! for let it be remembered, that Moses wrote the history of the creation of the world, as described in the book of Genesis, at between two and three thousand years afterwards; and at a place where there was not a particle of earthly evidence to provide him with the knowledge of the detailed account which he has written in The Book.— God can enlighten the re-born mind, far easier than we can enlighten ourselves by history and other means: for He can show to man a vision of the thing!

In this work, there will be found a true Chronology
of the Scriptures.   The dates which go to make up the
Chronology as heretofore published, are very defective:
the lapse of time between Adam and Christ, has been
hitherto put down at 4,004 years ; but I find, by unmistakable proofs which permeates the pages of Scripture,
the length of this period was 4,258 years.   This truth
was not arrived at by the study of the Scripture, however; but rather, was the result of a flash of light across
the Word and my perception at the same time, when
it was seen that certain passages which continued
on through the Scriptures, gave authority for certain
periods of time, to count consecutively ; these I followed up, and thus obtained a complete datum.   All
those who wish to check this Chronological statement,
will find chapter and verse for every event that has
been referred to, making things easy, and understood.

In some cases, I have deemed it expedient in des-
cribing an event of the future, to speak in the language
of present-tense : I have done this, in order to make the
picture of a more vivid character, and thus enable the
reader to realize the scenes portrayed.

Where there has been sufficient Scriptural information upon the subject to bear out the commentary, I
have not been assisted with any special inspiration :
but with the obscure subjects, I have been informed

by the Spirit of God, of the hidden meaning thereof.
I have therefore, in some cases, set forth the revealed
facts authoritatively : but in other, and most cases, I
have used suggestions by bringing to bear the arguments of the finite mind ; as well as adducing such
Scriptural evidence as it was deemed expedient to
make matters clear to the reader's mind, and thus
enable his perception to grasp the truth.

With regard to no man knowing "The day, nor
the hour," of Christ's second coming ; I have given
such an account of the subject in the body of the
book, as to render any preface remarks superfluous.

The 144,000 saints, who are to rise from their
graves just prior to the second Advent of Christ, are
those who have individually won the prize in the race,
as Paul puts it : "...Christ the firstfruits ; afterwards
they that are Christ's at his coming (these 144,000).
Then cometh the end, when He shall deliver up the
kingdom to God..."(i Cor. xv. 23, 24).—The raising up
of the full harvest unto the kingdom of God.

In cases where the language of the Revised Version
of the Scripture has been found to be plainer than
that of the earlier version of A.D. 1611 date, I have
made use of it for giving quotations ; in which cases,
the distinguishing letters, R.V., will be found at the end
of such.

With regard to what has been written about the Chapters xl—xlviii of the book of Ezekiel in connection with the Millennium ; I may state that I have received special information upon the matter, and know, that what has been stated will come to pass ; it is God's way of working !—As the religious aspect of the Jewish dispensation was ordained to become changed from the exclusive works of Judaism, to that of a more spiritual worship and faith, at the bringing of the Christian era : so must this same era expect, at the new, and Millennial dispensation, a modified religion to that of the present one.   For, as the Godhead then turned His face from the unbelieving—Judah-Benjamin— double-tribe Israelites, and went in search of His ten tribes, who had now become absorbed in, and known only as Gentiles : so will He upon the same principle at the Millennium, cease to strive with those of the Gentile races, who then reject the converted-Jew-doctrine of the established consummtion.—"...My Spirit shall not always strive with man," saith the Lord.   [It will be seen that I have nothing to gain, by laying the Millennial doctrine before the world but the goodwill of God : but, on the other hand, if the account I have herein given be not true, then, in that case, I have all to lose ! so that, my acts in this matter speak for themselves, and show, that what I have written, was at the dictation and will of God].

'Tis difficult, these things to perceive, I own :
But did He not say, all hidden things shall be made known ?

The 8888 which was shown me in bright golden-colour figures upon the wall of my bedroom, was the outcome of my seeking for information in earnest prayer, with regard to the final end of this earth.— There is no definite time given for the final end: all the Scriptures supply us with, is the information of the dates only to the end of the Millennium. Yet the Scriptures portray the taking place of events subsequent to this period: thus necessitating my asking further upon the subject, and which resulted in my being shown the above four figures.

As a great favour, I ask those into whose hands this work may fall, to peruse it unto the end; as they will be amply rewarded for sodoing, by meeting with some of those valuable messages which may be classified as diamonds in a field. This work must be considered historical, in a future sense; and will be found of an entertaining character. Nevertheless, I plead for extenuation of faults of imperfection in both style and expression,—for the work of man's hands must needs be defective! It is the opening of the hitherto figuratively-closed Revelations of God, and as such, is a work of instructiveness.

This work, as originally intended, was the Seventh part of a theological work of seven subjects, on which I had been engaged for some time: but having been directed by the Spirit, to send, as I have already said, the prophetic subject to the Tsar of Russia, I proceeded with this work forthwith; and was then so led on by the Spirit, that the work grew, and became of such a size, as to make it too large for its original position: I therefore resolved upon making it a separate book.

Although I have taken a firm stand at the prophetic Scriptures, it should be understood that it was by my searching the whole of God's Word, in the light of the Spirit; together with my seeing visions, dreaming dreams of a literal, and allegorical nature, and which portrayed the things it was desired to know: and the silent-whisperings of the indwelling, "STILL, SMALL VOICE," that I have been able to arrive at the truth, and portrayal, of the future events as contained in this work.

Hearken, ye who would have treasures foretold;
This commentary is of more value than gold!
Praise it not, as a literate compilation,
Yet praise it! 'tis written by inspiration.
                                        A.M.

TO THE END OF TIME.

CHAPTER I.

Truth, the equilibrium of society, creates the highest grade of nobleness; and, if spiritually discerned, is the basis of all godliness: but a written lie sends forth a poison, which multiplies in proportion to the number of its readers. How void of truth, however, are the many written expositions of prophecy! what a mistake expositors have hitherto made! They have confounded king Nebuchadnezzar's four-kingdom dream, portrayed to him in a man-image, with that of Daniel's four-kingdom dream.—They have made these two dreams to appear as if they were one and the same prophetic message, and thus have they robbed, so to speak, Daniel's dream of its truth, and the world of God's portrayed future. This has been done, by these men of letters putting-forth four Gentile kingdoms

only, instead of eight, which, without a doubt, the
two dreams plainly, although symbolically, portray
(see chaps. Danl. ii. and vii.).

Truth, however, must come to the front at the
time appointed, it being essentially stamped upon
God's written word, which, throughout its pages,
sets forth a perfect · revelation of His divine will.
In fact, time has worked out the truth : for we have
not only the evidence of the fulfilment of the four
kingdoms, portrayed in Nebuchadnezzar's dream,
which, from Babylon to Rome, as nations, grew
into mighty empires, and then dwindled down till
they ceased to exist, but we have also the rising up
of four other leading nations, two of which are already
in existence—Great Britain and Russia.   These are
the four nations which were set forth in Daniel's
dream (ch. vii.), and it is easy to perceive, were predicted to rise, and come into greatness subsequent
to the fall of the last nation belonging to the first
four, indicated by Nebuchadnezzar's image-dream
(Danl. ii.).   In the face of this, expositors, in order to
overcome the difficulty arising from the fact that six
leading nations, as answering to Scriptural symbol—
the four of the image, and the lion, and bear, of Danl's
dream—have been produced, and to still adhere to the
theory of the two dreams (Danl. ii.—vii.) forming one
message, have adopted the principle of stretching out
the fourth one of the dream-image (Rome), into a
continuous production of as many nations as the

present, and future, may establish. The grounds
upon which they work out this problem into a solution of feasibility, is, by their clinging tenaciously
to the symbolic " iron-legs " and " feet " (Danl. ii. 33.)
of the dream-image ; this " leg-and-feet " figure, the
fourth kingdom of Nebuchadnezzar's dream-image,
represents Rome. Thus they endeavour to continue
the existence of this nation, in other nations, which
have sprung up since Rome's decease. But this is
not teaching Scripture, as the word of a wise God !
Dreams and visions, which were given to men, are,
surely, of more value, and higher meaning, than that
of simply repeating already-known predictions, such
as we find portrayed in the first four-kingdom dream
(Danl. ii.), and which is made plainer by Daniel's
inspired interpretation (Danl. ii. 31—45.). There was
no necessity for a second dream to be put forth in
order to portray a former subject, which, expositors,
as I have said, have represented Daniel's dream as
doing. It is setting forth God's Word in a frivolous
light !—making Daniel's dream to appear as if given
for no other purpose than that of confirming king
Nebuchadnezzar's dream, which Daniel himself, by
giving an interpretation, proves to be otherwise.

God, in his wisdom, so worked out the TYPICAL
HISTORY of the world,—that period which extended
from the time of Noah's birth, down to the time of
Christ's first Advent—that expositors, although good
Christian men, are apt to get mixed in Scriptural

events, unless, indeed, it is the ordained "breaking-
of-seal" period ; but in that case, the expositor is
sure to be a " called," and " chosen," personal instrument.

Many writers avail themselves of the opportunity
of fitting in prophetic Scriptural incidents, which may
seem to the finite mind to bear upon each other ; ·
but this way of dealing with prophecy cannot adduce
anything more than mere feasibility, and a thousand
feasibilities does not establish a fact ! and the hidden
symbolic-Scripture facts, cannot be ascertained unless
the light of heaven illuminate the finite mind.

That there is a breaking-of-seal period, is evident,
by the angel telling Daniel to seal up his vision till
the time of the end (Danl. xii. 4.), signifying the age
at which the things he was then speaking of, would
take place.   Therefore, sealed prophecy cannot be
opened by fitting in events which may seem feasible ;
this principle is sure to produce the opposite of truth :
for instance, not a Jew, towards the time of the
coming of Christ, ever dreamt of the Messiah being
a Person of such poor circumstances as that of not
having " where to lay his head " : yet the Scriptures
portray Him as such ! The contrivance of man, in
those days, to establish the truth by feasibility, made
them expect something different to this, even a great
earthly king : this is seen in Herod, who, assuredly
thought, when he was told by " the wise men of
the East " of the Babe that was born at Bethlehem ;

it made him recon upon the lose of his kingdom ;
feasibility had painted upon his mind the Messiah
as a natural and mighty monarch on earth.

No, at the time of fulfilment of any prophesied
event, men will either be disappointed, inasmuch as
their expectations will not be realized, or else it will
cause sensation and wonderment : for conjecture of
Spiritual things can never be realized.

There ought not to be any doubt about these
two dreams being separate revelations : each dream
has its FOUR, SYMBOLICALLY PORTRAYED, KINGDOMS,
and it is quite plain that the last four, follows in
their several order, subsequent to the successional
wane of the first four. Thus, God has shown to
the world, that EIGHT GREAT GENTILE NATIONS
would come into existance from the time of the
starting with Babylon, down to the time of the
millennium. The knowledge of this, is of national
vitality. I will now show which are these EIGHT
CHOSEN KINGDOMS, dwelling somewhat upon the
latter four (Danl. vii.), and especially on the last two,
one of which, has not yet made its national debut,
although signes are not wanting which indicate its
coming into life :-

" *In the second year of the reign of Nebuchadnezzar,
Nebuchadnezzar dreamed dreams, wherewith his spirit
was troubled, and his sleep break from him. Then
Arioch brought in Daniel before the king in haste,
and said thus unto him, I have found a man of the*

captives of Judah, that will make known unto the king the interpretation. Daniel answered in the presence of the king, and said... THOU, O KING, SAWEST, AND BEHOLD A GREAT IMAGE. THIS GREAT IMAGE, WHOSE BRIGHTNESS WAS EXCELLENT, STOOD BEFORE THEE ; AND THE FORM THEREOF WAS TERRIBLE. THIS IMAGE'S HEAD WAS OF FINE GOLD, HIS BREAST AND HIS ARMS OF SILVER, HIS BELLY AND HIS THIGHS OF BRASS, HIS LEGS OF IRON, HIS FEET PART OF IRON AND PART OF CLAY. THOU SAWEST TILL THAT A STONE WAS CUT OUT WITHOUT HANDS, WHICH SMOTE THE IMAGE UPON HIS FEET THAT WERE OF IRON AND CLAY, AND BREAK THEM TO PIECES.   THEN WAS THE IRON, THE CLAY, THE BRASS, THE SILVER, AND THE GOLD, BROKEN TO PIECES TOGETHER, AND BECAME LIKE THE CHAFF OF THE SUMMER-THRASHINGFLOOR ; AND THE WIND CARRIED THEM AWAY, AND NO PLACE WAS FOUND FOR THEM. . . . *This is the dream ; and we will tell the interpretation thereof before the king. . . .* THOU ART THE HEAD OF GOLD. AND AFTER THEE SHALL ARISE ANOTHER KINGDOM INFERIOR TO THEE, AND ANOTHER THIRD KINGDOM OF BRASS . . . AND THE FOURTH KINGDOM SHALL BE STRONG AS IRON " . . . (Danl. ii. 1, 25, 27, 31—40.).

Now, it is plain, this symbolic figure has been fulfilled in four great nations :- Babylon, under king Nebuchadnezzar, was the " HEAD OF GOLD ": Cyrus, king of Persia, and Darius of Media, who, in their turn, became dynastic monarchs of a great Asiatic empire and leading power of the earth, were the "BREAST AND ARMS OF SILVER;" Alexander THE GREAT, of Macedonia and Greece, who, in Scripture-due course, overthrew Darius (the surviving arm of silver), and became the ** monarch of the Asiatic world, was the "BELLY AND THIGHS OF BRASS;" and the Roman empire, developed into a world-conquoring nation by Cæsar and others, the "LEGS OF IRON "and "FEET OF PART-IRON AND PART -‡CLAY."

But Scripture distinctly shows us, by the * Stone which was cut without hands, and which smote the image upon its feet and broke them to pieces, that THE IMAGE ENDS HERE.

Now, had the Stone been portrayed as striking any other part of the image than that of the "feet" (Rome), expositors might have had some ground for clinging to the theory of Rome being continuous : but the wisdom of God foresaw the likelihood of this misinterpretation, and did therefore so cause it to be written, that no legal doubt exists,—the Stone having struck the image-feet, or last nation, it is shown thereby that the end has come to these four Gentile nations. Does not this blow upon the feet of

---

** Alexander, when writing to the vanquished Darius, said : "henceforth, if you have any communication to make, address me · as the King of Asia. [Goldsmith's History].

‡ The Jewish nation, with Palestine, became a Roman province ; the Jews thus represent the "clay" of the "feet".

* Christ.

the image, which causes it to become like chaff
before the wind, indicate Rome's desolation and extinction? Does it not plainly show that, as chaff
blown away never returns, so shall it be with this
nation which is represented by the "feet,"—that no
posibility shall exist of Rome ever coming together
again? Italy remains, I grant! and a small piece
of ground belonging to the Roman Church, still
exists; but in all other respects, Rome has gone for
ever.

We have thus shown that the first four-kingdom
dream, was a distinct revelation, having no reference
to, nor portrayal of, the dream of Daniel. Now
let us take a view of, and prove what we have
said with regard to, the second four kingdoms of
Daniel's vision :-

"*Daniel spake and said, I saw in my vision by
night, and, behold, the four winds of the heaven strove
upon the great sea.* AND FOUR GREAT BEASTS CAME
UP FROM THE SEA, *diverse one from another.* THE
FIRST WAS LIKE A LION, AND HAD EAGLES WINGS :
*I beheld till the wings thereof were plucked, and it
was lifted up from the earth, and made stand upon
the feet as a man, and a man's heart was given to
it.* AND BEHOLD ANOTHER BEAST, A SECOND, LIKE
TO A BEAR, AND IT RAISED UP ITSELF ON ONE
SIDE, AND IT HAD THREE RIBS IN THE MOUTH OF
IT BETWEEN THE TEETH OF IT : AND THEY SAID
THUS UNTO IT, ARISE, DEVOUR MUCH FLESH. AFTER

THIS I BEHELD, AND LO ANOTHER, LIKE A LEOPARD, WHICH HAD UPON THE BACK OF IT FOUR WINGS OF A FOWL; THE BEAST HAD ALSO FOUR HEADS; AND DOMINION WAS GIVEN TO IT. AFTER THIS I SAW IN THE NIGHT VISION, AND BEHOLD A FOURTH BEAST, DREADFUL AND TERRIBLE, AND STRONG EXCEED-INGLY; AND IT HAD GREAT IRON TEETH: IT DE-VOURED AND BREAK IN PIECES, AND STAMPED THE RESIDUE WITH THE FEET OF IT: AND IT WAS DIVERSE FROM ALL THE BEASTS THAT WERE BEFORE IT; AND IT HAD TEN HORNS" (Danl. vii. 2—7.).

Here we have in symbolic portrayal, four other nations coming into existance subsequent to Rome's decline; and we know by the emblematic symbol, that two of them have already appeared, the first one (England) having risen to greatness. Let us now portray briefly, these four great nations, but dwelling more fully upon them further on :-

The first that Daniel speaks of, is the "*lion*;" he says, "THE FIRST WAS LIKE A LION, AND HAD EAGLE'S wings." Now, what nation, or nations, answer emblematically, to the lion? and mark, we have the angel's authority (Danl. vii. 23.) for stating the lion signifies a nation! What nation, again I ask, is emblematic of lion?—I imagine I hear a multitude of voices exclaiming, England! and this, I need hardly say, would be proclaiming the truth. Everyone knows that England fulfils this emblem! The lands, which it is her lot to possess, proclaim it

by animal nativity! India for instance, claims the
lion as a native: and, it is said, the land of her
own small Isles, in the earliest days, were inhabited
by lions. And does not this nation float the lion
boldly as her national emblem upon her national
flag?—Even the coin of her realm glitter with this
emblematic sign! The lion, then, which Daniel
was shown, signified the emblem of the coming
great nation of England.

I am aware that, to the tribe of Judah, in the
capacity of a Jewish nation, the lion-emblem was
first predicted—"*Judah is a lion's whelp: from the
prey . . . he couched as a lion, and as an old lion:
who shall rouse him up?*" (Gen. xlix. 9.)—but during
the period of the Jewish national decline and decease,
England stepped in as Judah's substitute ("*young
lion*"); and there is no doubt whatever in my mind,
that the people, from ages past, are also Jews, but
of lost identity; and this is not hard to understand,
if we perceive that many Jews availed themselves
of the opportunity afforded to immigrate to Britain
during Cæsar's, and other military expeditions
against that nation: the three thousand who were
converted by Peter's Sermon (Acts. ii. 37—41), for
instance; these would be likely to embrace this
opportunity, in order to escape from Jewish persecution, and so formed part of the foundation of British
community. These lost-to-identity Jews, under a
special prolific-seed blessing, would gradually gain

in numbers over those of Britain's original race; and this accounts for the early Christianization of England. Scripture somewhat bears out this theory:- "Behold, the people shall rise up as a great lion (Judah, under king David), and LIFT UP HIMSELF AS A YOUNG LION (England) : he shall not lie down until he eat of the prey" (Judaic-England's conquest of her ordained portion of the world). Num.xxiii.24; xxiv.9. Under these conditions, with regard to the symbolic emblem, England may be counted the lion in a Judah-emblematic sense, as well as that of her ordained national sign.

The next question to be considered, with regard to England being the predicted "beast - lion," is, the "LION'S EAGLE-WINGS" (Danl.vii.4.) :-

Eagle's wings, being the largest limb-appendage of any that is found upon the animal life of this world, and England's possessions being the largest of any among the nations, it is plain that this symbol is the figurative portrayal of England's extensive national appendages throughout the world. If we take an imaginary view of these possessions—India, Australia, Canada, and the intermediary lands which are in her possession, we shall see that whilst ENGLAND PROPER, REPRESENTS THE BODY OF THE LION, HER POSSESSIONS, which extend to the extreme ends of the world, are so situated, each side of England, that, comparatively speaking, THEY FORM, AND FULFIL, THE POSITIONAL PORTRAYAL OF SPREAD

EAGLE-WINGS (see page 14.). The vision-dream of Daniel, however, tells us that the "lion" is to be PLUCKED OF THESE WINGS (Danl.vii.4.), which the dullest of perceptions can see, signifies England's wane, and the suffering of the loss of at least a portion of her wing-like possessions. This is no new thing either: for national growth unto pinnacles of greatness, and then the wane and fall, can be traced in history to all nations of any note, which have come into existence since the world began.— It is national maturity and death, a principle which not only governs all nations, but which also takes place with every other thing of growth. It was so with Edom; the Israelites in the time of Solomon, took their turn of rising to national immensity; Assyria realized her national importance; Babylon rose to the pinnacle of greatness; Persia became a great empire; Greece, under . Alexander, conquered the world; Rome swept the earth and ruled its people: but where are all these nations now? have they not all fallen?—have they not, with one or two exceptions, vanished from the face of the earth? It is true, Persia exists; but, comparatively speaking, only in a name: and Greece, by breaking away from the Turkish yoke, in A.D.1830, enjoys, also, a national name, the empire of Alexander however, has gone: even Rome, the greatest of them all, where is she? Italy, as we have said, exists, but Italy is not that nation which was built upon the foundation-

stone of Romulus, and which became the famous
city of four million inhabitants: no, Rome has
vanished! and like "chaff before the wind," is not
found. It is a significant fact, that England's seed
was sown during the days of Rome, and became
tributary to that nation: but growth unto maturity
could not be stopped—She had to traverse the path
of ascedency! and, therefore, the yoke was removed
by the hand of destiny causing the people, whilst
Rome was sinking under her magnificence, to rise
up as if by general consent and vindicate their freedom. The Romans, about 448.A.D, having withdrawn from British soil, leaving the Britons to govern
themselves, England grew, and became a mighty
nation until she reached a greatness which surpassed
all other nations under the sun. But, as we have
seen, she is to be "plucked:" England therefore,
from the end of the nineteenth century, (which is
deduced by the rising into power of the second
nation of Daniel's prediction. Danl.vii.5.) must *wane
and fulfil Scripture by the "lion" being reduced, or,
as Daniel puts it, becoming "as a man" (Danl.vii.4.).

---

* I here solemnly declare, by the light of heaven, that, from the
end of the nineteenth century, when Russia will be brought in, as
answering to the figure of the "second beast" which is symbolized
as being like unto a "bear", England has been her own instrument
in determining the date of her wane, by her "FALLING AWAY"
as predicted, [ii Thess.ii.3.] from the simple truth as it is found in
Jesus. They have gone over to ritualism, or, what some are pleased
to call, high Church; also, by ministers disapproving, yea, in some
cases, ridiculing, open-air preaching by dissenters, saying, "you

Thus, the first nation of Daniel's dream, and which is THE FIFTH great Gentile nation since Babylon, has been fulfilled in the kingdom, and possessions, of Great Britain.

The following map, represents the "LION WITH EAGLE'S WINGS, and undoubtedly proves the claim of England to the fulfilment of the symbolic prediction, by the geographical position of her possessions, each side of Great Britain.

The next figure of Daniel's dream which we have to consider, is the "BEAR;" he says:- "*And I beheld another beast, a second,* LIKE TO A BEAR AND IT RAISED UP ITSELF ON ONE SIDE, AND IT HAD THREE RIBS IN THE MOUTH OF IT BETWEEN THE TEETH OF IT: AND THEY SAID THUS UNTO IT, ARISE, DEVOUR MUCH FLESH" (Danl. vii. 5.).

Let us look closely into this symbol:-

When God caused Daniel to be an instrument of instruction by visions and dreams, He knew the land of these future nations which He was then portraying under symbol to the world, would be

---

have not been ordained, and therefore, have no right to preach!" In addition to this, the police, in nine cases out of ten throughout the country, drive away men, whom God has sent forth to preach the Gospel in the streets of its Cities; instead of fostering such men, by protecting them from the interruption of ungodly men. Also, by the permission which is given to secularists to preach poisonous and blasphemous doctrines in London parks; these things have caused the Jews to take courage in London, by interfering with open-air work of Christians. Once, I say, these things became the rule, and grow into

[For the remainder of this foot note, see page 26.]

N–I**ernsey. C–Jersey. D–Gibraltar
O–B**. West Africa–1. Massina. 2. Sen-
T–N**gambia. 3. Guinea. 4. Sokoto.
**olony–1. Natal. 2. Bechuanaland.
X–J**frica. L–Cyprus. M–British East

productive of certain animals, and that each of these four nations would select one of its own native animals as an emblem of the nation, or, as in the case of the Russian-bear, be emblematically known, and recognised by, this sign.—Who takes up the paper called "PUNCH" and does not at once recognise the BEAR in its cartoon to SIGNIFY RUSSIA? There is no misunderstanding this emblem!—Everyone knows that the bear is emblematic of this nation! This being so, let us consider the next point of Daniel's prediction :-

"IT RAISED UP ITSELF ON ONE SIDE "(Danl.vii.5.).

If any eye can foresee, surely it is that of God! Here we have in the shape of the territory of Russia, a land which forms a great OBLONG; and the foresight of God, in order to point out the direction which He would permit this nation to accomplish great victories, made use of this OBLONG-SHAPE symbol to indicate the aforesaid direction. Thus it pleased Him to ordain that, the arms of Russia shall go forth to battle, and shall accomplish great conquest at a certain date, in the direction of its oblong-side —" it raised up itself on one side. "

Spiritual promptings have already taken place ; —Do we not know that Russia for ages past, has had her eyes drawn towards Constantinople, and other neighbouring places that lay in the direction of her side,—and by her vast length, which extends from Findland to the sea of Okotsk, no doubt whatever

exists as to the direction in which her side does lay
—and that she would be only too willing to extend
her possessions, and control, as far as the mediterranean sea, enabling a pent fleet to have an outlet,
which, alone, makes a nation great and powerful.
Well then, the "raising up of itself on one side,"
is the prediction of Russia, *sweeping* the country in
the direction of Egypt, with a lateral splay as far
as *the sick man's house :* but more of this anon.

> Why should great ships territorially keep?
> Tho' gold is, every marksman's butt!
> A pent Fleet! when Scanderoon has water's deep:
> And the Dardanells cry, open! never more shut.
>   A.M.

The next stage for our consideration in connection
with the predicted Russian-symbol, is :-

"AND IT HAD THREE RIBS IN THE MOUTH OF it
BETWEEN THE TEETH OF IT" (Danl.vii.5.).

This part of the prediction, although set forth in
figure, is, at our present day, quite clear: it is a
similar expression as that of a man saying, when
speaking of someone he has within his power, "*ive
got him under my thumb.*"—We know that Russia
has succeeded in the iron-grip of one nation (Poland),
—this is one "rib" *between her teeth*—and that Turkey,
who has been firmly grasped by the war indemnity
of 1878, through Russian conquest of that nation,
and which she will never be able to pay, has given
her sufficient power over Turkey, to form at any

time, the subject to realize another "rib,"—that
Russia is to make this the basis wherewith to close
her teeth upon this second "rib."

The third "rib," which is of the distant future,
will be in connection with Korea, which, of course
means a slice off China. Well then, God has made
known to Russia, through Daniel, that she is to
overthrow Turkey, and another nation; not necessarily to annex them in the entirety, yet, nevertheless,
lay such hold of them, as to be sufficient for national,
and strategical purposes, and thus enable her to rise
to supremacy which, in her turn, it is ordained she
shall reach.

The "bear," so the symbol goes on to say, is
to "DEVOUR MUCH FLESH" (Danl.vii.5.).

This prediction of the future action of Russia,
calls for no explanation except, the pointing out that
it refers to her going forth and accomplishing great
conquests, the three "ribs" being her leading display.
But all these events will be fully dealt with further on.

Before we go into the details of the third great
nation which it is predicted will rise up unto power,
let us mark the opening words of the prediction (Danl.
vii.6.); it states, "AFTER THIS I beheld,". . . now,
the words, "AFTER THIS," signify the duration of
time which will elapse between the second and third
event,—the time between Russia's "devouring much
flesh," and that of the rising up of the third ("leopard-
beast") great nation. This must obviously take place

because the predicted third nation is not in existence at the time when Russia, the predicted second nation, is flourishing.

"AFTER THIS I BEHELD, AND LO ANOTHER, LIKE A LEOPARD, WHICH HAD UPON THE BACK OF IT FOUR WINGS OF A FOWL; THE BEAST HAD ALSO FOUR HEADS; AND DOMINION WAS GIVEN TO IT." (Danl. vii.6.).

Now, what land, throughout the world, for we are about to interpret the above passage of Scripture, claims the leopard nativity ?—Is not its origin that of (Abyssinia) Africa ?—Does not its very appearance suggest a country inhabited by black, white, and every intermediate shade among races of men ?—and this variety of humau colour may be found upon African soil. However, the leopard being a native of Africa, it is ordained that this shall be the emblem of an African, and third great Daniel-predicted nation. It now behoves us, prior to the explanation of the leopard-symbol appendages, to take a glance at Africa, and briefly review the history of its people, in order to ascertain who were the aboriginals :-

Until recently, this portion of the Globe, comparatively speaking, was lying dormant : by the signs of the times, however, it is evident that God is stirring up this country as a preliminary movement, previous to His nationally moulding it as a piece of machinery to carry out the fulfilment of Scripture-historical events. The original African race are very ancient ;

contrary to the common theory, they are the offspring of Esau, who, upon leaving his father's home, founded a great city on Mount Seir, in Edom. Generation after generation springing up, the posterity of Esau spreading very rapidly, the venturous would, I have no doubt, wander farther afield into the interior of Africa, in search of fertile land ; whilst others, in small ships, may have been driven at various times, into the open sea, and finally reached African shores, where, in course of time, they would spread abroad.—Esau's skin, together with the early portion of his progeny, being covered with hair, and, therefore, reasonably different from other men's skin, and the African clime, being hot, nature dictated to them the needlessness of their extra (hair) clothing ; this would cause *nature, by lessening her exertion in the direction of hair culture, to gradually cast it off, until, after generations, the skin would become bare, but, alas ! the black skin no longer hidden. And was not this thing ordained to be so ?—Was it not part of God's plan to make a CHOSEN PEOPLE OUT OF ONE BROTHER (Jacob), and a black-slave race of the other ? otherwise, what is meant by the written Word, which says : —" *and the Lord said unto her (Rebekah), two nations are in thy womb, and two manner of people shall be separated from thy*

---

* Nature is ever building up the system in the direction of our desires : so that, if we would change the course of our nature, we may do so, by bringing strong desires in the required direction, which has the effect of turning the blood-builders from the old energy.

bowels; and the elder (Esau) shall serve the younger."
Gen.xxv.53. This has a trumpet-like voice in the
matter: no need for further evidence: for we know
that Africa has been the *slave-product country*, and that
no white man's posterity have as yet borne the slave
yoke; we have, however, more evidence to adduce in
this direction, which, not only strengthens the argument unto establishing the identity of *Esau with
that of the father of the slave and black race, but also,
that of the portrayal of the African aborigines :-

When, let me ask, did Esau's race serve Jacob's
race, if it was not in the capacity of a black slave?
and we have the written Word of God to show that
they were to serve thus :- *"Isaac answered and said
unto Esau, behold I have made (Jacob) him thy lord"*...
(Gen.xxvii.37.). Scripture thus lays it down, and the
language is unmistakable, that Esau is the origin of a
great slave community, and therefore, of the black
race. This is proved by the prediction, that a time
will come when the slave yoke shall be broken,—*"It*

*I am aware that the compilers of maps have placed in Ethiopia,
the name of Cush : this, I suppose, signifies that the Aboriginals of
that part of Africa descended from the man of that name ; but
Cush being the son of Ham, who dwelt at Ararat [Armenia], was
not likely to travel from that place to inner Africa, in order to obtain
more acreage or better land, when every acre of land along the route,
would be better than that of Africa. Moreover, Cush begat Nimrod,
and this man founded Babylon [Babel], and, it appears, went uo further
SOUTH, but NORTHWARD in the neighbourhood of the Jordan ; and
some went EAST [Gen.x.8,11,19,30.]. Thus, there is no foundation for
making the offspring of Cush, the African aboriginals ; neither were
they black people.

shall come to pass when thou shalt have the dominion"
("third-beast" kingdom) "*that thou shalt break his
yoke from off thy neck*" (Gen.xxvii.40.). This passage
of Scripture clearly portrays Esau's progeny as slaves,
but redeemable at some distant period—the African
predominant kingdom. Now, by the coming into
power of an Esau-African nation, the yoke of slavery,
although put down by several Christian governments,
will be finally broken. And do we not see the prelim-
inaries of African ascent going on ?—exploring, laying
railway tracks, colonizing, and gold finding which,
with other precious things, only require the will of
God to point them out to the miner, and Africa will
become rich, rapidly peopled, and powerful : for, is it
not a fact, that wealth can raise the smallest of nations
into kingdoms of the highest degree and power ?
Thus we see the aboriginals of Africa, and their future
greatness, symbolically predicted. But we must now
get back to the African-prediction symbol, in order to
give its interpretation :-

"A LEOPARD WHICH HAD UPON THE BACK OF IT,
FOUR WINGS OF A FOWL" (Danl.vii.6.).

As wings, are not the natural parts of a leopard,
we perceive, these wings are foreign appendages that
have come upon him. Now, THE LEOPARD BEING
EMBLEMATICALLY THE REPRESENTATIVE OF AFRICA,
the "wings, " or foreign appendages, must also represent some foreign colonising settlements upon African
soil—wings not being the natural limb-product of a

leopard, these settlements, or colonies, in Africa, will
not be the national-populace product of that country.
To put it in other words : Africa, signified by a leopard,
is to have settlements of four foreign colonies, 'which
will subsequently become four national independencies
upon that land, and, eventually, form a confederacy
with the future African kingdom, the whole becoming
a great African empire.   These four, are designated
fowls wings : now, as eagle's wings denote in Scripture,
something very great, so, fowl's wings, signify something small ; therefore, these colonies are to be small,
when compared with the size of the African territory,
which exceeds twelve millions of square miles.   This
is the true interpretation of the "leopard" with "four
wings of a fowl."

It is somewhat difficult at the present date, and
whilst the scramble for this land is going on, to def-
initely pick out from the many permanent settlements
that are already in Africa, which will comprise these
"four wings ;" but if I have understood clearly, the
gleam of light upon this particular point, the four
successful nationalities, which will answer to the call
of the symbolic "wings," may be stated as follows :-

     I. BRITISH TONGUE :- Cape colony (south) ; Mata-
                          bele land, and Bechuanaland
                          (east central) ; Sierra Leone
                          and Ashantee (west).—One,
                          or a combination, of these.

2. GERMAN TONGUE :- East, South, West, and the
Cameroon, colonies.—One,
or more of these combined.
3. FRENCH TONGUE :- Congo settlements.
4. PORTUGUESE TONGUE :- The Boers, joined, perhaps, with the East, and
west, settlements.

These, as republic states, may be considered the
"four wings" at the time of Africa becoming a great
empire, of which, they will form part, in regard to
military strength, and national power. I shall have
something more to say about this empire further on.

THE "BEAST" (leopard) HAD ALSO, "FOUR heads"
(Danl.vii.6.) :-

The head of a leopard, unlike that of wings, being
a natural appendage, and this fact is not altered by
there being four of them, and, as we have shown, the
leopard being representative of Africa, the "head" of
this symbolic-leopard, must mean an *African head*, or
ruling monarchy; and as the "leopard" was seen in
possession of "four heads," so must there be included
in this monarchy, four African kingdoms, the whole,
together with the "wings," forming one great African
empire. These four kingdoms, however, will not be
foreign settlements: because, like the "heads" of the
"leopard," they are to be natural, or, in territorial
phrase, native appendages, and we mean by this,
kingdoms whose subjects consist of African races.

The whole figure is intended to convey to our minds

the fact, that Africa, in its ascendency, will consist of four crownhead-kingdoms, and four foreign republic states, as a great empire. As to who these four crown-head kingdoms will be, the same difficulty presents itself, as that which exists in the case of the "four wings," viz : the uncertainty of which of the present nations, and tribes of Africa, will survive, through the changes which will take place in matters of overthrow and raising up into existence, of nations, in a country of such vast territorial dimensions, during a period of several hundred years.—War and strife, are bound to swallow up some, whilst others, will gain footing ; so that, most of the nations and tribes which are now prominent, may, four hundred years hence, be nil. Nevertheless, I feel *persuaded that, the four victorious "*heads of the leopard,*" will be as follows :-

   1. EGYPT.

   2. BARBARY-MOROCCO, AS A MOORISH KINGDOM.

   3. ABYSSINIA-ETHIOPIA.

   4. A CENTRAL-AFRICAN TRIBAL-AMALGAMATION, FORMED INTO ONE MONARCHY.

These, or similar kingdoms which, at that period may have taken other names, is the interpretation of the "four heads of the leopard."

The "leopard" of "four wings" and "four heads," then, is the emblem of an African empire, which will consist of four foreign republic states, and four

---

  *I have only been shown one of the surviving kingdoms, that of Egypt.

kingdoms of African races, the greater of the eight, which may be that of Abyssinia, filling the position of ruling monarch, or EMPIRE SOVEREIGN.

"AND DOMINION WAS GIVEN TO IT" (Danl.vii.6.) :-

Here we are given the assurance of the amalgum nationalities, as a population of Africa, becoming a national power;—dominion is here literally applied to this country : and therefore, it is impossible to misunderstand the meaning of this portion of the "third-beast" prophecy.—A conscription like that of France, or Germany, would supply a mighty army in this immense country. The prediction (Danl.vii.6.) is self affirming, and shows that the African people, together with four foreign colonies, will, at the ordained period, become a combined national power, and, for a time, have pre-eminence over the nations of the earth.

It is here, Esau fulfils the prediction of his *father— " And by thy sword shalt thou live ;. . . and it shall come to pass when thou shalt have the dominion, that thou shalt break his yoke from off thy neck " (Gen.xxvii.40.).

Now we come to the "fourth beast," the symbol of the fourth great nation, which, Scripture has shown us, will come into existence, and have great national power, subsequent to the "third beast's" kingdom (Danl.vii.7, 19.) :-

---

*It will presently be shown that, the lost ten tribes of Israel [Jacob's progeny] are, at the present day, the Gentile races ; therefore, with one exception, the nations of the earth will be the actual offspring of Esau's brother.

"AFTER THIS I SAW IN THE NIGHT VISION, AND BEHOLD A FOURTH BEAST, DREADFUL AND TERRIBLE, AND STRONG EXCEEDINGLY : AND IT HAD GREAT IRON TEETH : IT DEVOURED AND BREAK IN PIECES, AND STAMPED THE RESIDUE WITH THE FEET OF IT : AND IT WAS DIVERSE FROM ALL THE BEASTS THAT WERE BEFORE IT : AND IT HAD TEN HORNS.   I CONSIDERED THE HORNS, AND, BEHOLD, THERE CAME UP AMONG THEM ANOTHER LITTLE HORN ". . . (Danl.vii.7,8.) :-
This is the same representative symbol, as that which is written by John, in Revelation xiii.1,2. ; the "little horn, " spoken of by Daniel, being that of the "second beast, " in the eleventh verse.   Paul, also speaks of this ("fourth beast ") reign, as a terror in the latter times (see, ii Thes.ii.) ; and I shall have a lengthy account to give of these two "beast "- rulers, further on ; for they represent the fourth great kingdom of distant future.   Nevertheless, I will now lay before the reader a synoptical portrayal of the figure, in order to establish its interpretation.   First, however, let me point out that, the same words, "AFTER THIS, " occur in this case, as in the case of the "third beast, " which, in

---

[The first part of this foot note, is to be found on pages 13 and 14.]
strength, The Spirit of God, which, hitherto, had guarded the interest of the nation, saw that He was no longer valued, nor accredited, and, as might be expected, would yield up His guardianship to the more called-for influence and power of Satan.
England was born, matured, and made great by her Christianity! but if He who gave birth, sustained, and raised up unto eminence, depart, the nation is deprived of its life ! It must die '

both cases, signify the duration of time that will elapse between the last event, and the one he is then setting forth. This gives us a clue as to how long the third kingdom will stand, from the time of its becoming an empire, to the period of the forth kingdom's supersedure : for, as the words, " after this, " is applied to both second and third kingdoms, it gives an equal duration of time to both of them ; and, as we will presently prove, there being over thirteen hundred years, from the time of the second kingdom's (Russia) power, to the declining period of the third kingdom (Africa), it will obviously give the African kingdom an empire duration of between six and seven hundred years. The wane of Russia, will be the first empire-ladder rail of the African nation. But what I wish to point out mostly, is this : the " fourth beast," which the Lord has shown me is the monarch of Egypt at a distant future, by snatching the " third-beast " African empire from its then-ruling emperor, will usurp himself, along with Egypt, into a matured, and mighty empire, of over six hundred years standing : this he will do, by proclaiming himself and Egypt, at the head of the African empire. Hence the same emblematic symbol is applied to the " fourth beast," as that which applies to the " third beast, " viz : the " leopard " (Danl.vii.6. Revl.xiii.1.), except, that the latter has " seven heads " and " ten horns ; " and this usurping of a ready-made empire, explains why it is, that the " fourth beast " is only to reign, and his kingdom have power, "forty

two months (Revl.xiii.5.): for, it will be seen, he is not
only saved the tediousness of an up-hill task of national
growth, but, by obtaining a ready-made empire, is
equivalent in national power, to other kingdoms which
may have lived longer, but in weakness during their
growth from national childhood.

   * The "fourth beast" as monarch of Egypt, by
usurping this kingdom, will change himself and Egypt,
from one of the "four heads" of the "leopard" (of the
third kingdom), to that of the *"leopard" itself*: to do
this, he will of course, issue a proclamation throughout
the land, go forth and conquer the capital city, and
thus overthrow the SOVEREIGN-RULER of the "third-
beast" kingdom.   In other words, the monarch of
Egypt, by a supernatural power from an indwelling
satanic spirit which he and the false prophet are to
possess (Revl.xiii.2,4,11—15.), will gain over the people; he then being the caliph, who is able to exercise
more power over the mohammedans than that of any
national monarch, will easily step into supreme power,
proclaim Egypt the capital of the African empire, and
himself, the caliph of all mohammedans throughout
the world.   This is to be the principle upon which the
"fourth beast" will proceed, and thus, by the Africans,
and all mohammedans, giving him allegiance, he, at
once, raises both himself and Egypt into a dominant

---

   * The events of the "fourth beast" being fully explained further
on, when the thread of Scriptural predictions call him in, we have
here, only explained the symbolical figure.

power, which fulfils the predicted coming into existence of the "fourth-beast" kingdom.

"IT DEVOURED AND BREAK IN PIECES, AND STAMPED THE RESIDUE WITH THE FEET OF IT" (Danl.vii.7.) :-

It does not require deep perception to understand the meaning of these words ! Have we not seen the Turks indulging in a little of it already?—Thousands of Armenian inhabitants have recently been massacred by these bloodthirsty people, for no other reason than that of the Armenians being Christians. This supplies the knowledge which enables us to form adequate ideas of the principle on which the "residue-stamping" mohammedans of the "fourth beast's" time, will carry on in their endeavour to wipe out Christianity.

"IT WAS DIVERSE FROM ALL THE BEASTS THAT WERE BEFORE IT"(Danl.vii.7.) :-

The "fourth beast's" empire, with Egypt for the Capital, is to be a MOHAMMED-RELIGION nation, held together by virtue of the Egyptian monarch being the caliph or supreme head of their church, together with the false-prophet antichrist ("little horn") as a king's counsellor and high priest of the nation ; both being in satanic power and guidance unto miracle working.—Not a kingdom which comes within the political circle and national constitution only; but a kingdom in which will be annexed all mohammedan races throughout the world, for purposes of religion and national strength, which, by the sword, as heretofore creed-established,

will create a great multitude of religiously-welded fanatics, ready at all times for purposes of war. *Hence
the difference* ("diverse") *from all other kingdoms.*

"AND IT HAD TEN HORNS :-"   .

As we give a full account of the "ten-horn" symbol
on pages 146—150, the thread of future events then
calling for it, I refrain from any explanation at this
stage, except to state, that these "ten horns" refer to
the ten lost tribes of Israel, who have been marvellously
guided by God, in fulfilment of His ordained plan.

It is now necessary for us to take a glance at Daniel's
visions as written in chapter viii, in order to convey
our minds along the path of true events, which lead
up to the actual reign of the "fourth beast," and, eventually, to the end of this present world.   In this chapter
(Danl.viii.), it is figuratively pointed out that Alexander
THE GREAT, was the seed sower of the future "ten
horn beast," and "antichrist-false-prophet," kingdom.
This chapter also carries us in two directions, the paths
of which we will follow, in order to have a clear perception of the wonderful way that God has taken, in
order to secretly guide predicted events to the end of
time.   These two eventful paths, however, run into
each other, and then form one main path of threaded
events.   If, then, we follow these two by-paths, we
shall reach by the one, England at the pinnacle of
her greatness : and by the other, the crumbling doors
of the Turkish nation.   This will open the reader's
perception more fully, and enable them to grasp the

events which are to follow.

The eighth chapter of Daniel opens with the event of Alexander going forth to meet the Persians, under the figure of an "he goat" :-

"I saw in a vision . . . I was by the river Ulai. Then I lifted up mine eyes, and saw, and behold there stood before the river a RAM which had two horns: and the two horns were high: but one was higher than the other, and the higher (Darius) came up last. And as I was considering, behold an HE GOAT came from the west . . . and the goat had a notable horn between his eyes. And he came to the ram that had two horns . . . and run into him in the fury cf his power. And I saw him come close unto the ram, and he was moved with choler against him, and smote the ram, and break his two horns : and there was no power in the ram to stand before him, but he cast him down to the ground, and stamped upon him : and there was none that could deliver the ram out of his hands. Therefore the he goat waxed very great : and when he was strong, the great horn was broken : and for it came up four notable ones towards the four winds of heaven."(Danl.viii.2.3.5—8.).

We are further enlightened upon this passage of Scripture, by the explanation of the angel unto Daniel, and which reads as follows : " *and I heard a man's voice between the banks of Ulai, which called, and said, Gabriel, make this man to understand the vision. So he came near where I stood : and when he came, I was afraid, and fell upon my face : but he said unto me, Understand, O son of man : for* AT THE TIME OF THE

END *shall be the vision.* — THE RAM WHICH THOU SAWEST HAVING TWO HORNS, ARE THE KINGS OF MEDIA AND PERSIA; AND THE ROUGH GOAT IS THE KING OF GRECIA : AND THE GREAT HORN THAT IS BETWEEN HIS EYES, IS (ALEXANDER THE GREAT) THE FIRST KING. NOW THAT BEING BROKEN, WHEREAS FOUR STOOD UP FOR IT— FOUR KINGDOMS SHALL STAND UP OUT OF THE NATION, BUT NOT IN HIS (ALEXANDER'S) POWER." (Danl.viii.16,17,20—22.).

> History, the pendulum of prophecy carries,
> And will surely oscillate its fulfilment !
> A.M.

Cyrus, who turned the Persian settlement into a great empire, left some of his glory to others : Darius Codomanus of Median seed, being one of them. These two monarchs, as the FIRST and LAST rulers of this empire, stand, in Scriptural portrayal, for the whole of the many-king Persian dynasty; and which are symbolically set forth as a "ram with two horns :" but the last (Darius) of these "two horns, " is, Scripturally, the representative of the whole dynasty of the Persian empire.

The "he goat, " which represents Alexander of Macedone-Greece, is here ordained to overthrow his Persian neighbour, who, at this time, had predominance over the Asiatic world. Let us glance at the "he goat" before we follow him to the great battle :-

The history of Greece, or ancient Grecer, is not
so much the history of any particular kingdom ; but
rather, of a number of small independent states, whose
government somewhat resembled republicanism.   One
of these, however, that of Macedonia, had formed, and
kept up, a monarchical government.   At the period
when the prophecy concerning the "he goat" was
about to be fulfilled, the father of Alexander and king
of this Macedonian state having been traitorously
killed, Alexander, who was about twenty years old,
came to the throne, but saw himself surrounded
with many dangers connected with other nations.
His first warlike act, was against the barbarians, when
he defeated the king of Triballi.   A short time afterwards, he virtually conquered the republic states of
Greece, by marching an army against the Thebans,
a Greek State of no mean order, and razing this city
to the ground.   Alexander might have then proclaimed
himself Monarch of all Greece ; but it seems, in cases
of victory, there was no necessity for him to proclaim
himself king on these occasions, because, his sovereignty ascended to him by virtue of his general conquest :
he was, nevertheless, the "king of Grecia" (Danl.viii.).
Alexander gloried more in the military rank of a
nation, than that of monarchy : and he took the
highest Military Rank, that of Generalissimo of Greece,
in which capacity he commanded his army in battle.
We will now follow him as the symbolical "he goat,"
with an army of about 35000 men, on his way to fight

Darius, king of Persia, the symbolic "ram," who,
commanding an army of 100000 men, had already
marched forward to meet him. These two moving
masses of destroying intent, were travelling towards
each other, Alexander passing from Europe to Asia,
and Darius, over the Cilician mountains, history tells
us, made a halt at Issus. Here Darius awaited his
antagonist, little thinking that he was about to perform
that part, in which the symbolic ram, "had no power,
and there was none that could deliver him" (Danl. viii.).

Alexander now came in sight of the Persian army,
who seemed eager to engage in battle. Alexander,
history tells us, exposed himself to danger like the
meanest soldier in the ranks. He wounded Darius's
equerry with a steel-pointed spear, and the king himself would have shared the same infliction and most
likely have been killed by Alexander, had he not saved
himself by flight. The Persians being now defeated
at all points, they also took to flight, but were hotly
pursued by Alexander's forces; Alexander himself, in
whom is now realized the "he goat   coming with
choler against the ram," rode after Darius as far as a
place called Arbela, but he managed to reach Media
where, it is said, a secret design was entered into by
a commander of the Bactrians, to capture and hand
him over to Alexander; the enemy, however, being in
close pursuit, and the traitors fearing for their own
safety, fled, but not before they had thrust Darius
through with their spears, from which he died. Thus

did Darius fulfil the ram-symbol even to the extent of
there being "none to deliver him" from death.   The
whole proceedings were so completely displayed by
Darius, and carried out by Alexander, that it is almost
impossible to view the circumstances without perceiving the hand of God fulfilling his predicted purpose :
Goldsmith describes the display, as an Inventory of
MATERIAL, WEALTH, and POWER, being handed over
from one RULER to ANOTHER on completion of office ;
and the following portrayal is given by hin :-

" King Darius with a mighty army displaying mag-
.nificence in every quarter, advanced ; over his tent was
exhibited the sun in jewels, silver altars were carried
on which lay fire, three hundred and sixty five youths
were clothed in purple robes, ten chariots adorned with
sculptures in gold and silver, then came a body of
horsemen composed of twelve nations, next to these
marched the Persians called immortals amounting to
ten thousand who wore golden collars and gold-cloth
robes with sleeves covered with precious stones, then
came fifteen thousand in vain pomp of dress, then the
cloak bearers and the king, who now followed in the
magnificence of gold and jewels and chariot enriched
with various images of gold escorted on each side by
two hundred relations with two thousand pikemen
following.   The rear-guard consisting of thirty thousand infantry, behind which were four hundred of the
king's horses being led.   About a hundred yards further behind came Darius's mother and his consort,

both seated on thrones and with numerous female
attendants riding on horseback followed by fifteen
chariots in which were seated the kings children,
closely followed by those who had the care of their
education, and then a band of eunuchs. The next to
swell this moving mass of life and wealth were the
kings three hundred and sixty concubines in the equi-
page cf queens, followed by six hundred mules and
three hundred camels, which carried the kings treasure,
guarded by a large body of Archers. After these came
the wives of the Crown officers, and Lords of the
Court in chariots; then the sutlers, servants, and other
followers. In rear were a body of light-armed troops
and their commanders." Such was the pomp and
splendour of king Darius and his multitude, which were
brought to fight, or be handed over to, Alexander and
his well trained forces, which, without a doubt, completely fulfilled the "ram's" overthrow, as the prefigured "he goat." So noteworthy of predict-fulfilment is
this event, that, the night before the battle was fought,
Alexander exclaimed, in answer to General Parmenio's
remark of surprise at his calmness, "how can I be otherwise than calm when I see that the enemy is come to
deliver himself into my hands!" Alexander shows
by this, he was not lacking that Spiritual discernment
which is needed in a man who goes forth as an instrument of God in the fulfilment of prophecy.—He looked
upon this display of power and weakness on the part
of the Persians, as being quite as inevitable, as that of

his taking over the kingship of Macedonia. There is not, however, any greater proof of the divine workings in the matter of the instrument, than that of the immediate decease of Alexander, as soon as he had dealt the crushing blow to the Medo-Persian power ;—here, the instrument of fulfilment, having accomplished the task, has no further service upon this earth. No one ever truthfully knew the disease that caused his death.

Alexander left no definite instructions with regard to the disposal of his empire,—here again we see the DIVINE FINGER pointing towards Scripture (Danl. viii. 8, 22.)—the principal officers of his army, however, decided to crown Philip Aridaus, a weak minded half brother of Alexander, with Perdiccas as protector ; and were there not prophecy to be fulfilled, there is little doubt but what Philip would have become king: as God's " word shall not return unto him void," however, we find that several appointments of Governorship to the various provinces, took place.— Antipater, and Craterus, took the whole charge of the Grecian States; Lysimachus, was set over Chersonese and Thrace ; Eumenes, had Paphlagonia and Cappadocia; Ptolemy, took Egypt ; Antigonus, obtained Phrygia the Greater, Lycia, and Pamphylia ; Seleucus, governed Babylon. All this, however, was man's arrangement : God's decree had yet to proceed and fulfil Gabriel's words to Daniel, which were, that " FOUR KINGDOMS SHALL STAND UP OUT OF THE NATION "—not four usurpers, nor four kings : but rather, " four kingdoms." The result of Alexander's conquest and death, therefore, was predicted to bring forth out of his empire, and establish :-

1.—GREECE.
2.—SYRIA ; now the enlarged Turkish empire.
3.—EGYPT.
4.—PERSIA.

Whilst all others were swept away, THESE FOUR were ordained to stand, and are still standing at the present day.

Samuel Sharpe, in his history of Egypt, states: a treaty between the victorious four of these Generals, by which it was agreed that each should keep the country that he then held, was to the effect that, (1) Cassander, should govern Macedonia until Alexander Ægus, the son of Alexander, should be of age ; (2) that Lysimachus should keep Thrace, (3) Ptolemy Egypt, and (4) Antigonus, Asia-minor and Palestine. But God had ordained that Alexander's empire SHOULD "BE PLUCKED UP, EVEN FOR OTHERS BESIDE THESE" (Danl.xi.4.), which, as we have shown, was, eventually, fulfilled in the above described four kingdoms, and are now known by the names of, PERSIA, EGYPT, GREECE, and TURKEY. It being necessary for us to follow two of these nations, those of Syria-Turkey and Egypt, which are the two by-paths previously mentioned ; it is wise, in order to produce to the reader a true interpretation, to deal with Scriptural-predictions as written in the eleventh chapter of Daniel, verse by verse ; let us, therefore, carry out this maxim in dealing with the chapter in question.

We will first, however, give a few explanations :-

Although Daniel xi is written, comparatively speaking, in language other than that of figure, there is a certain amount of obscurity about it which can only be overcome by Spiritual light : this is because the characters therein have reference to kings, rulers, and armies, yet, do not plainly say so ;—God, in His wisdom, has deemed it expedient to so word this chapter, that while the verses are readable, they carry sufficient obscurity to make it impossible to finitely-discern which king, army, or country, the, " he," " his," "arms" &c., mean ; to read it, therefore, literally, would be to apply the several distinctions therein to one," king," "army," or "country ;" for it indiscriminately makes use of the words, " HE shall scatter ; arms shall stand on HIS part ; THE KING shall do according to his will ; thus shall HE do in the most strongholds ;" but no definite person, army, or country, is stated : this leaves one to think it means the one and the same person &c., whereas, under heaven's gleam in which the perception opens, it is seen that the words, "he," "his," "armies " &c., mean different "kings," "rulers," "armies," and "countries," in almost every case.— One verse,—Danl.xi.31.—which seems to refer to one king only, has, in reality, reference to two kings, and two distinct powerful-events : for the words," *and they shall place the abomination that maketh desolate,*" in the

after-part of the verse, refer to, hundreds of years
after the events signified in the first part of it.   The
wisdom of all this is obvious ! because, by it not giving
any particular king, country, or period, sufficient obscurity is maintained, which, by preventing premature
interpretation, enables the fulfilment at the ordained
date.   It is easy to see, on the other hand, that God is
able to point out the meaning to a chosen servant, by
giving him a gleam of light which will enable his perception to pierce the obscurity and produce the interpretation in plain language, at the time appointed.
The "he" &c., then, have reference to kings and
armies of Egypt, Syria, Jerusalem, Rome, Russia,
Turkey, and the Mohammedans of the distant future.
But let us now proceed with the verses in this (xi)
chapter, starting with the fifth, the first four having
been dealt with already, and we shall then be in one
of the by-paths :-

Danl. xi. 5—13.   *"And the king of the south (Egypt)
shall be strong, and one of his princes; and he shall be
strong above him, and have dominion; his dominion shall
be a great dominion.   And in the end of years they shall
join themselves together; for the king's daughter of the
south shall come to the king of the north (Syria) to make
an agreement: but she shall not retain the power of the
arm; neither shall he stand, nor his arm: but she shall
be given up, and they that brought her, and he that begat
her and he that strengthened her in these times.   But out
of a branch of her roots shall one stand up in his estate,*

*which shall come with an army, and shall enter into the
fortress of the king of the north, and shall deal against
them, and shall prevail : and shall also carry captives
into Egypt their gods, with their princes, and with their
precious vessels of silver and of gold ; and he shall continue more years than the king of the north. So the king
of the south shall come into his kingdom, and shall return
into his own land. But his sons shall be stirred up, and
shall assemble a multitude of great forces : and one shall
certainly come, and overflow, and pass through : then
shall he return, and be stirred up, even to his fortress.
And the king of the south shall be moved with choler,
and shall come forth and fight with him, even with the
king of the north : and he shall set forth a great multitude ; but the multitude shall be given into his hand.
And when he hath taken away the multitude, his heart
shall be lifted up ; and he shall cast down tens of thousands : but he shall not be strengthened by it.* FOR THE
KING OF THE NORTH SHALL RETURN, AND SHALL SET
FORTH A MULTITUDE GREATER THAN THE FORMER,
*and shall certainly come after certain years with a great
army and with much riches."*

Verse 5. Egypt is here designated the "SOUTH,"
it being southern to that of its adversary—Syria ; and
the king therein spoken of, is Ptolemy Lagus, one of
the Generals who "STOOD UP" out of Alexander's
empire ; he changed his name to Soter. Ptolemy first
established himself in the City of Alexandria, annexed
Egypt and its environs, and became king. He reigned

from 322 to 285 B.C., when he abdicated in favour of his son, Ptolemy philadelphus, and died at the ripe age of close upon 83 years.

Verses 6—9. If the following points are carefully noticed, it will be seen how accurate the above quoted prophecy has been fulfilled. History tell us, that Ptolemy Philadelphus, in order to put a stop to the disputes between Egypt and Antiochus, king of Syria (" NORTH "), offered his daughter Berenice—THE KING'S DAUGHTER OF THE "SOUTH"—with a large sum of money. Antiochus accepted Ptolemy's daughter to wife, although he was already married to Laodice, by whom were two children (Seleucus and Antiochus), but he cruelly divorced her, to suit his purpose. After the death of Ptolemy, however, Antiochus, again put on the dogskin garb, and drove Berenice and her young son away from him, and recalled his first wife Laodice. But she distrusting him, and, perhaps, a revengeful spirit possessing her, together with the making sure of the Syrian throne for her elder son, had her husband unsuspectingly murdered,—" HE THAT BEGAT HER "—and her son, Seleucus, then became king of Syria. Ptolemy Euergetes, the son of Ptolemy Philadelphus and brother to Berenice, who was now upon the throne of Egypt, upon hearing of the treatment his sister and her son had received from her husband, Antiochus, marched with an army without delay into Syria, but was too late to save his sister and her son from death, which took place as follows :-

Antiochus, the husband of Laodice and Berenice, having been murdered, and his younger son by Laodice having succeeded his elder brother to the throne of Syria, a body of men was sent after Berenice who was returning to Egypt, with orders to put her and her son. to death.

It will be seen by these events, that Scripture was fulfilled in Berenice, " THE KING'S DAUGHTER OF THE SOUTH, COMING TO THE KING OF (Syria) THE NORTH :" she did not retain the " POWER OF THE ARM," because the king put her away, and her son, therefore, did not come into possession of the Syrian throne. " NEITHER SHALL HE STAND," was also fulfilled in (Antiochus) the husband of Laodice and Berenice, being murdered. By the body of men which was sent from Syria to murder Berenice, she was," GIVEN UP ;" also the escort that brought her, by suffering the same fate ; and her father, " HE THAT STRENGTHENED HER " by giving her in marriage, had died : these events, together with Ptolemy Euergetes, the brother who came to avenge his sister, going forth and making havock of some of the Syrian possessions, placing an army of occupation in the capital, and taking possession of about forty thousand talents of silver, two thousand five hundred vases, AND THE STATUES OF GODS, WHICH WERE BROUGHT AND PLACED IN THE EGYPTIAN TEMPLE WITH GREAT POMP, was Daniel xi. 6—9. minutely fulfilled. For the " ROOTS " of Berenice, must be Ptolemy Soter : and a branch of her " ROOTS " would

be her father ;. now, her brother who came forth to
avenge her, being also of that branch (Danl.xi.7.),the
whole picture is complete unto a perfect fulfilment of
this portion of the prophetic Scripture.

Verses 10—12 . Through treachery on the part of
the garrison which the king of Egypt had left in the
Syrian Capital, young *Antiochus, the son of Antiochus
(verse 10.) and grandson of Laodice, retook the Syrian
possessions from the sway of Egypt ; and, on marching
his army against Egypt proper, was met by Ptolemy
Euergetes and the Egyptian forces, whom he overthrew, and placed his son Ptolemy Philopator, on the
Egyptian throne.

Verse 13 . After a few years, Antiochus Epiphanes,
the son of Antiochus THE GREAT, who had ascended
the Syrian throne, came against Egypt ; Maccabees
states :- "*Antiochus thought to reign over Egypt, that he
might have the dominion of the two realms : wherefore he
entered into Egypt* WITH A GREAT MULTITUDE, *with
chariots, and elephants, and horsemen and a great navy,
and made war against Ptolemy king of Egypt, but Ptolemy
was afraid of him and fled ; and many were wounded to
death" (Mac.1.16—18.).* These events, which were
foretold in the hearing of Daniel by an angel, over 300
years previous, ends the figures " north " and " south,"
with regard to Egypt and Syria.

Geographically speaking, the position of Jerusalem
during the strife of these two nations, placed the Jews

*This Syrian king, became ANTIOCHUS THE GREAT.

in the centre of war-planes, by being exposed to the violent collisions which took place between these two forces : thus, while the king of Syria was striving for mastery over Egypt, Jerusalem became a prey to this king's terrible rule ; and this, we perceive, was permitted by God : for the hand which had hitherto guarded the Jews, was now withdrawn from them, on account of their great transgression. This unfortunate nation of intermediary position, was sometimes belonging to Syria, and at other times to Egypt, giving rise to a state of things, both national and religious, which tend to overthrow stability : the high-priesthood was bartered to the highest bidder, and numbers of Jews deserted their own religion for that of Greek idolatry. Things went on from bad to worse, until Jerusalem became subject to the worst of tyranny, by Antiochus Epiphanes, king of Syria, endeavouring to wipe out the Jewish religion ; he forbade the daily sacrifice, defamed God's Altar in the worst conceivable manner, and then carried on, by plundering the city and temple of its golden vessels and ornaments, for a period of 2300 days (evenings and mornings, Danl.viii.14.R.V.). Much of the severity of the persecution, however, arose from the fact that, the king being exalted after his victories over Egypt, felt the sting of the Jews, who were rejoicing at a report of his death ; on this occasion, he sent an army against them, who plundered Jerusalem, slew 80000 persons, sold half as many into slavery, and took of prisoners, nearly 40000. History tells us that, in less than two years, this cruel tyrant, by his army plundering the houses and massacring the people, Jerusalem was abandoned to heathen idolatry.—Whosoever refused to do according to the king's command, the decree stated, he should die (see i Mac.i.). These terrible events lasted from the time of the * invasion of the Syrian army, until the death of Antiochus, a period of six years : but atrocities began some months before this, by a Jew and brother of the high priest, who took the Greek name of Jason, and who strove hard to undermind the Jewish religion and bring in that of Greek idolatry. The whole of the Jason-Epiphanes business of evil, was carried on between the dates, 172, and 165, B.C., which fulfils the Scriptural prediction period of 2300 days.

As there are different opinions, however, in the matter of fulfilment of the predicted 2300 days (Danl. viii.14,26.), some believing it to be yet an event of the future, while others have applied it to the event which took place between Jerusalem and Rome at the date A.D. 70, I will endeavour to point out the landmarks which will enable the reader to see that this event was the persecution of the Jews by the king of Syria,

---

* As we are treating with a country, the climate of which is very hot in summer, we must allow ourselves to be guided, in the matter of time of year when the invasion of Jerusalem took place, by the general wisdom and discretion that is used by governments on such occasions.—Wisdom would lead the king of Syria to send his army against Jerusalem at a time of the year best suited to promote the health of the troops, and success of the expedition ; this would be

assisted by Jason, which took place between the dates, 172—165 B.C.

First, let us take a look at three great events of persecution which overtook the Jewish nation, from the time of the reign of Antiochus Epiphanes :-

1. Defilement of the Jewish Temple, by Antiochus Epiphanes, king of Syria, about 171—166 B.C.

2. Destruction of the Jewish Temple in the year 70 A.D., by the Romans.

3. The invasion of Jerusalem in A.D. 637 by the Mohammedans, and the appropriation of the JEWISH-TEMPLE SITE, by them.

Now, the first of these three events being the only occasion on which the temple, or sanctuary, was left standing, it is the only event that fully answers to Daniel's prediction—"*And an host was given to it together with the continual burnt offering through transgression; and it* (Syrian nation) *cast down truth to the ground, and it did its pleasure and prospered. Then I heard a holy one speaking; and another holy one said unto that certain one which spake, How long shall be the vision concerning the continual burnt offering, and the transgression that maketh desolate, to give both the*

---

about the month of January. Therefore we must count the whole of the first year of Epiphanes' persecution period ; and also the whole of the last year, which was decided by the king's death : for the historian tells us [i Mac.iv.52.], the cleansing of the sanctuary was finished in the month of CASLEU, which, in the Jewish calendar, is the ninth month ; and this answers to the thirty days that is between the middle of November, and the middle of December, of our calendar.

vision concerning the continual burnt offering, and the transgression that maketh desolate, to give both the sanctuary and the host to be trodden under foot? And he said unto me, Unto two thousand and three hundred evenings and mornings; then shall the sanctuary be cleansed"(Danl. viii. 12—14. R. V.)—because it states, "THEN SHALL THE SANCTUARY BE CLEANSED;" this shows us, plainly, that whenever this defilement of the temple came to pass, the building must have been LEFT STANDING : otherwise, how would it be possible to subsequently cleanse it ?—to enable a building to be abused for a certain period, that building must necessarily remain standing ; for it would be impossible to continue the abuse for 2300 days if, at the outset, the building was demolished ! And at the second Jew-persecuting event (A.D.70.), the temple was the first building the Romans destroyed, and it has never been rebuilt. Moreover, Scripture states, this persecution and defiling event, should last for " 2300*EVENINGS and MORNINGS :" this admits of no deviation from 2300 twentyfour-hour days. But above all, having received special light, and information from a Spiritual source, with regard to this subject, I am in a position to state positively, that the event in question has been fulfilled in the acts of Antiochus Epiphanes towards Jerusalem, his death ending the predicted period ; for the sanctuary could not be counted cleansed, although the

---

* Evenings and mornings, is the truest rendering of the original Scripture, and has been adopted in the Revised Version.

altar was rebuilt, whilst he, who was determined to wipe out the Mosaic rites and law, was living.

Having described the atrocities of the king of Syria towards Jerusalem, in order to prove the fulfilment of the predicted 2300 days; we will now continue the thread of our discourse :-

The word " SOUTH," or " NORTH," as used in Scripture predictions, is not figure ; but rather, a term used to signify in a measure, the country it is intended to portray ; and as these countries, which prophecy has marked out and which allude to two nations being at strife, vary in position, in cousequence of it being sometimes these two nations, and at other times, another two ; the reader will unaerstand that what was " north" to its adversary at one time, may, by change of a more northward-to-itself adversary, become " south :" thus, Jerusalem is NORTH of Egypt, and would be so designated if these two countries were at war with each other ; but let Egypt cease hostilities and Rome take up national strife with Jerusalem, and this country immediately becomes " SOUTH. " The " north, " and " south," then, signify the geographical position which one nation stand to another, when at war. We have been dealing with Daniel xi 5—13, this referred to Egypt and Syria ; the scene now changes to that of Jerusalem ("south"), and Rome ("north"):-

Verses 14—17. At this time, Rome was begining to grasp the nations which made her become worldwide famous,—Macedonia was the first that fell into

her hands ; then Pompey (of Rome), seeing an opportunity of reducing Palestine, ordered the rival brothers,
Hyrcanus and Aristobulus, sons of Alexander Jaddæus
who were in dispute about the succession of the Crown
and Priesthood of Jerusalem, to appear before him ;
Aristobulus, not being satisfied with Pompey's decision, made preparations for war with Rome : this,
realizing the anticipation of Pompey, he soon put his
favourable opportunity into practice, by marching an
army into Judæa.   Aristobulus was taken prisoner,
about twelve thousand Jews were put to the sword,
and Judæa reduced to the conditions of a province of
the Roman Empire.   This took place in the year 63
B.C. ; Judæa, however, was subsequently divided into
five provinces under an oligarchal-republic government, Herod becoming governor of Galilee about ten
years later ; but, eventually, he became the sole ruler
of Judæa. THIS RULE, WOULD ACCOUNT FOR THE
CORRUPTION WHICH IS SPOKEN OF IN VERSE 17; the
whole business, however, fulfils, as the "north" and
"south," the prediction of Daniel xi.14—17.   The
Romans thus became "THE ROBBERS OF THE (Jewish)
PEOPLE," but who are, as the fourteenth verse predicts,
now FALLEN THEMSELVES.

Verses 18—20 . A threefold government composed
of Julius Cæsar, Crassus, and Pompey, which was
called the Triumvirate, at this time existed in Rome ;
and Cæsar deliberated with his confederates upon the
subject of sharing the foreign provinces of the empire

among them ; the result was, that the province of Gaul
fell to Cæsar. With a large army, history tells us,
Cæsar then fought and subdued both the Gauls and
Britons in an expedition which lasted eight years, the
Britons being so terrified at Cæsar's power, that they
sent to desire peace ; this was granted to them, and
some hostages delivered, about the year 55 B.C.

Here we see the fulfilment of the words, he shall
" TURN HIS FACE UNTO THE ISLES " (verse 18.) : the
latter part of the eighteenth verse, however, that which
speaks of the REPROACH TURNING UPON HIM (POMPEY),
was subsequently fulfilled in the events which follows:-

Pompey was afraid of Cæsar's great ambition,
now that he had risen in popularity and power ; he
therefore, persuaded the Roman Senate, to withdraw
from him a large portion of his army, and then to recall Cæsar himself; Cæsar, however, perceiving the
artifice of Pompey, sent word to the effect, that he
would resign his command, if Pompey would do the
same thing. The senate then ordered Cæsar to lay
down his government ; this caused a rupture, and he
marched, with secret intentions, his army back to
Rome. Cæsar soon brought his arms to oppose
Pompey, and, after some hard struggles overthrew
him, reconquered a number of Roman provinces, and
then became the ruler of Rome. So that the secret
" REPROACH " of Pompey towards Cæsar, TURNED
UPON HIMSELF : for he not only lost his part of the
kingdom, but the loss of his life resulted also. Thus,

were al. the events of the eighteenth verse fulfilled.

Verse 19 . By Cæsar returning to Rome as above described, he was "TURNING HIS FACE TOWARDS THE FORT OF HIS OWN LAND ;" also the following events, which realizes the "STUMBLING AND FALL, AND NOT BEING FOUND," is very plainly fulfilled :-

Cæsar little knew what a short time he would live to enjoy his conquest—he did not dream of the tragic event, in which he was to be the victim, was so near at hand ; which not only filled the world with astonishment, but also left a deep stain upon the nation to which he belonged. A deep conspiracy had been laid against Cæsar ; no less than sixty senators had agreed to carry out his death, by attacking him upon his entering the senate house. No sooner had he taken his place, than the conspirators approached, under pretence of saluting him, and stabbed him to death, by no less than twenty-three wounds.

By the WILL of Julius Cæsar, Octavius, the grandson of Cæsar's sister was made heir, with permission to take the name of Cæsar, which, eventually, he did, and became AUGUSTUS CÆSAR and Rome's first Emperor. This is he of whom Scripture speaks as "A RAISER OF TAXES" (verse 20),—Augustus had ordered the taking of sensus, or enrolment, of the people of Rome's vast dominions, with a secret view of levying a tax ; the Jews were registered, not where they happened to be living at that time, but at the place where their families originally belonged. This led to

Joseph, and Mary, going from Nazarith to Bethlehem the city of David—"*Now it came to pass in those days there went out a decree from CÆSAR AUGUSTUS, that all the world should be enrolled: this was the first enrolment made when Quirinius was †governor of Syria* (Luke ii. 1,2. R.V.)." This taxing event, fulfils the first part of verse twenty; the second part of the verse is fulfilled in the following acts of triumvir Antony :•

The government of Rome had been carried on by ‡Lepidus, Antony, and *Octavius; but in figurative language, this triumvirs government, is counted as one monarch: and in setting forth prediction it is designated, "HE," just the same as in the case of a unit sovereignty. Now, on this principle, the "he" in the twentieth verse, is made to serve two purposes: it has kept this part of the Scriptures obscure until the time appointed for its revelation, and it enabled two distinct events to be portraid, that of Octavius as a tax raiser, and Antoney the destroyer of his life, under prophecy. The enrolment took place during the time that Octavius and Antony were in triumviri office, but the tax was not raised until the triumvirate had decreased to one, that of Augustus Cæsar; and this is what the twentieth verse is setting forth, by its stating, "HE SHALL BE DESTROYED," the "HE" referring

---

† It is now concluded that Quirinius was twice governor of Syria, and that the enrolment took place during his first term of office.

‡ Lepidus had been deposed, prior to this date.

* Subsequently, Augustus Cæsar.

to Antony, for, by his death, Augustus Cæsar became Emperor of Rome.   But let us now identify Antony with the predict-words, "destroyed, neither in anger, nor in battle."   Antony lived, after taking over trium-vir power, about ten years ; this period compared with the fifty-five years of Augustus, in prophetic language, would be classed as a day : therefore the destruction of this individual (Antony) is set forth to take place "WITHIN FEW DAYS."   Furthermore, who can dispute the fact of Antony taking his own life by a stab when staying in Egypt ?—Here is a man, and brave soldier, whom God foresaw would die by the deed of his own hands, and so, portrayed him as "being destroyed, neither in anger, nor in battle ;" in Antony, therefore, is this part of the twentieth verse fulfilled.

Verses 21,22 . *"In his estate shall stand up a vile person to whom they shall not give the honor of the king-dom "*(*verse 21.*):-

So far as it concerns the first part of this verse, the fulfilment is like holding up a looking-glass in front of king Herod : for every reader of history will agree with me in saying, there could not be a man more fitted to answer to the character of a vile person, than this king was ; the very fact of his ordering the massacre of all the male infants of Bethlehem, in his endeavour to kill one particular Babe of whom he was afraid would be his supplanter, is, of itself, sufficient guilt to stamp him with the brand of the vilest of monsters that it is pos-sible for nature to produce.   As regards the second part of the predict in this twenty-first verse,—Herod, whilst being cruel in the extreme, was none the less a flatterer : he married Mariamne who belonged to the Asmonaen family so highly esteemed by the Jews, and placed Aristobulus, her brother, in the priesthood, in order to gratify the Jewish people ; he also rebuilt the Jewish Temple, and petitioned the Roman authorities for certain privileges for foreign Jews ; all this, according to history, was done under duplicity. But prior to this, Herod, who had been forced from the governorship of Galilee by the Parthians who were then rising into power and contending with Rome for the eastern empire, fleeing to Rome, found, in Antony, a ready instrument unto bribery, and flattery.—It was by Herod's flattery and bribes, that this man (triumvir Antony) warmly espoused his cause, and PLACED HIM, with the concurrence of Augustus and the senate, SOLE RULER OF JUDÆA. So that, we have no difficulty in identifying Herod with the flatterer, of whom it was predicted (verse 21) would obtain the (Jewish) kingdom under that artifice, and therefore, void of "honor."

The first part of verse twenty-two, is also fulfilled in Herod, by subsequent visitations, which took place during the fifth year of his reign ; Bannister states :- "an earthquake had destroyed several thousand individuals, a raging pestilence swept away multitudes, and, three years afterwards, a famine, followed by another pestilence, desolated the country." Thus we see, "*with the arms of a flood*," they, Herod's subjects,

were to be "*overflown from before him* (verse 22), and
Herod made to taste of the fear which the Almighty
arm had fulfilled in judgment upon an erring nation,
and its vile king.

Let us now take the latter part of verse twenty-two,
which deals with the " PRINCE OF THE COVENANT ":·

Antipas, Herod's son, by continuing the same line
of rule as his father, together with his being of the
same dynasty, is Scripturally counted the same vile
person ; and it was during this king's reign, that " THE
PRINCE OF THE COVENANT," Jesus Christ, was crucified—The completing act in the Herod-drama of evil.

As we Scripturally prove, in this written work, the
second Advent of Christ, we will here adduce some
testimony to show that He who laid down his life at
Calvary was Deity, and, therefore, "the Prince of the
covenant."

In Daniel ix. 20—27, the angel Gabriel is portrayed
as giving Daniel the glorious news of which the following is a portion :-

"*Seventy weeks are determined upon thy people and
upon thy holy city, to finish the transgression, and to
make an end of sin, and to make reconciliation for iniquity, and to bring in everlasting righteousness, and to
seal up the vision and prophecy, and to anoint·the most
Holy. Know therefore and understand,* THAT FROM
THE GOING FORTH OF THE COMMANDMENT TO RE-
STORE AND TO BUILD JERUSALEM UNTO THE MESSIAH
THE PRINCE, SHALL BE SEVEN WEEKS, AND·

THREESCORE AND TWO WEEKS: *the streets, and wall, shall be built again, even in troublous times. And after* THREESCORE AND TWO WEEKS SHALL THE MESSIAH BE CUT OFF, BUT NOT· FOR HIMSELF "... (Danl.ix.24—26.).

It is a settled question, that in many instances of prophecy, the word days, is used to signify years; this rule, we must perceive, is applied to the prediction which sets forth the coming of the Messiah in the above quotation: we may therefore, without further comment, count the above named 70 weeks thus, 70 x 7 = 490, years.

Now, the date upon which this 490 years commenced, was decided by somebody giving "the command to restore and rebuild Jerusalem." Who was it that gave this command? Let us ascertain—WHEN ARTAXERXES, KING OF PERSIA, SANCTIONED LEAVE OF ABSENCE TO NEHEMIAH, AND *COMMANDED THAT HE SHOULD PROCEED TO JERUSALEM, IN ORDER TO RESTORE THE CITY BY THE REBUILDING OF ITS WALLS, THE SETTING UP OF THE GATES, AND THE RENEWING OF THE STREETS WITH BUILDINGS, THE COMMAND IN QUESTION WAS GIVEN: (Neh.i.1—4; ii.1—9.) AND THIS TOOK PLACE IN 446 B.C.; we have, therefore, **69 weeks to account for, between·the date

---

*The events of both first and second chapters of Nehemiah, took place in the same year, that of the twentieth year of Artaxerxes's reign [446 B.C.].—See the first verse of each chapter.

**One week was cut off from the 70 weeks, in order to confirm the covenant [Danl.ix.27.].

B.C. 446, and the death of the Messiah, Jesus Christ. (Danl.ix.25.).   But this 69 weeks is divided into two periods, viz : "seven weeks," (49 years) and, "three-score and two weeks" (434 years).   If we look at verse twenty-four, we shall see that it speaks of sealing up the vision, and prophecy, or, as it is in Hebrew, seal-ing the prophets, i.e., the ending of the old custom of public-acknowledgment of prophets.   Now, from B.C. 446 (Artaxerxes's command), to the last acknowledged prophet (MALACHI), whose date of office was 397 B.C., exactly 49 years elapsed ; this fulfilled the "SEVEN WEEKS" of year-days.   we have now "threescore and two weeks," or, 434 year-days, to account for be-tween the last prophet, Malachi, (397 B.C.) and the death of Jesus—the date of the Messiah being cut off.

Now, by the birth of Jesus Christ taking place at a date, †FOUR YEARS BEFORE the common account called ANNO DOMINI, we have from this date, to Malachi, 397 years ; so that the account stands thus : 434–397=37.   Jesus died the death of crucifixion at the date ANNO DOMINI 33, and, by His birth taking place four years before the ANNO DOMINI commenced to count, He must have been 37 years of age, at His death.   Thus, we see the complete fulfilment of the (69 weeks) 483 years, which was predicted to elapse between the date of the COMMAND of Artaxerxes, and the Messiah being "CUT OFF."

†See marginal heading of Luke ii., of a marginal Bible of the authorized version.

There is yet the seventieth week, which, having little or nothing to do with the fulfilment of the Messiah
prediction, has, nevertheless, to be accounted for. If
we look at verse 27, we shall see that the seventieth
week was ordained to be set apart for the purpose of
confirming the covenant ; but what is this covenant ?
We have it here;—" *Behold my servant, whom I uphold ;
mine elect, in whom my soul delighteth . . . Thus saith
God the Lord . . , I the Lord have called thee in righteousness,. and will hold thine hand, and will keep thee,* AND
GIVE THEE (JESUS CHRIST) FOR A COVENANT of
THE PEOPLE, FOR A LIGHT OF THE GENTILES " (Isa.
xlii.1,5,6.). We see, by this passage of Scripture, that
the " COVENANT " was the giving of Jesus, whose Blood
cleanseth from sin, to be Sacrificed and thereby bring
in everlasting righteousness, which, flows therefrom.
The " COVENANT," then, was the Blood of Christ—
"This cup is the NEW *COVENANT IN MY
BLOOD" (i Cor.xi.25. R.V.). It therefore, follows,
that the SEVENTIETH WEEK, was ordained to be de-
votedly applied to the confirming of the Gospel of the
blood of Christ—energetic-preaching, and exhortation
of the Disciples, for THE FIRST SEVEN YEARS ("one
week " of year-days) immediately after His death.
This was carried out : and the " new covenant," as
a gift of Grace to those who believed, immediately
reached the hearts of 3000 (Acts.ii.) ; and the Gentiles
were also brought in. (Acts.x ; xi.1,18. Tim.i.11.).

*Revised Version.

From date of ARTAXERXES'S COMMAND, TO
    THE PROPHET MALACHI, = 49 years.

—"—   MALACHI, TO THE BIRTH
    OF JESUS CHRIST, =   397 years.

—"—   BIRTH OF JESUS, TO THE
    ACCOUNT CALLED ANNO
    DOMINI, =   4 years.

—"—   ANNO DOMINI EPOCH, TO
    THE DEATH OF JESUS, = 33 years.

(right margin: 7 wks. 62 weeks, of years.)

TOTAL   483 years.

Having laid the true interpretation of the 70-week prediction before the world ; let us add proof to knowledge, by adducing evidence in support of Jesus being, not only the Messiah and Prince of the covenant, but also, actual Deity :-

A. Jesus said, when speaking of John the baptist, "THERE HATH NOT RISEN A GREATER THAN JOHN THE BAPTIST : NOTWITHSTANDING, HE THAT IS LEAST IN THE KINGDOM OF HEAVEN IS GREATER THAN HE." (Matt.xi.11.). Now, does not these words prove Jesus to be the possessor of Divine Perception, and knowledge of heaven, beyond the reach of the finite mind ?

B. Moses, on mount Sinai, when being shown the Lord and his Glory, must have seen the vision of Jesus Christ, portrayed in the ordained structurally-formed Spirit-manifestation, (Exod.xxxiii.19—23.) for, God being Spirit (John.iv.24) and having no distinguishable parts, could not have shown Himself to Moses otherwise : and Scripture states that he would be shown the back part of the Lord.

C. The devil said unto Jesus, and surely he has supernatural power enough to discern who a person is, ..."IF THOU BE THE SON OF GOD, cast thyself down from hence "(Luke iv.9.). Now, as Jesus had not yet asserted his Sonship, this high title was not called for ; this fact proves, that the challenge of Satan who addressed Jesus as the Son of God, was the fruit of his knowing of Jesus being God : and who was, in subtilty, striving to gain obedience of the Deity.—He wanted to overcome God, who was now in structural form.

D. By Jesus saying,"I AND MY FATHER ARE ONE" (John x.30.), and, "HE THAT HATH SEEN ME HATH SEEN THE FATHER " (John xiv.9.); also, when individ-ually tempted, "THOU SHALL NOT TEMPT THE LORD THY GOD," is, indirectly, calling Himself God ; and He who died in truth's cause, could not lie (Titus i.2.).

E. It is written, "I WILL NOT GIVE MY GLORY TO ANOTHER " (Isa.xlviii.11.). Now, by Jesus possessing "ALL POWER ... in heaven and in earth " (Matt.xxviii. 18.), this glory has been given to Him ; for all power, must mean Glory ! This absolutely proves, that He who said,"I WILL NOT GIVE MY GLORY TO ANOTHER," was the same Being, as He who had received "ALL POWER," otherwise there would be a lie in the matter: there is no lie, however, but simply the Deity in a sec-ond form — a portion of the Spirit-God becoming structural, and the transferring of management-power from Spirit-self to Structural-self (Isa.ix.6.).

F. If the risen Christ who appeared to his disciples in the Person of the crucified Jesus, had not been Deity, how could He have given them the Holy Ghost out of his breath (John xx. 22.)?—we have the evidence of a Disciple-jury, that he did do so.

G. John the Baptist said, when speaking of Jesus, "ONE MIGHTIER THAN I COMETH, THE LATCHET OF WHOSE SHOES I AM NOT WORTHY TO UNLOOSE" (Luke iii. 16.). Now, if Jesus had been nothing more than a man, John would have been the greater of two! because it is written, "AMONG MEN THERE HATH NOT RISEN A greater than John" (Matt. xi. 11). This proves, absolutely, that Jesus was more than a man: and, as the Scriptures state, He not being an angel, it follows, that He who was thus structurally formed, was God manifest in the flesh.

H. Jesus said, when speaking of the end of the world, "THAT DAY AND HOUR KNOWETH NO MAN, NO, NOT THE ANGELS OF HEAVEN, BUT MY FATHER ONLY" (Matt. xxiv. 36.): to assert this, a statement which none but The Deity could have knowledge of, proves that He was of the omniscient Spirit, and therefore, Deity.

K. Prefigured typical-Scripture, was the method which God adopted in some instances of prediction: a prophet carried out a certain event, which typically represented, and foretold of, a similar but greater event of the future. By this principle, Isaiah, who was the author of a prefigured birth, was able to wright the prediction, "UNTO US A CHILD IS BORN, UNTO US A

SON IS GIVEN...," in phraseology which expressed the present tense, but which did not apply till near seven hundred years afterwards. This enabled God to set forth in Scripture, a positive fulfilment of the Messiah Advent, during the prophet-age. The wisdom of this is obvious : for it not only kept the prediction obscure, but it also leaves a living record through the ages of the Christian era of the Messiah-advent having taken place, leaving the Jew, and other unbelievers, no loop-hole to justify themselves in the looking forward to a yet promised Messiah.

L. If Jesus was not the Divine Being that Script-ure represents Him to be ; what meaning is their in the words, "O JERUSALEM...HOW OFTEN WOULD I HAVE GATHERED THY CHILDREN TOGETHER, EVEN AS A HEN GATHERETH HER CHICKENS UNDER HER WINGS, AND YE WOULD NOT"(Matt.xxiii.37.) ! Does not this prove a pre-existing care, on the part of Jesus, of a date prior to his natural birth ? And this is affirmed by his words, "I AM NOT OF THIS WORLD ; I AM FROM ABOVE"(John viii.23.).   •

M. When Jesus was in the house of Simon the leper at Bethany, "there came unto him a woman HAVING AN ALABASTER BOX OF VERY PRECIOUS OINT-MENT, AND POURED IT ON HIS HEAD, AS HE SAT AT MEAT (Matt.xxvi.7.). By this act of ANOINTING JESUS, the *Messiah, the Scripture of Daniel ix.24., was fulfilled ; for it was the custom to anoint kings in

---

*Messiah, in Hebrew, means ANOINTED.

this way (i Sam.x.1 ; ii Kings.ix.3.).

N. By the portrayal of God The Omnipotent Spirit (Psalm cxxxix.7—10; Jere.xxiii.24.), who concentrated Himself on mount Sinai (Exod.xix.1—18.), to the terror of the Israelites who trembled at the glory of God which appeared like devouring fire of furnace-like brightness, and which caused the mount to quake greatly (Exod.xix.18 ; xxiv.17.), these Israelites were shown the fact of God-in-Spirit being too great for the finite mind, and sight ; and points out to us, the necessity of God taking upon Himself a form of lesser degree than that of His mighty Spirit, for, this earth's people being a structural family, it needed a similar,or structural God. This, in due time, was supplied in the form of Man, and not only brought the Omnipotent Spirit to a more applicable form, but also, enabled the giving of Himself up a RANSOM for this fallen race.

Do we require any further evidence, or more powerful logic, than the above Scripturally adduced statements ?—Are they not thoroughly convincing to any impartial mind ?   Well then, in Jesus Christ, we perceive, "The mighty God," the promised Messiah, and "The Prince of the covenant."

· Jesus having been brought before Herod (Luke xxiii.6—11.), and then " broken "(crucified), Daniel xi. 22., was fulfilled.

The predicted events which we find in Daniel xi. 23—35, are, with one exception, incidents of perfidy so interwoven, and obscurely set forth, that it behoves us to 'take' these verses collectively, and follow the thread, as history produces each fulfilled event :-

Verses 23—35. In the first place, we have (verse 23) a league of deceitfulness, one of the parties becoming prosperous.—Herod Agrippa had fallen into disgrace, and was thrown into prison ; but he managed to league himself with Caligula, who had succeeded Tiberius to the Roman throne, who then releaced Herod from prison, gave him the Tetrarchy of Trachonitis, Gaul- onitis, and Batanæa, and allowed him to take the title of king.   Herod so grew in power that he became sole king of the Jews, fulfilling to the letter, the predict, "HE SHALL COME UP, AND SHALL BECOME STRONG WITH A SMALL (Jewish) PEOPLE. " Claudius, who had become emperor of Rome, fulfilled another portion of this man's predicted lot, by adding to Herod's pos- sessions, Abilene, Judæa, and Samaria,—THE "FAT- TEST PLACES OF THE PROVINCE." Thus, the first part of verse twenty-four, is fulfilled, the other part being subject to the death-roll change which never waits for any man's will ; for Herod Agrippa having died, and his son Agrippa having been judged incapable of taking charge of his father's dominions, they were united to Syria, under Longinus, who was made prefect (A.D.45). Jerusalem, with a portion of Judæa, being now under the procuratorship of Albinus, things grew into a state of terror : he allowed the chief priest, who was a sort of vassal to him, to encroach upon the rights of the lower priests, by sending his servant to the "thrashing

floors" and "taking away by force, the tithes, which
belonged to the common priests ;" this was doing THAT
WHICH HIS FATHERS HAD NOT DONE (verse 24), for the
tithes were always counted the property of the diocesan
priests. Florus having now succeeded Albinus, matters
ripened into that stage which fulfilled the part of the
twenty-fourth verse, which speaks of "SCATTERING
THE PREY AND SPOIL ... AND FORECASTING DEVICES
AGAINST (Jerusalem) THE STRONG HOLDS." These
devices, which Florus put forth for the purpose of
stiring up the people unto the scattering of the spoil
among the Roman soldiers, and to his own gain, were :
the protecting of all robbers who would divide their
spoil with him ; the throwing into prison a petitioning
party of Jews, who, through quarrels between them
and the Cæsarians, had transferred their sacred books
from the temple at Jerusalem to Narbata, for safety ;
and Florus sending to demand seventeen talents from
the sacred treasury of Jerusalem, for the use of
the Emperor. These things so ripened matters that
a tumult was incited, and insults were cast upon the
procurator. The desired effect having now been produced, Florus ordered his Soldiers to march upon the
city to force his demands, when, he becoming enraged
at the unfavourableness of matters, ordered his men to
plunder the upper market, which was carried out to the
extent of pillaging private houses, and massacring the
inhabitants. Many men of rank were dragged before
Florus, and by his orders were scourged and crucified.

This cost the Jews between three and four thousand lives. Now, Agrippa, king of this Roman province, happened to be away at Alexandria, at this time : he returned, however, in order to make enquiry into these disquieting matters, but, on his attempting to persuade the Jews to be obedient to Florus until his recall from the procuratorship, they drove him out of the city, menacing him with stones. The fire of rebellion had now been so fanned, that no persuasion could stay the impetuosity of the people ; the whole country rose up and directed their fury against their rulers, and, on the fifth of July 66 A.D., killed the Roman troops of Jerusalem garrison. This so exasperated the Roman army, that " HE " (Emperor of Rome) WAS STIRRED UP AGAINST JERUSALEM ("KING OF THE SOUTH") AND, WITH A GREAT ARMY (verse 25.), eventually, fought the Jewish nation. The Jews having incurred war with Rome, gathered together the whole nation, which, naturally, produced "THE VERY GREAT AND MIGHTY ARMY " which the twenty-fifth verse predicts ; but " HE "(the Jews) " SHALL NOT STAND." We know that the Roman army ("they that *feed of the portion of his meat ") were victorious, and therefore, fulfilled the predict-words, " SHALL DESTROY (Jerusalem) HIM, AND HIS (Jewish) ARMY SHALL OVERFLOW : AND MANY

---

* The Roman Soldiers who were stationed in this Judaic Roman-province, and who subsequently formed part of the army that invaded Jerusalem, were provisioned ["portion of his meat"] from Jewish taxation. Thus, this portion of the twenty-sixth verse was fulfilled.

SHALL FALL DOWN SLAIN"(verses 25,26.).   This prediction is practically carried out, however, as set forth
in verses 29, to the begining of 31.   In the meantime,
it speaks of (verse 27) mischief and lies going on—this,
it should be seen, is not portrayed in the name of the
perpetrators, but rather, is set forth in the name of the
responsible men to whom the perpetrators are, nationally, servant and subjects.—Florus, and the Jews,
were the actual transgressors, but they are each representative of a nation (Jerusalem and Rome), under the
Scriptural figure of "kings"(verse 27.).   The "LIES,"
refer to the evidence which was given at the court of
enquirey ;—what sort of evidence ought we to expect
from such a man as Florus?   Knowing what we do
of his character, we are justified in concluding that he
would "SPEAK LIES" AT THE "TABLE" OF THE CON-
VENED court.   The Jews also, if we consider that
while they were looked upon as being the culprits,
were in high dudgeon at the terrible treatment they
had received, would give evidence full of untruth.   It
is only fair to perceive, that evidence of self-justification would be adduced from both sides, Florus throwing the blame upon the Jews, and the Jews vindicating
their character and cause.   Thus, did these kings, under proxy, "SPEAK LIES AT ONE TABLE," and fulfil
the prediction of the twenty-seventh verse.

Verse 28.   Vespasion, the Military Commander,
who had returned from an expedition against the Ger-
mans, and Britons, rich in honour and possessions,

had thus fulfilled the Scripture-predict," RETURNING
INTO HIS LAND WITH GREAT RICHES "(verse 28). He
being made prefect of the Roman province of Syria,
and, having entered upon an expedition against the
Jews—" THE HOLY COVENANT "—in 67 A.D., at which
40000 were slain and 1200 taken prisoners, again, in
full glee over these " EXPLOITS, RETURNED TO HIS
OWN LAND "(verse 28). This time, however, to take
the place of the emperor Vitellius : for his army had
proclaimed him Emperor of Rome. These events,
fulfilled the twenty-eighth verse to the letter.

Vespasian did not complete the subjugation of
Judæa ; and Jerusalem had not yet been overthrown,
only that of Galilee and Jotapata, together with a few
other cities, which did not oppose the Roman arms.
Therefore, " AT THE TIME *APPOINTED, He (the army
of Rome) RETURNED, AND CAME TOWARDS (Jerusalem)
THE SOUTH."—Neither the army, nor its commander,
however, were the same as that of " THE FORMER "
INVASION, because, the invading army under the command of Vespasian (A.D.67), belonged to the emperor
†Nero, whereas, the RETURNING invaders in A.D. 70,
to complete the subjugation of Judæa, belonged to

*" The time appointed," was forty years from the time of Jesus
commencing his ministry ; as prefigured in the proclamation of
Jonah at Nineveh [Jonah i.1,2 ; ii.1-4.]. This, Jesus publicly declared
would come to pass, and warned the people of the wrath they were
bringing upon themselves ; and their temple, He predicted, would not
be left with one stone standing upon another.

†Galba, Otho, and Vitellius, ascended the Roman throne after Nero's
death; the whole three, however, did not reign much more than one year.

Vespasian, the newly ॒enthroned Emperor: and in place of Vespasian being in command, Titus, his son, now held that position : so that, they were not "AS THE *FORMER" invaders.   The predictions of the twenty-ninth verse, were thus accurately fulfilled.

Verse 30. "FOR THE SHIPS OF CHITTIM SHALL COME AGAINST HIM."   According to Peter Oliver's Scriptural Lexicon,"ships of Chittim" means,"THOSE THAT BRUISE ;" this prediction, therefore, is fulfilled in the following events :- Vespasian, having taken at the first invasion the strong places which covered Jeru-salem, was preparing to attack this city, when, through the death of Nero, the subsequent dissension with regard to the choice of a successor, and the German-legion now bringing forth Vitellius to fill the imperial throne, not only " GRIEVED " him, but, suspending his operations at Judæa, he, (Vespasian) in concurrence with his army who had proclaimed him Emperor, also, marched against Vitellius.   Arriving at the walls of the Roman city, this army was met by Vitellius and his arms—in figure, the "ships of Chittim"—who were determined to defend the city against this expedition-ary branch of the Roman army ; and thus, by the ensuing battles, the "ships of Chittim " was fulfilled.

Having enthroned Vespasian, this army returned to the seat of action outside the walls of Jerusalem in the year 70 A. D., in order to carry out to a full and

---

*The true rendering of the latter part of Daniel xi.20., is : " but it shall not be in the latter time as it was in the former"[Revised Version].

complete measure, the "INDIGNATION AGAINST THE HOLY COVENANT "(JEW), and Jerusalem. History tells us,,that many of the better class Jews, "FORSOOK THEIR HOLY COVENANT," which means, their having given up Judaism, and embracing CHRIST'S HOLY "COVENANT:" this, naturally, caused them to peaceably receive the Roman soldiers, who spared their lives. Upon this transaction, the Romans fulfilled the completing part of verse thirty, in which it was predicted that "he," the Roman army, would "HAVE *INTELLIGENCE WITH, *or have regard unto*, THEM THAT FORSAKE THE HOLY COVENANT."

ARMS DID STAND ON HIS (Rome) PART, as the thirty-first verse predicted; but oh, what a terrible slaughter of human life, and edificial destruction !— The assault now having commenced, by the battering-rams dealing tremendous blows against the walls of Jerusalem, a cry of terror arose from the inhabitants of the city. The first two of the three walls which enclosed the inner city having been breached, the Romans brought to bear their strength against the Temple; not to destroy however, only to take possession of it, but JEHOVAH had marked out its total destruction, and who can stay His hand ? The zealous army of Jews who held the temple, and who where willing to die in its defence, made it a difficult task to gain an entrance; but one of the Roman soldiers

---

*The true rendering of this passage of Scripture, is, " and have regard unto them that forsake the holy covenant [Danl.xi.30. Revised Version].

settled the question by casting a firebrand through the communicating-appartment window of the Sanctuary, whereby the whole edifice became one mass of flames.

The cry ot dispair of the Jews now rent the air: every Jew the soldiers encountered was cut down, blood flowed down to the lower court, and the inner court was thickly covered with dead bodies. Subsequent to this struggle, and when the resistance of the Jews had grown feeble, a breach was made in the inner wall; this enabled the Romans to possess the Upper City, the inhabitants of which were put to death, except the male-vigorous and female-beautiful who were taken captives. The city having been set on fire and many Jews who were in hiding burned, the soldiers set to work to demolish the buildings.— Houses, walls, towers, and the *temple, were razed to the ground; three towers only, and a portion of the western wall, being left standing in honour of the conquerors. The destruction of Jerusalem having been accomplished, Lucilius Bassus, the following year, was sent with an army to subdue the remaining revolters of other parts of the country; many of the Jews of these smaller cities, however, were already agreed ,as we have said, to embrace Christianity, and had therefore, "forsook their holy †covenant" and "fell" from Judaism to become raised in Christ, in order "TO PURGE, AND TO MAKE THEM WHITE." This fulfilled

---

*Christ said, "there shall not be left here one stone upon another."
†This is the Scriptural method of expressing Judaism.

in a remarkable manner, the predicted words of the thirty-fifth verse.

Here then, we see the complete fulfilment of the destruction of the Jewish nation " BY THE SWORD, AND BY FLAME, BY CAPTIVITY, AND BY SPOIL," in accordance with verse thirty-three ; the captivity being obvious, seeing that many of the Jews were taken to Rome in order to grace the returning conquerors.

The prediction also speaks of their becoming " CORRUPT BY FLATTERIES :" now, when we consider that the female-beautiful of Jerusalem were reserved for calamities worse than death, we shall easily see the meaning, and the fulfilment, of this prophetic passage of scripture ; yet some of these preferred the suffering of martyrdom sooner than be dishonoured, which, by thus " DOING EXPLOITS," completed the predict of the thirty-second verse.

By a large number of Jews fleeing into the open country at the time of the Roman invasion, and who were then destitute, together with every other indigent of the time, God caused it to be written for their knowledge, that they were to be given " A LITTLE HELP "—verse 34. This ends the Jewish overthrow, and the fulfilment of all the predicted events, up to the time of the appearance of Mohammed, we therefore proceed with the events of that date :-

It may have been noticed, that the last part of the thirty-first verse was passed-over : this paragraph— " AND THEY SHALL PLACE THE ABOMINATION

THAT MAKETH DESOLATE "—requires to be pointed
out, in order to show that it is a separate paragraph,
and has reference to other events, than that of the first
part of the verse.—The words, "AND THEY SHALL,"
which occurs twice, does not refer in both case, to the
same army, event, nor date.   This verse is so obscurely written, that the two events appear as one, and yet,
they are so distinct, that nearly six hundred years
stands between them—the one referring to the pollu-
tion of the Sanctuary with the blood of the slain in
A.D. 70, and being finally demolished, while the other
refers to the placing of, in 637 A.D., "THE ABOMINATION
THAT MAKETH DESOLATE."

Omar, the third caliph from Mohammed invaded
Palestine, and established in Jerusalem *an abomination
that made it desolate*; it was desolate enough before :
but this man placed the one needful thing to seal its
desolation in God's sight.   I need not state the particulars of the "abomination" at this juncture, because
it is more appropriate with other events, further on ;
what I wish to point out now is, that although the event
which took place in the year 70 A.D. (first part of ver 31),
was a literal desolation, it was not until the Mohammedan Caliphs made their appearance, that the desolation, both Spiritually and literal, became absolute.
For up to the time of Omar, there was a possibility
of another Jewish temple being built ; this gave to the
desolation a retrievable character, and would remain
so while the consecrated ground was standing vacant.

Even a tent on the principle of the ancient *tabernacle, would retrieve the desolation in a religious sense! But once the ground became irretrievably occupied, then, and not till then, was the desolation final. I know there was a time when it would have been impossible for the Jews to have rebuilt their temple, in consequence of Adrian who came to the Roman throne in 117 A.D., issuing a decree which exterminated the Jews from Jerusalem, and prohibited their return. But then, it was altered again by Julian, who restored them. The Persians also invaded Palestine and took Jerusalem, but did not hold it long, for the Emperor Heraclius, in the early part of the seventh century, wrested it from them. The Jews were thus in a state of fluctuating-desolation until the rising of the mohammedan impostor, when, by the acts of his earliest caliphs who erected "the abomination," they became absolutely desolate.

Before we can go into a most interesting and momentous subject, which deals with Mohammedism and the overthrow of Turkey, it behoves us to briefly pass along the second by-path in order to prove that Mohammed was the predicted "little horn," in whose caliph-dynasty we have the future antichrist, and the "beast" of "seven heads" and "ten horns :-"

Daniel viii.9,10,11,23,24. These five verses were

---

*The reader will perceive that these remarks are not intended to convey appreciation of Judaism, but rather, to show that the desolation which is spoken of in Daniel xi.31., was not fulfilled until A.D, 637.

pᴜrposely omitted at our previous comment, to enable.
the account we lay before the reader to be as clear as
possible.—Ptolemy Soter, who, it will be remembered,
was one of Alexander's officers, had usurped Egypt ;
this city was one of the four kingdoms of Alexander's
divided empire, and the one from which MOHAMMED,
the "LITTLE HORN," arose.   We have very little
record to show the exact boundary of the Egyptian territory at the time of Ptolemy's reign, but we
have every reason to believe that he was the Monarch.
of certain portions of Arabia adjoining Egypt: for.
Ptolemy was an ambitious man, otherwise he would
not have been an usurper, and this is sure to have lead
him to become the sovereign ruler of these neighbouring lands.   Anyway, Arabia must have stood in some
relation to Egypt, even if only under a protectorial :
otherwise it would be difficult to account for the absence of invaders, during the years of conflict which
went on among those who were endeavouring to
obtain the land of Alexander's empire.   These arguments are strengthened, when we consider that it was
Ptolemy who retained his power, and held his position
in Egypt from the begining.   All we require, how-.
ever, with regard to the matter, in order to realize
the Scriptural prediction (Danl.viii.8,9.) in the birth
of Mohammed within the boundary of Egyptian
territory, is that Mecca, and Medina, were under
Egyptian suzerainty.—Andrew Grichton states, in his
history of Arabia :- "When the Macedonian empire

was partitioned into four kingdoms, Arabia was indeed
included as a province in that which fell to the inheritance of Ptolemy, but the name is evidently applied
mearly to the regions that bordered on Egypt and
Palestine." Now this, surely, proves Mecca to have
been within the sphere of Egyptian rule, and, in fact,
by her possessing the doors of the country, Arabia
was, virtually, an Egyptian province. We do not
require any further evidence as to the extent of the
province, because that portion which borders upon
Egypt—Mecca and Medina—is the only part of Arabia
that affects our subject, and this part is doubly assured:
for history again tells us, that Ptolemy Euergetes, king
of Egypt, made himself master of the Arabian coast
of the Red sea ; and this locality embraces both Mecca
and Medina. Having adduced sufficient evidence in
support of Mecca being within the Egyptian quarter
of the divided empire, I will now produce the "little
horn," in the person of Mohammed :-

Mohammed was born in the city of Mecca, it is com-
puted, in the year 569 A.D. ; it is believed that he died,
about 632 A.D., having first become the founder of
mohammedism. Now, how do we know that Mohammed fulfils the predicted "LITTLE HORN ?" In the
first place, let us see what the prediction says about
it :- " AND OUT OF ONE OF THEM (Egyptian quarter of
Alexander's empire) CAME FORTH A LITTLE HORN
WHICH WAXED EXCEEDING GREAT, TOWARDS THE
SOUTH, AND TOWARDS THE EAST, AND

TOWARDS THE PLEASANT LAND"—Judæa
(Danl. viii. 9.).

Now this signifies that, the man whom the "little
horn" prefigures, shall make his name nationally
great and powerful, in the direction of three distinct
points of the mariner's compass—SOUTHERN, EAST-
ward, AND TOWARDS JUDÆA. Now, I assert that no
man except Mohammed, has ever fulfilled these conditions. It must be understood that this greatness,
is to be spread in these three directions only, and
that each direction, as laid down in the prediction,
must be counted from the stand-point of the "little
horn's" native place. And to be able to comply with
this, it will be found necessary to produce the "little
horn" representative, in, or near, Arabia : but let us
portray, and thus prove, Mohammed's case :-

Abu Baker, the first caliph, invaded Bosra and
Damascus, and eventually, the whole of Syria was
conquered by these mohammed-creed fanatics ; and
Bannister states, in his Survey of the Holy Land, "they
carried their religion, if not accepted in peace, by force
of arms, OVER THE GREATER PART OF THE EAST,
AND SOUTHERN LANDS. The Caliph Omar,
the third from Mohammed, INVESTED THE
HOLY CITY (*the pleasant land*), which, after ... a
protracted siege, surrendered on terms of capitulation
in the year 637 A.D." Now, no one will dispute the
fact, that mohammedism from the time of the first
invasion, has fulfilled the "little-horn" prophecy by

their occupancy of these parts of the globe—Africa, which is the "SOUTH," is undoubtedly a great center of mohammedism ; the inhabitants in the "EASTERN" direction, as far as India, have also adopted this creed, and followed Mohammed ; also Turky, of which JUDÆA, "THE PLEASANT LAND" forms part, have adopted it. Mohammedism did not spread to the North, neither did it come to the West, but took the exact course that Scripture had predicted ; therefore no other case of prophecy-fulfilment is so plainly de-fined as this one of the "little horn," in prefigure of Mohammed spreading his fraudulent creed towards the "SOUTH, EAST, AND PLEASANT LAND"—JUDÆA.

We have now arrived at that stage which neces-sitates the breaking of the seal of a great Scriptural secret, inasmuch as it is the key that opens the door of Daniel's dates, and reveals the period of fulfilment of all the future great events :-

When Jesus said, in speaking of his second Advent and the end of the world, "THAT DAY AND HOUR KNOWETH NO MAN, NOT THE ANGELS OF HEAVEN, BUT MY FATHER ONLY "(Matt.xxiv.36.), He did not know the date upon which HIS SECOND COMING would take place ; why was this ? Here we have one of the mysteries of prophecy : to be revealed, however, in "THE TIME OF THE END" (Danl.xii.4.), in which period we are now living. The mystery lay in the fact that God had so arranged the wording of Daniel's predicted dates (xii.11,12.), that they were made to

depend for their commencement to count, upon a
certain event; the date of this event, which the foreknowledge of God saw, would be decided by the birth
and subsequent acts of a certain child at some time
during the Christian era, and performed by his succes-
sors; this not being likely to take place for at least
500 years after the death of Christ, it will be seen,
there was no information to enable any one to
know the actual date of His second Advent, it being
ordained for Him to *come at the expiration of Daniel's
predicted period of year-days (Danl.xii.11,12), which
did not commence to count until the event in question
took place.   The individual who was to consist of this
new birth, was the child Mohammed; and the event
which was to be performed in his name, was the placing of "THE ABOMINATION" in the city of Jerusalem.
When this had come to pass—from this satanically
eventful date, did the predicted periods of Daniel, we
repeat, commence counting, and thus decide the date
of the second Advent of Christ.   Every thing, then,
depended upon the date of the placing of the "abomination," to enable the predicted 1290, and 1335, years
to go on; for the prediction remained dormant and
an unfathomable mystery, until the date of this epoch
arrived.   Jesus, knowing these things, quoted their
signs for the information of the world; He said :-

---

*The question which Christ was deciding, when referring mankind to
the "abomination" of desolation of Daniel's prediction, was the sign
of His second coming, and the end of the world [Matt.xxiv.3,15.].

"WHEN YE SHALL SEE THE ABOMINATION ...
*STANDING IN THE HOLY PLACE"... (Matt.xxiv.15.);
or, as Mark gives it, "WHEN YE SHALL SEE THE
ABOMINATION OF DESOLATION, SPOKEN OF BY DANIEL
THE PROPHET, STANDING WHERE IT OUGHT
NOT" (Mark xiii.14.). But the key to the date of this
"abomination not having been understood by man;
until it actually transpired and men saw the thing standing, it was impossible to know the epoch to Daniel's
predicted dates. We have not only the testimony of
Jesus to this effect, but the very words from the mouth
of the Angel spoken to Daniel (xii.11.): Jesus, therefore, whilst showing the obscurity of things eventful
of the future, actually revealed the epoch, which is the
key to the whole matter. The most astonishing thing
is this, that every one seems to have shut their eyes
to the epoch, in place of looking out for it !—Did not
Jesus in Spirit, leave the Holy Realms in order to
bring The Father's message, and carry out His will?
and yet to this message, which He seems to have attached the highest importance, no one, all these ages,
as so much as gleamed its essential truth. But their !
the reasons are as I have stated them in the begining.

The abomination is made plainer by its being
localized : the words of Matthew being—"STANDING
IN THE HOLY PLACE," while that of Mark, shows the
"abomination" as being that of something "STANDING
WHERE IT OUGHT NOT;" now, if we put these two

*Revised Version.

together, and form one paragraph, it will give us the
true message, and will read as follows :-

"THE ABOMINATION STANDING IN THE
HOLY PLACE, WHERE IT OUGHT NOT."

Now what is this "abomination" that is "standing
where it ought not ?"—

In all ages, Jerusalem has been acknowledged the
holy City : and the holiest of places, was that one spot
upon which stood Solomon's Temple, and where God
honoured the earth with His continual presence, as
was his wont, at the mercy-seat (Exod.xxv.17—22.).
This temple having been built upon an ever-sacred
piece of ground, the holy place I need hardly say, is
Jerusalem, while the spot, where the "abomination"
ought not to have stood, is this sacred piece of land.
This, until Christ came, was the dwelling-place of
God (i Kings ix.1—9.), but which had been completely
swept away; and now, to complete that desolating
event, the caliph Omar, having conquered Jerusalem,
in the latter part of 637 A.D. built a mosque (mohammedan temple) upon the very same sacred-site as that
on which God's Temple once stood.

While Rome held Jerusalem, although colonized
by Christians, there was a possibility of the Jews rebuilding their temple : but now that the mosque stood
upon this sacred site, no chance whatever exists for
the Jews to re-occupy this land; desolation is therefore fixed, and the antichrist party become masters of
the situation until the time appointed.   Scripturally

speaking, by the word "abomination," is signified idolatry (i Kings xi. 5,7.): —" Solomon went after . . . milcom (idol) the ABOMINATION of the Ammonites; then did Solomon build an high place for chemosh, the ABOMINATION of Moab, in the Hill that is before Jerusalem ; and for molich, the (idol) ABOMINATION of the children of Ammon"— therefore, what greater offence could be offered to God, than the idolatrous act of building a temple upon His piece of sacred ground, for the purpose of honouring, and worshipping, an imposter who strove with all his might to exalt himself above Christ Jesus : yea, so much so, that he cast down the true Messiah, in the assumption that he himself was the Messiah ? Nothing can be of greater abomination to God, than the erection of an edifice wherein men lift up their hearts unto a mear man whose bones have crumbled into dust and lie with the earthy, creating an ever growing stumblingblock to the community for whom Christ shed His precious Blood, in redemption. It was an abomination in the truest sense ! and sealed the desolation of the Jewish people. And still it stands there !—This hallowed spot which God had chosen to place His seal, and to plant His standard of identity as the Monarch of the earth, is still occupied and defiled by this building, the unholy sound of which, echos through the realms of heaven, and cries, as with a loud voice, ABOMINATION! Desolate indeed, is the aspect of Jerusalem !

In A.D. 637, then, all was made clear ; the fingerpost of Christ's erecting, has justified itself: for the given-date epoch is a reality, and was the acceptable truth unto revelation. The secret epoch-seal having been thus broken, it has been standing open to man's perception and gaze to enable him, by the aid of Daniel's given periods, to ascertain the exact time of the "WOUNDING" OF THE "BEAST" (Revl. xiii.3.); THE ANTICHRIST REIGN —"SON OF PERDITION "(ii Thess.ii.3—9.); THE GLORIOUS TWO ADVENTS OF THE LORD :-

1. To overthrow the antichrist (ii Thess.i.7—9; Revl.xix.11—21),and to bring in the Millennial Age, as a righteous dispensation.

2. To judge mankind, and to take the righteous home (Revl.xx.11—15 ; i Thess.iv.14—17.).

All we have to do, in order to become acquainted with the dates of these events, is to bring Daniel's year-day periods (Danl.xii.11,12.), and place them against the epoch thus :-

The epoch, 637 A.D.   Daniel's periods, 1290, 1335.

Date of the "death-wound" overthrow of Turkey, equals :- 637 A.D., added 1290,----------------A.D. 1927.

Date of destruction of the "ten-horned-beast" king and mohammedan power, by Christ; and the setting up of the Millennium :- to 1927 A.D., add 1335---A.D. 3262. This will be the second Advent ; but more of this anon.

His "handy-work," for "He sleeps not," is kept to the mill !
Maidens gambol ! but penitence, strikes the line-marked face :
"Golden bowls break, silver cords loose," all must fulfil !
For the EPOCH now moves predict-periods apace !   A.M.

Having arrived at the end of the two by-paths, we now glide into the main course of future events ; and in doing so, we absolutely keep in the thread, and truth of Scripture. We have a few more verses of the eleventh chapter of Daniel to follow, which are the predictions of events which will take place subsequent to our present time :-

Daniel xi. 36. "AND THE KING SHALL DO ACCORDing to his will ; AND HE SHALL EXALT HIMSELF, AND MAGNIFY HIMSELF ABOVE EVERY GOD, AND SHALL SPEAK MARVELLOUS THINGS AGAINST THE GOD OF GODS, AND SHALL PROSPER TILL THE INDIGNATION BE ACCOMPLISHED : FOR THAT THAT IS DETERMINED SHALL BE DONE."

This passage of Scripture is, undoubtedly, speaking of Mohammed,—predicting his exalted audacity : for mark the analogy between the above quotation, and that passage quoted below, which, without a doubt, is speaking of the "little horn,"—Mohammed ; and therefore, by the analogy, we are justified in concluding that the above passage is speaking of him also :-

Daniel viii. 10, 11 : " AND IT WAXED GREAT EVEN TO THE HOST OF HEAVEN . . . HE MAGNIFIED HIMSELF EVEN TO THE PRINCE OF THE HOST. . ."(Jesus Christ).

Now, if the reader will go to the trouble of reading the koran, or mohammedan book of faith, he will see that the mind of Mohammed was so lifted up in self-exaltation, as to warrant the above quoted predictions; especially, when it is seen how he trampled upon the name of Jesus, and put himself forth as the Messiah, and thus magnified himself above the Prince and God.

Daniel xi. 37—39. "NEITHER SHALL HE REGARD THE GOD OF HIS FATHERS, nOR THE DESIRE OF WOMEN, NOR REGARD ANY GOD: FOR HE SHALL MAGNIFY HIMSELF ABOVE ALL. BUT IN HIS ESTATE SHALL HE HONOUR THE GOD OF FORCES (or fortresses): AND A GOD WHOM HIS FATHERS KNEW NOT SHALL HE HONOUR WITH GOLD, AND SILVER, AND WITH PRECIOUS STONES, AND PLEASANT THINGS. THUS SHALL HE DO IN THE MOST STRONG HOLDS WITH A STRANGE GOD, WHOM HE SHALL ACKNOWLEDGE AND INCREASE WITH GLORY: AND HE SHALL CAUSE THEM TO RULE OVER MANY, AND SHALL DIVIDE THE LAND FOR GAIN."

These additional self-raised features of earthly glory, are attributable to the success of growth and power of mohammedism; and is Scripturally counted to be the acts of Mohammed, although for ages, have been continued by his Caliphs: the interpretation is, therefore,—1. Mohammed having sprung from the Arab race who are Ishmaelites, and who, in the time of Abraham worshipped the true God, "THE GOD OF HIS FATHERS," it was seen, would be disregarded by these "abomination" worshippers. 2. As every mohammedan believes in his sword as being part of his religion, it was foreseen that he would honour and worship this weapon, as "THE GOD OF FORCES;" for if a mohammedan die in battle, he is led by the koran to believe, in the certainty of his going to paradise.

3. The mohammedan is so enamoured with the mosque which stands "IN HIS ESTATE," that in his infatuation, he will honour it with gifts to the extent of often depriving himself;—so sacred does he hold this idolatrous building of marble walls, gilded ceiling, and handsom columns, that it is death to any Christian to pass its threshold. This mosque, then, is the predicted "STRANGE GOD IN THE MOST STRONG HOLDS," which is Jerusalem. 4. "HE SHALL DIVIDE THE LAND FOR GAIN;"—The mohammedan caliphs, the present one being the Sultan of Turkey, have ever divided, and taxed, the land in every conceivable manner, since their coming into power; even at the present period, it behoves every pacha of a pachalik of Palestine, to remit to their Constantinople master a good money supply, which is obtained from this source, otherwise they soon find themselves withdrawn from office, and others, who are more wily in draining wealth from the land, appointed. Even the Jews are forced to pay heavily for the privilege of burying their dead in an allotted piece of land, which, alone, fulfils the prediction of "DIVIDING THE LAND FOR GAIN;" yet this is but a drop of water from the troubled sea!

CHAPTER II.

The germ of the slimy ophidia,
Assum'd the biped-shape ;
And grew, till he reach'd the pinnacle of blood !
But alas ! 'twas the blood of an assassin.   A.M.

Turkey is to fall ! The *"deadly wound"* to the mohammedan nation whose Sultan is the caliph of Mohammed, is sealed !

Who is to deal the *sword thrust* against this long tolerated blood-thirsty kingdom ?

Russia !

And in *1927—8 A.D., it is ordained, this overthrow shall take place.

Most people who have a fair knowledge of Script-ure, are agreed in the matter of the events which are recorded in the old Testament, being typical of those recorded in the new, and especially those of the Apoc-alypse, which, contain the whole cymbolically-hidden future.   This being so, and it having been shown me

---

*It has been shown me that the actual overthrow of Turkey will not be accomplished until 1928 A.D., although Daniel's predicted 1290 years, added to the epoch 637, makes only 1927 : I conclude, therefore, that the building of the mosque [the epoch] did not take place till the end of 637 A.D., and as war between nations is not settled in a day, the year 1928, must, necessarily, be broken into.

that the first Advent of Christ was the center of time, I perceive, apart from the two great events which the given periods of Daniel enables us to portray, that we may ascertain, approximately, the dates of the smaller future-events, by simply studying the old Testament with the light of the Spirit, and finding therein as the typical part of God's word, the prefigured events that are laid down in the new Testament to take place subsequent to Christ's death. We could not do this, however, if it were not for the Apocalypse, and Daniel's compass, to steer the future-event craft. On this principle, the Apocalypse is made to supply us with a threaded narrative of futurity ; but, as the old Testament chronology is wrongly numbered, it is essential that we should produce a Scripturally-true chronological account, so as to arrive at the true date of the world at the time of the birth of Jesus, and thus gain the knowledge of the CENTER OF THE TIME of this world's existence from Adam down to the judgment seat. Also the true dates of the typical events, to guide us in the framing of the Apocalypse futurity ; the decision in finding the events themselves, must be the work of Spiritual discernment : for instance, the first Advent of Christ, as the center of time, together with the second and third Advents, require Scripturally-recorded type.—Noah is the type of Jesus in the aspect of the first Advent ; the analogy being bound up in the inspired message which was sent forth to the people at the birth of Noah, and which said,

"*this same shall comfort us concerning our work and toil
of our hands . . .*"(Gen.v.29.); which meant, the child
Noah, upon growing to manhood, would open a way
of escape (the ark) from physical destruction (the flood);
but as none of the people would pay any attention to
what he said to them during the ark's construction,
whereby they virtually refused the means supplied to
them for the redemption of their natural lives, so, on
the same principle, does Jesus open a way of escape
from SPIRITUAL destruction, and his message has also
gone forth unto mankind that He is the way of escape from the *flood* of fire. Jesus, then, is the prefigured Person, and His first Advent is the fulfilment
of this type ; mark how similar is the language in connection with both of these births :-

"AND HE CALLED HIS NAME NOAH" (Gen.v.29.).

"AND HE CALLED HIS NAME JESUS" (Matt.i.25.).

King David is the type of Christ, under the second
Advent aspect ; but we speak of him when dealing with
this subject later on.

Adam, is the personal type of Jesus, as well as that
of the third-Advent aspect : Adam prefigures Jesus in
his own likeness, he having been made after His
(structural God) image—see Gen.i.26. ; i Cor.xv.45-47.
Adam instituted a millennial curse (Gen.iii.17;viii.21.),
he is also the parent of this earth's structural race.
Jesus is to institute a millennium of blessing (Revl.xx.
1—3.), and is the Parent of heaven's future structural
race, who will be produced at the third Advent.

A TRUE CHRONOLOGY OF SCRIPTURE :-

	Years	Months	Days
From Adam, to birth of Noah (Gen.v.29),	1056	.	.
From Noah's birth, to the close of the flood (Gen.viii.13,14.),————————	600	1	27
From the end of the flood, to the birth of Abraham (Gen.xi.10—26.),————————	292		
From the birth of Abraham, to the birth of Isaac (Gen.xxi.5.), ————————	100		
From the birth of Isaac, to the birth of Jacob (Gen.xxv.26.), ————————	60		
From the birth of Jacob, to the time when he and his offspring (70 souls, Gen. xlvi.27.) settled in Egypt (Gen.xlvii.9.), —	130		
From the date of the Israelites settling in Egypt, to the date of Exody (Exod.xii.40,41),	430		

From the date of the Exody, to the DIVIDING of the LAND—the reaching of Mount Sinai, 3 months (Exod.xix.1) ; further events, 10 months (Num.i.1.) ; DO, DO, 19 days (Num.x.11.); DO, DO, 3 days (Num.x.33); flesh supplied for ONE MONTH (Nnm.xi.20-23) during which period the Israelites marched to Hazeroth and Paran (Num.xi.35 ; xii.16.); DO, DO, 40 days (Num.xiii.25.) ; DO, DO, 40 years, by sentence, in the Wilderness from this date (Num.xiv.33. ; Joshua v.6.) ; land dividing &c., *5 years (Joshua xiv.10.),——

	Years	Months	Days
	46	4	2
Carried forward	2714	5	29

---

*The difference between 40, and 45, years spent in the Wilderness.

Brought forward 2714 5 29

From the dividing of the land date, to
the end of the Judgeship rule, which includes
Samuel (Joshua xiv. ; Acts xiii. 20.),——— 450

King Saul's 40 years reign (Acts xiii.21.);
David 40 years (i Kings ii.11.); Solomon 40
years (i Kings xi.42.); Rehoboam 17 years
(ii Chron.xii.13.); Abijah 3 years (ii Chron.
xiii.1,2.); Asa 41 years (i Kings xv.9,10.);
Jehoshaphat 25 years (i Kings xxii.42); Jeho-
ram 8 years (ii Chron.xxi.5.); Ahaziah 1 year
(ii Chron.xxii.2.); Athaliah 6 years (ii Kings
xi.3,16); Jehoash, or Joash, 40 years (ii Kings
xii. 1. ; ii Chron. xxiv. 1.); Amaziah, or
Uzziah, 29 years (ii Kings xiv.1,2.); Azariah
52 years (ii Kings xv.1,2.); Jothan 16 years
(ii Kings xv.32,33.); Ahaz 16 years (ii Kings
xvi.1,2.); Hezekiah 29 years (ii Kings xviii.
1,2.); Manasseh 55 years (ii Kings xxi.1.);
Amon 2 years (ii Kings xxi.19.); Josiah 31
years (ii Kings xxii.1.); Jehoahaz, or Joahaz,
3 months (ii Kings xxiii.31.); Jehoiakim 4
years (Jere.xxv.1,11 ; †Danl.i.1.)——— 495 3 0

From the begining of the 70 years captivity (Jere. xxv. 11,12.) which ended during
the first year's reign of Cyrus (ii Chron.
xxxvi.21.23 ; Ezra i,ii.) who released whosoever desired to go back to Jerusalem,
the Temple-rebuilding having been ordered, 70

Carried forward 3729 8 29

---

†Although the invasion was made at the latter part of the third year
of Jehoiakim's reign, Nebuchadnezzar did not prevail unto the captivity,
until the fourth year of this king upon the throne of Jerusalem.

Carried forward   3729 8 29

From (Cyrus' first year) the end of the
70 years captivity, to the time of king Artaxerxes Longimanus' command to rebuild
Jerusalem (Nehem.i,ii.), in his twentieth year
(Nehem.i.1. ; Danl.ix.25.) — Cyrus, 7 years ;
Ahasuerus and Artaxerxes (Ezra iv.6,7.), 7
years ; Darius (Ezra vi.1.), 36 years ; Xerxes
12 years (see Rollins ancient history) ; Artaxerxes Longimanus 20 years—————   82

Daniel's 69 weeks of year-days (483 years)
which commenced at the twentieth year of
Artaxerxes' reign (446 B.C., Nehem.i.1.), to
THE BIRTH OF JESUS CHRIST, which took
place four years before the common account
called Anno Domini ;—483 minus 37, the
age of Jesus at death, leaves 446 years———   446

The total length of time of the whole
period Before Christ, as the typical part,— 4257 8 29

The period of four years, which was between the date of Christ's birth, and the
Anno Domini epoch—————————   4

Total date of the World, down to the
time of the Anno Domini epoch————4261 8 29

TOTAL, IN ROUND NUMBERS— 4262 years.

[See page 240 for the remainder of this Chronology,
which deals with the Christian-era part, and which
gives the dates of the future great events of this
world's creation, down to the taking place of the
"lake of fire"].

By this CHRONOLOGICAL TRUTH, together with the
epoch for Daniel's periods, we have a wise, yet obscurely set forth plan ; this, enables the Apocalyptic-written-
events to be portrayed in their proper order, and thus
form one complete, and comprehensible narrative of
future-historic events, down to the end of time.   Well
then, the typical period of this world's time having
occupied 4258 years, to which we must add four years,
(the period which elapsed between the date of Christ's
birth, and the Anno Domini epoch, it not having been
accounted for, or included in the annals of, either the
B.C., or the A.D., periods of time) making the total 4262
years, the other half, or Christian-era of time, must
also be 4262 years.   And by Christ's second Advent,
preceding this 4262 A.D. date a thousand years(the millennium), the date of OUR LORD'S COMING will be 3262
A.D.   Now, behold the exactness of prophecy :-

Daniel's 1290, and 1335, year-day periods, added
to the epoch date, A.D. 637, brings us exactly to the
same date, viz, 3262 A.D.   These are not statements
of an ordinary character, neither are they calculations
based upon feasibility, but rather, are Scripturally laid
down truths, and gives us a complete data.   I now proceed along the path which leads to the END OF TIME :-

THE FIRST "SEAL"(Revl.vi).—Jesus said,"*It is
expedient for you that I go away : for if I go not away,
the Comforter (holy Spirit, John xiv.26.) will not come
unto you ; but if I depart, I will send Him unto you*"
(*John xvi.7.*).   Now, the first "seal-opening," which

produces the figurative "WHITE HORSE," is the fulfilment of the above promise; the white, denoting purity, and the horse, signifying power. Thus, the pure and powerful Spirit, descends to whosoever will truly accept Jesus during the Christian era, becomes indwelling, overrules Satan who is within until this time, and thus destroys the evil power that is over the individual's will.—*"The Son of God was manifested, that He might destroy the works of the devil"(i John iii.8.).*

THE "SECOND SEAL" (Revl.vi). This "seal," also portrayed in symbol, but as a "RED HORSE," signifies, national wars throughout the Christian-era period; in wisdom it has been thus ordained, the purpose being, that of conquest unto civilization and better rule.—England has taken a leading part in this direction, and has carried out the will of God in establishing a procedure of justice on these occasions, which is the object of the "third seal."

THE "THIRD SEAL" (Revl.vi) is that of a symbolic "BLACK HORSE," and has for its purpose, the setting up of a system of true justice on the part of the conqueror in matters of national war, so that, with other things, the local interests of the vanquished may not be crippled.—The symbol demands justice. These three seal-events have no set date of accomplishment, but are continuous, being fulfilled in every act of the above specified character.

THE "FOURTH SEAL" (Revl.vi). This event, which is symbolized by a "PALE HORSE," and which denotes plague, famine, and death, has been shown me, was fulfilled in the ARMENIAN MASSACRES of this period; famine and plague among the mohammedans of India in retribution to the race of which the perpetrators belonged, having been predicted under this seal to be the forerunner of the overthrow of the guilty nation, whose caliph-monarch had bathed the land with the blood of Armenian Christians. [It is very difficult as yet, to obtain the correct number of those who have died during the Indian famine and plague, which took place at the end of the Armenian massacres, and which, a very significant fact, touched scarcely any of the European population, whilst the mohammedan people were dying of this scourge at the rate of near 2000 a week ; but the following statements, which were extracted from the Times Newspaper, will somewhat show the magnitude of the visitation :-

"*At no one moment before has a combination of misfortunes befallen India since it passed under British rule. The evil against which the Litany prays for protection—war, pestilence, and famine—have come upon it ; and an earthquake of terrible magnitude has devastated Assam." A large number of the mohammedan population has succumbed to it, but the number of sufferers is not as yet known. Information was given by LORD GEORGE HAMILTON on the eighth of January 1898, that"the distressed subjects would

*The "Times" of December 31st 1897 ; and of January 1898.

cost the Indian Government six millions sterling for
the barest necessaries of life," and that, "the total cost
of the famine in direct relief and loss of revenue, could
not be estimated at less than £10,000,000 ;" this will
give us some idea of the extent of this visitation.   But
more serious than even this, is the "bubonic plague" of
Western India : this terrible epidemic disease, after a
deadly ravage of more than a year, up to January 1898,
is still going on].

"The death rate is now 95·29 per 1000 inhabitants ;" this is near a tenth part of the millions which
inhabit these parts.   Thus, has judgment come upon
these people whose creed bids them thirst for Christian blood.—"I will repay saith the Lord."

Openions, as to the conduct of the Sultan and his
advisers, have been freely advanced, and the outcome
of thought has expressed itself to the effect, that the
complications with Constantinople might end in the
deposition of Abdul Hamid ; but this cannot take place
at present, because, his "hour is not yet fully come ;"
there are progressive parties who would deal with
him in a similar way as other rulers of Turkey have
been dealt with, were it not otherwise ordained : the
cup of iniquity of this nation must bubble over, and
then, by a severe *hug of the "bear*," will matters change.
This cup, nevertheless, is in no way wanting in its
measure at the present period ! which, it will be seen,
the following statements of the press at the time,
do very ably testify :-

"*Reuter's agency has received the following telegram, signed by a number of Armenians at Constantinople, and dated the 6th instant :- Armenia is at her last gasp. Work of extermination continues. The number of massacred reaches one hundred thousand. Five hundred thousand survivors have taken refuge in forests and mountains. Hunger and cold have begun to make great ravage. In the name of humanity and Christianity save us."

A "Times" *correspondent*, telegraphing from Urumiah on December the 10th, says :- "It is now certain that the Hamidieh Cavalry have DESTROYED TWO HUN-DRED VILLAGES in the province of Van, and 50,000 homeless people are flocking into the city of Van. The Turkish Government is doing nothing to prevent outrages."

Thus, the "fourth seal," which indicates HELLISH proceedings on the part of the Turkish nation towards their Christian subjects, has been "*opened*," and the events thereof fulfilled in the "*sword, hunger*, and *death*," as specified in verse 8 of the 6th of Revelation. And these fulfilled-predictions bring us to the present period of 1895-6. A.D., which is, 1367 years †B.C.S.A.

THE "FIFTH SEAL" (Revl. vi.), which is representing the martyrs of the various dates including those who have suffered death at the hands of the mohammedan people, is calling upon God to avenge

---

*Western Evening Herald, Plymouth, 12th December 1895.
†BEFORE CHRIST'S SECOND ADVENT.

their spilt-blood : the symbol is a similar one to that
which is set forth in Genesis vi. 10., and which speaks
of the blood of Abel crying unto God.   There is to
be an immortal Government of a 144000 well tried
saints ; these will, necessarily, consist of the martyrs
of all ages, but not having arrived at the full predicted
number, cannot yet be raised from their graves ;
and therefore, "IT WAS SAID UNTO THEM THAT THEY
SHOULD REST YET FOR A LITTLE SEASON, UNTIL
THEIR FELLOW-SERVANTS ALSO AND THEIR BRETH-
REN, THAT SHOULD BE KILLED AS THEY WERE,
SHOULD BE FULFILLED" (Revl. vi. 11.).   It is at these
times, when the mohammedan unsheathes his knife,
that the spirits of these dead-in-Christ martyrs, are
crying unto God : and the answer which was given to
them shows us, that there are more deeds of blood to
follow ; but a full retribution is to come upon these
mohammedan fiends who delight in such diabolical
acts ; in the meantime, Russia is intrusted with the
victors-arm to curtail them by at least one nation, and
thus curb their ferociousness when they go forth in
His name, to :-

> Sweep the gory land, of its fire-brand;
> And thus, cleanse its wretched state !
> To give Armenia life, abolish Jewish strife,
> In nineteen twenty eight.   A.M.

A national overthrow !   This will mean death to
THE SIXTH HEAD OF THE "BEAST."— Scripturally
speaking, the "beast's" SEVEN HEADS (Revl. xiii. 1.)

consists of SEVEN CALIPHS, or seven successive mohammedan rulers, who, it has been ordained, shall be
permitted to rule over Israel's possessions, which contain THE SEVEN SACRED MOUNTAINS (Revl.
xvii.9.),—seven mohammedan caliph-emperors were
to come into existence CONSECUTIVELY, annex Palestine, and each of them in their turn, rule over this land
for a period. The following are the names of these
seven sacred mountains :-

1. LEBANON.—It is well known that Lebanon
is a great Scriptural mountain, being famous for its
cedars, and other incidents of note.

2. CARMEL.—Mount Carmel was a great resort
of Elijah's: he seems to have been able to closely com-
mune with God when at this place, which, in many
ways, is a great Scriptural mountain ; but, for some,
probably - figurative, purpose, it was blighted at the
top (Amos i. 2 ; Isa. xxxiii. 9.).

3. TABOR.—Mount Tabor was a sort of counsel
plateau at the place where, it is believe by the ruins
which now stand there of three sacred bnildings,
Jesus met in counsel with Moses and Elijah, and
where, at the time of the Transfiguration, Peter said,
" Let us make three tabernacles, one for Thee, and
one for Moses, and one for Elijah " (Luke ix. 33,).

4. QUARANTANIA, or, by its Scriptural name,
Rock of Rimmon (Judges xx. 47.).—This mountain is
understood to be the place of Our Lord's temptation,
and where He spent most of the forty days of fasting.

5. MOUNT OF BEATITUDES.—It was here, upon this mountain, that Jesus delivered His great Sermon, which will be found written in Matthew, v., this being one of the Scriptural-seven mountains of God.

6. MOUNT CALVARY, which is part of mount Moriah.—This place being the scene of Our Saviour's Crucifixion, is the most sacred of all the mountains.

7. MOUNT OLIVET.—This mountain seems to be the point of connection between heaven and earth ; it was from here that Christ Jesus ascended to heaven, and, according to the statment of two angels, it will be upon this mountain that Christ will again descend at His next Advent (Acts i.11.), for the angel's words, "*come in like manner*," must have reference to the place, as well as to His personl appearance.

These are the seven mountains of Palestine which were ordained to be given into the hands of the mohammedan "beast," until it shall have passed through the rulership of seven different mohammedan caliph-sovereign dynasties, figured in Scripture as "SEVEN HEADS" of a "BEAST."

Now, SIX of these caliph-sovereign heads-of-the-beast have already transpired, the sixth one completing his term of office in A.D. 1928 ; the SEVENTH HEAD, will not be in a position to have dominion for some centuries yet to come; but we deal with him further on. The following are these six mohammedan dynasties, five of which have past away, and Turkey is the sixth:-

1. THE ARABIAN SARACENS, under the first

beast-head caliph Omar, who, in the name of Mohammed, invaded the land of the seven sacred mountains,
and became its ruler for more than 400 years; but,
owing to the division of the empire into petty sov-
ereignties, it became subverted, and :-

1. THE SELJUKIAN TURKS from Tartary,
who gradually conquered Palestine and took dominion
over the "seven mountains," constituted the SECOND
of the "SEVEN HEADS" of the "BEAST."

3. THE EGYPTIAN SARACENS were next;
they, by taking advantage of the Turkish disunion,
expelled the Turks from Judæa, and then became
the THIRD-HEAD-OF-THE-BEAST ruler of the "seven
mountains" of Palestine; they were, however, themselves conquered by the Christian Crusaders.

4. SLADIN, the victorious Sultan of Egypt, then,
as the FOURTH CALIPH-HEAD of the mohammedan
"beast," wrested the country from the Christians
who had held it for abont ninety years, and became
dominant of the land of the seven sacred mountains
themselves.   Then :-

5. THE MAMELUKES, about 1250 A.D., took
possession of Palestine, and fulfilled the position of
the FIFTH-HEAD of the "BEAST," and held dominion
over it for about two centuries and a half, until 1517
A.D., when the :-

6. OTTOMAN TURKS became possessed of the
"seven mountains" of this land, and they remain at
the present day its ruler; Abdule Hamid, the SIXTH

HEAD of the mohammedan " beast," is therefore, quite unknowingly, fulfilling that part of Scripture which predictively states, "THERE ARE SEVEN KINGS; FIVE ARE FALLEN, AND ONE is (Turkey), AND THE OTHER IS NOT YET COME "(Revl.xvii.10.). By a side light, which was put forth by an angel to St. John, we perceive that Turkey, the sixth beast-head, is that stage of mohammedism in which it was seen to contain a full cup of iniquity, and therefore, ripe for a figurative wound, or overthrow;—when the angel invited John to " come hither "(Revl.xvii.1—3.)and see the capital city of a great mohammedan empire, he was laying before the minds of the future readers of the 17th chapter of Revelation the fact of his taking John, not to a city then in existence, but rather, to a city belonging to a race of evil fanatics which it was fore-seen would spring up at a future period,—showing the world, through John, the dominion of the moham-' medan " beast." It is the whole of the mohammedan rule over Palestine throughout time, that constitutes the " seven heads:" and the cup of iniquity is to flow over at the time of the existence of the seventh one, which, being the last scene in the mohammedan drama, the whole of the iniquity of these "seven heads" is to be centred and accredited thereto, and classed, Scripturally, the " abomination of the earth " (Revl. xvii.4,5.); this, however, is yet of the distant future, and is here set forth in due course. It is with the sixth " head,"or Turkey, that we are now dealing, in order to point out that Russia is ordained to invade and overthrow, and perform such acts, as will become the golden history of the age.

In 1927-8, then, being the date of fulfilment, the doors of Russian right-of-way will open, and she will marshal her arms and go forth to vanquish the no longer tolerable misrule of a blood-besotted nation, and thus climb to the summit of national pre-eminence: she will then have dominancy over the Palestine province of the present Turkish possessions; and there will be other arrangements, which the overthrow of a nation must necessarily entail, the details of which will rest largely upon circumstances at that date. The deposition of the sixth caliph-head "beast," together with a general crippling of the nation, is sure: it has been symbolically spoken by the foreknowledge of God to Daniel, whereby he was enabled to prophesy these things, and it has been told to me that this event will come to pass. Ye Armenians, deliverance is nigh! The Ottoman Empire is doomed!

Daniel vii.5. "AND BEHOLD ANOTHER BEAST, A SECOND LIKE TO A BEAR (Russian emblem) AND IT RAISED UP ITSELF ON ONE SIDE, AND IT HAD THREE RIBS IN THE MOUTH OF IT BETWEEN THE TEETH OF IT: AND THEY SAID THUS UNTO IT, ARISE, DE-VOUR MUCH FELSH."

Here we have the symbolically written order for Russia to rise unto national pre-eminence: the first exalting movement being that of "RAISING UP ITSELF

ON ONE *SIDE ;" (see page 15) — By conquering the country in the direction of her side, Russia will be adding a second "rib" (Turkey) to BETWEEN HER TEETH, to that of Poland, the first "rib;" or, in plainer language, having Turkey within her power, and annexing a portion of her territory, including that of Palestine. The rupture, by which this will be brought about, is obvious, seeing that Turkey has already been placed within the grasp of the "bear," by the war-indemnity of the treaty of Berlin, and which, Turkey will never be able to pay : together with provocation to Russia, by fresh outbreaks of Christian massacring, who, in a geographical point of view, has the right to interfere, when deeds of such a horrible character are transacted ; these, and other things, will open the Dardanell *gates*, wrest from the sixth-head "beast," Palestine and its sacred mountains, and, allot to the Jews for their exclusive right of settlement and free possession, the land of Edom. —This will be the outcome of the part played by Russia, in the predicted events of the near future.

There is no doubt, as to who the task of this event is ordained to fall upon : God has so made use of his foreknowledge, with regard to the *geographical po-sition, and the shape of Russia, as to point her out

---

*By the geographical position of the Russian country, which stretches out from Finland to China and which may be designated her length, Turkey, including Palestine, forms one side, or south boundary, of her, and it is in this direction, the figure of "raising up itself," is pointing.

very clearly in Scriptural predictions :- "Thus saith the Lord, behold, A PEOPLE COMETH FROM THE NORTH COUNTRY, and a great nation shall be raised FROM THE SIDES (or, uttermost parts) OF THE EARTH" (Jere.vi.22.) — ". . . Like to a bear, and it raised up itself on one side . . ."(Danl. vii.5) — "Lift up your eyes and BEHOLD THEM THAT COME FROM THE NORTH . . ."(Jere. xiii.20.).

Now, does not Russia in Europe fulfil, above any other country on the face of the globe, the geographical position of "north country?"—her very boundary, on the north side, is that of the Arctic ocean : and, positionally compared with Turkey, is north also of that country.   Russia, then, is the ordained country to move southward ; but let not the victor hesitate in the fulfilment of his part with regard to Edom, lest he be "weighed in the balance and found wanting:" but rather, let him afford that portion of land which it is ordained "shall escape out of his hand," even *EDOM : . . . "I WILL SAY TO THE NORTH, GIVE UP . . ."(Isa. xliii.6.)—the Jews, that they may settle in Edom ; for, "Thus saith the Lord : behold, †waters rise up out of the NORTH, and shall be an overflowing flood, and shall overflow the land, and all that is therein ; the

---

*This Edom, or Idumæa, is that of old Testament history, and which lay to the South of Judæa.

†The word WATER, in many instances of Scripture, is figure for people — See Revelation xvii.15.

city, and them that dwell therein : then the (mohammedan) men shall cry, and all the inhabitants of the
land shall *howl "(Jere.xlvii.2).—[Although this passage of Scripture was spoken in the time of the Philistines, it is, like most of the old Testament Scripture,
predictive of the mohammedans, who are prefigured ·
by the Philistines.— By the first verse, (Jere.xlvii.)
Pharaoh, of Egypt, is about to smite the Philistines,
but Egypt, it will be seen, was situated SOUTH of the
Philistine country, whereas, the above quoted prophecy states,—"OUT OF THE NORTH" shall come
the "overflowing flood :" the type, then, is of Egypt,
but the predicted fact, refers to Russia].

According to the prediction, the Russian conquest
will not be a very hard task :—" At the time of the
end (1927 A.D.) shall THE KING OF THE SOUTH (Turkey)
PUSH AT (provoke) HIM : AND THE KING OF THE NORTH
(Russia) SHALL COME AGAINST HIM LIKE A WHIRL-
WIND, with chariots, and with horsemen, and with
many ships ; and he shall enter into the countries,
and shall overflow and pass over. HE SHALL ENTER
ALSO INTO THE GLORIOUS LAND (Judæa), and many
†countries shall be overthrown : but these shall escape
out of his hand (not retained,) even Edom, and Moab,
and the chief of the children of Ammòn. He shall
stretch forth his hand also upon the countries : and

*This does not signify severe rule on the part of Russia, but rather,
on account of the Christian conquest over the mohammedans.
†This word, countries, not being in the original, is misplaced.

the land of Egypt shall not escape.   But *he* (the sovereign of Egypt) shall have power over the treasures
of gold and of silver, and over all the precious things
of Egypt : and the Libyans and the Ethiopians shall
be at his steps.   But tidings out of the east (probably
Japan) and out of the NORTH (Russia) shall trouble
him : therefore he shall go forth with great fury to
destroy, and utterly to make away many.   AND HE
SHALL PLANT THE TABERNACLES (Russian churches)
OF HIS PALACE BETWEEN THE SEAS IN THE GLORIOUS
HOLY MOUNTAIN ; yet he shall come to his end, (like
all other nations, wane and fall) and none shall help
him"(Danl.xi.40—45.).

This is the outline of the future programme of
Russia, who is to rise unto predominancy and remain
pre-eminent for, probably, not less than 500 years; then
will come, like every other great nation since the world
began, the wane and fall.   The internal disturbance
will hasten external matters : and deep down in the
Eastern national eruption, will be discovered the realm
of Corea, hiding from the " bear;" but the third "rib" is
sure, for the prediction must be fulfilled.   The preliminary to these things can be perceived now, and Russian
national glory looming a-head, by the mystic and unseen hand, slowly, but surely, paving the path for the
spirit of prophecy which is moving apace : the alliance
with France ; the permanent establishment of a Russian legation in Abyssinia, which is a narrow-gauge
line reaching to the fulfilment of Daniel xi.43. ; and

the Russo-Chinese treaty (Manchuria right of way), which, by a greater significance than that which is seen upon the surface, may prove a formidable weight in the ally-scale thirty years hence, are instances : and which are diplomatic achievements of no mean order, as a national worth. The sixth head-of-the-beast caliph, then, shall have his misruled possessions wrested from his grasp, and Edom shall be full of rejoicing at the above stated ordained date.

It is now essential for us to take a perception-flight into the innermost part of our spiritual gleam, and there see behind the scene of the chosen people in connection with the ten lost tribes, and we shall discover a wise, and true, working purpose unto the fulfilment of the promise to Abraham, and to Jacob, of these lost-identity Israelites unconsciously playing their part into the hands of the inevitable. In order to create in the reader's mind a smooth course, which will enable their perception to keep free from any impediment to its grasping power, I will ask him, or her, to fully comprehend the following passage of Scripture :-

"AND GOD SAID UNTO HIM (Jacob), I AM GOD ALMIGHTY : BE FRUITFUL AND MULTIPLY ; A NATION AND A COMPANY OF NATIONS SHALL BE OF THEE ..."(Gen.xxxv.11).

Now, one part of this Scriptural-passage we know to have been fulfilled, by the progeny of Judah and Benjamin having become " ONE NATION :" but where are the " COMPANY OF NATIONS," which it was said,

"shall be of thee?"—This I am about to show, by adducing sufficient Scriptural evidence and realized
facts, as will establish the truth of the existing nations
upon earth being, (with the exception of the Chinese
race) or will be before the antichrist period arrives,
composed of ABRAHAMITES, of Arabia and neighbouring districts, the offspring of Hagar; Edomites, the
progeny of Esau; and the Israelites: but mostly of
the last of these three, which consists of the unrecognizable ten tribes, and the recognised Jew of Judah-
Benjamin progeny.   This need not, in the least, be
wondered at: for if it is considered by what hand the
chosen race has been guided, in respect to fruitfulness
of procreation during the march of time, and also,
that they were ordained to populate the wide world
in the form of many nations, it will be understood
that, as nothing is impossible of Him who has said,
"*My word shall not return unto me void,*" the ten lost
tribes of Israel in sure progress, has been producing
the present, so called Gentile races.

For ages past, the subject of the ten lost tribes has
been in men's mind, but while they have read, and
understood the promise of God to Abraham, they
have never given it a thought as to the manner in
which it would be carried out: and thus a blindness
laid hold and shrouded the question.—So blind has
men been in this matter, that the fact has never struck
them, that, the MULTITUDES WHICH THEN COMPRISED
THE TEN LOST TRIBES OF ISRAEL, and who were

scattered throughout the land, losing their identity, must, by the ordinary ratio of propagation, be at this period, at least some millions in number : and therefore, they must be occupying the places of Gentile men upon the face of the earth. Could it be otherwise ?—Could millions of people be living upon earth, and yet hidden away from the rest of the world ? This being not at all likely, let me ask, WHERE ARE THESE MILLIONS OF THE TEN-TRIBE HEBREWS ?—If they were not absorbed as Gentiles, and then, by procreant supersedure became the present population of this world, again I will ask, WHERE ARE THEY ?—When the promise which was given to Abraham that, " THOU SHALT BE A FATHER OF MANY NATIONS "(Gen.xvii. 4,16.), is implicitly believed, then the realization of of this truth will dawn upon men's mind : at present, it is as a dead letter.

When the ten tribes of Israel revolted against Rehoboam, king of Judah, and chosed Jeroboam to be their king (i Kings xi.29—32 ; xii.20—24.), God made them acquainted with the fact, THAT THIS THING WAS DONE OF HIM (i kings xii.24.): this gives us a great light upon the ten-tribe subject, and clears away the mystery attached to the abandonment of the ten-tribe Isralites :- God wished to people the earth with Abraham's seed ; but the people themselves, kicked against the process which He had adopted to make them obedient to his will. This necessitated their being curbed, and taken captive, by other nations ; and

by these destroying agencies, were kept in a state of
minority, a thing which God in no wise desired, seeing
that it prevented their carrying out the conquest of
the world.   These things did not upset God's plans,
but simply called forth another procedure, which,
necessarily, was less advantageous, in a spiritual sense,
to the Israelites themselves.   This plan was shortly
to be put into execution ; in fact, was put into execution at the time when God said, " THIS THING IS FROM
ME," for He had, from that date, " cut off" these ten
tribes from David's inheritance of the chosen race ;
it was only a matter of time, and they would be spread
over the face of the earth as a Gentile community.
The manner in which this was to be brought about, is
this : these ten-tribe Israelites must be scattered among
other nations, lose their identity by becoming absorbed in the Gentile races, and thus, people the earth
as Christians of individual-conversion, like unto the
Christians of a Christian country, or, left in their "gall
of bitterness," they must remain under the power of
Satan and become the "abomination of the earth,"
such as the mohammedans, atheist, and others, who
believe not in the ATONEMENT of Jesus Christ (Hosea
i.9 ; iv.17 ; Revl.xvii.5.).

Now, at the numbering of the people, by order of
king David, it was ascertained that the number of the
ten tribes of Israel were 800 000 valiant men (ii Sam
xxiv.9., of which 70 000 were destroyed by pestilence,
(ii Sam.xxiv.15),leaving 730 000 ; this number however,

must be multiplied fourfold, in order to account for the wives, parents, and children: this will bring the number up to 2 920 000. But, 500 000 of this number, some years afterwards, were slaughtered at a great battle (ii Chron.xiii. 17.) ; this amount we will deduct from our last total, and we shall then have 2 420 000 of a ten-tribe population.

In order to arrive at a true calculation of the number of these ten tribes at the time when they lost their Hebrew identity, we will further reduce this total, in consequence of famine, and invasion, of life-destroying character, having overtaken these people :-

For a three years famine, during Elijah's time, (i kings xviii. 1,2) which we may safely say swept away many, we will deduct *one tenth*, and this will leave us 2 178 000 ; then again, the famine of Elisha's date, which was very grievous (ii kings vi. 24—30.), calls for a further reduction of *one tenth* ; we now have a ten-tribe population of 1 960 200.

In the year 724. B.C., Shalmaneser, king of Assyria, invaded Samaria, the country of the ten-tribe Israelites, and besieged it for three years : now, this would mean death to at least *one fifth* of the population ; if we, therefore, deduct this number from our last total, there will remain 1 568 160. This will be the number that were taken captive by king Shalmaneser, and were scattered throughout the Assyrian empire (ii kings xvii. 1—20.), and thus, losing their Hebrew identity, have not, since that date, been found. It is only reasonable, however, to suppose that at least *five eighths* of this multitude, who were thrown among foreign people of antagonistic countries, would die prematurely in consequence of the hardship and suffering attending this exceptionally trying occasion of national overthrow, and captivity, by a cruel monarch. We have, therefore, the number of 588 060 to work out a resultant progeny for a subsequent period of more than 2 600 years, which has elapsed since their national obliteration and Judaic decease.

In order to get an approximate period, in which a given population will double themselves in number, we will be guided by statistics :-

According to the statistics of 1861—71, England Scotland and wales increased on a ratio of doubling their population in about 79 years; but, as medical and sanitary science were things hardly known at the date of the ten-tribe scattering and subsequent period, but were, on the other hand, in a state of perfection at this statistical date, we may, in order to be within the boundary of the possibility of erring, safely take the treble of this number (237) of years, as the period within which the ten-tribe people went on doubling their number. We have, therefore, 588 060 people at the date of 724.B.C., who multiply to double their number in every 237 years, for a period of 2607 years ; this gives us a propagated result of 1 204 346 880 people of the scattered and lost-identity ten-tribe Israelites, living on the face of the earth to-day.

Now, recent statistics, gives the number of the Judah-Benjamin-tribe Jews, at EIGHT MILLIONS of people.—The Chinese, who are outside of the Abraham progeny, we will take at half of the Buddhists population of five hundred and two millions ; this will leave the Chinese number, at TWO HUNDRED AND FIFTY ONE MILLIONS : if we add together the Jews, and the Chinese numbers—259 000 000, we shall have the population of those, other than the ten-tribe progeny— 1 204 346 880, or Gentile Abrahamites. Now these two numbers, and a comparative-few yet remaining of Abraham's seed other than by Isaac, ought to be equal to the present population of the world, and show, who, and where, the ten tribes of Israel are.

By the Royal Geographical society in January 1891, the population of the world, in 1890, was estimated to be 1 487 600 000 ; our calculations, therefore, show that the ten lost tribes have grown, with the exceptions named, into nearly the present Gentile population of the world :-

Chinese, and Jewish, population,—— 259 000 000
Offspring of the ten lost Tribes,——— 1 204 346 880
Other Gentile population,———— 24 253 120

Population of the world,—— 1 487 600 000

This is conclusive evidence, and is in accordance with the promise of God to Abraham, and to Jacob, that they should be "the fathers of many nations."

But it might be said, "what about the Gentile

races that existed before the Israelites were scattered?"   Naturally, this question arises, and it is only
reasonable to suppose that it is these who have grown
into the present population of the world : but do not
let us forget two things :- THE PROMISE OF GOD TO
ABRAHAM, which could not be broken, and that, "ALL
THINGS ARE POSSIBLE WITH GOD."—When Jacob
kept the flock of Laban, his father-in-law, God wrought
a work whereby He showed to the world the type of
His purpose, with regard to the increase of the children
of Israel, and His checking the growth of the Gentile
people ; He then permitted man to witness His power
over all creature progeny, by His making Jacob's own
flock, which were but few at starting, and which was
figure for the Hebrew race, growing into a number
far above that of Laban's flock, which represented the
Gentile community (see, Gen.xxx.28-32 ; xxxi.7-12.).

The whole thing prefigured the people of the earth
being guided by God with regard to propagation.
Nothing was easier than for God to bring together,
in marriage, the right Jewish couple, in order to produce fruit of the greatest prolificacy ; and to carry out
the opposite principle with regad to the heathen ;
and this is the meaning of the saying, "marriages are
made in heaven."   This being so, the lost tribes of
Israel have been generating with prolific results since
they were scattered, while the original heathen, has
so degenerated by this slow, but sure process, that, in
the course of ages which has elapsed, this part of the

world's population with the exceptions named, have
been brought to extinction. May it not be said, and
admitted, that through the instrumentality of Esther,
the Persians of to-day are the resultant growth of the
Hebrew settlers of that land, but lost to man's iden-
tification? Also, may we not conclude, by the prominent feature which is observed upon the face of the
Roman race, that this is the result of God's secretly-
guiding hand increasing the Jewish people, by causing this once flourishing, and universally-spread nation
to have sprang from a territorially-seeking Hebrew?
Who was Romulus?—He who founded the great city
of Rome, who was he? dare we say he was not an
Israelite?—But I say, by tbe sanction of the Spirit of
God, that he was an Israelite!—and one of God's
secret-hand leading. From whence came, also, the
smelling-organ which the Turks possess?—Is this not
another instance of the fruit of the seed which was
scattered by king Shalmaneser, some of whom, in the
first instance, wandered and increased until we find
them under the name of Tarters, and from whom the
Turks sprang? Even the Greeks, although in existence before Shalmaneser's time, have sprung from the
Israelites!—History tells us, that "Corinth lay in ruins
till it was rebuilt by Julius Cæsar, who sent a colony
thither:" and by the Romans having descended from
Hebrews, this colony would consist of the lost-identity
sons of Israel; and, by their prolific growth, would out-
number the original Greeks, until, in the course of

ages, they would have completely supplanted them, and become the inhabitants of the present cities and villiages of Greece.   In many ways, and under various circumstances, the Israelite progeny has been spread abroad unrecognizable,—The seed of Esau, which produced the black race ; and also, by their intermarrying with white people, the various shades of skin which is met with throughout the globe were produced ; the incidents of propagation which took place between the seventy-year-captive Israelites, and the heathen inhabitants (Ezra x ; Nehemiah xiii.23—28.) ; together with the following intermarriage-event,— *"And the children of Israel dwelt among the Canaanites, Hittites, and Amorites and Perezzites, and Hivites, and Jebusites : and they took their daughters to be their wives . . ." (Judges iii.5,6.)*, are instances of the hidden growth of the Israelites, to supersede the Gentile races.

It is quite plain and easy to see, the way in which God has been carrying out His promise to Abraham : "THIS THING IS FROM ME," said He to the Israelites of Rehoboam's time, who were scattered and became absorbed as Gentiles, and who grew into many of the nations—He intended to wipe out the heathen from the face of the earth.   So that, whilst the ten-tribes have been almost forgotten, and certainly not perceived to have been forming the present nations, the mysterious march of time has been fulfilling God's will.—"THE NUMBER OF THE CHILDREN OF ISRAEL SHALL BE AS THE SAND OF THE SEA . . ." (Hosea i.10).

For the Lord had said," HE WOULD INCREASE ISRAEL
LIKE TO THE STARS OF THE HEAVENS." (i Chron.
xxvii.23.). These people had no power to alter matters : for once the plan of God had been decreed,
it would stand irrevocably sealed ;—He changes not !
Therefore, whilst men have been keeping their minds
indifferent to this subject, the ten-tribe progeny has
brought our very selves into existence ! And must go
on increasing, until they have replenished the earth.
Does not the prophetic Scriptures, which speak of
Israel's destiny, clearly show the ingathering of the
outcast from among the gentiles ?—I do not allude to
the recognisable Jew, which is found in every town
and country ; but rather, to an ingathering of the non-
identified-Israelite into the kingdom of God, by individual conversions of the so called Gentile races, " for
the kingdom of God dwelleth in you." If it is not so,
why was St. Paul, when at Corinth, spoken to in a
vision by one who said, " I HAVE MUCH PEOPLE IN
THIS CITY " (Acts xviii.10.) ? Paul was not sent to
administer to recognisable Jews, but to the Gentiles ;
and to give him a Divine message such as we have
quoted, would not have any meaning, unless it referred to some particular class of men : therefore it is
plain to be seen, the message, " I have much people
in this city," meant the scattered ten-tribe "lost *sheep*
of Israel" who were then as Greeks in this city of
Corinth. The founders of the Russian nation, it is
clear to me, were also of the lost-tribe Israelites :—

when scattered, and they saw that there was no hope
of ever getting back to their own country in conse-
quence o: the Assyrians being in possession of Samaria,
a great number of them freed themselves from the
Assyrian yoke : among other directions, some moved
Northward, re-crossed the Euphrates at the curve of
the river which lies in the direction of Armenia from
Assyria, and, not only laid the foundation of Armenia
(Turcomania), but also, by some wandering still further
North, founded the present great Empire of Russia.
In order to evade apprehension in case of persuit,
or subsequent detection, they would, naturally, clear
away all possible Judaic sign, and, for further safety,
give up their Hebrew custom ; and thus destroy all
national identity.   The Ephraimite tribe, moved in a
Southern direction,—" EPHRAIM... THEY CALL TO
EGYPT... They shall not dwell in the Lord's land;
but EPHRAIM SHALL RETURN TO EGYPT ..."(Hosea
vii. 11—16 ; ix. 3.).   By this event, together with the
fact of the city of Alexandria receiving a large portion
of its population from Jerusalem, during Ptolemy's
dynasty, warrants our conclusion of Egypt having
had the seed-growth permeation of unrecognizable
Israelites, and settles the question of that country being
to-day composed of the progeny of the Ephraim tribe,
and a percentage of · the races of Judah-Benjamin
tribes.   No matter how small the number of the first
settlements were in these cases, The Lord, we may
be sure, has so promoted their prolificacy, as to

supersede in the course of time, the original inhabitants, who would be made to degenerate and die out.   Take the case of Egypt, for instance : the number of ages this nation has been in existence, if things had not been as I have stated, this realm would have been as numerously populated as that of China : whereas, by the checked course, we find it, comparatively speaking, a mere city of a handful of *men.   This principle of secretly populating the world with Abraham's seed, was typically set forth in the act of the Hebrew-serpent which was produced from Aaron's rod, and which swallowed up the heathen-serpents (Exod.vii.9—12.).

Being lost to identity, did not prevent God from seeing the hidden race, although not circumcised : they are still looked upon as the chosen people of Israel (Hosea v.3), and the seed of Abraham (Isa.lxi.9), who, with the exception named, may be counted the father of us all (Rom.iv.16.).   It was on behalf of this hidden-Israelite community that Jesus was speaking, when He said, "Other sheep I have, which are not of this fold : them also I must bring, and they shall hear my voice ; and there shall be one fold, and one Shepherd "(John x.16).—This is being practically carried out by Gospel-spreading unto individual conversion (Acts xi.18 ; xxii.21 ; xviii.11), and we, as the ten lost tribes, are being rescued.

Having plainly set forth both argument and proof,

*By the Census of 1897, Egypt consisted of 9 700 000 population [London Evening Standard June 16th 1897].

to show that the present civilized world are the people
of Hebrew progeny, and particularly those of the ten
. lost tribes of Israel, it being essential for me to do so
in order to show the true meaning of the "beast's"
"TEN HORNS" which will shortly be spoken of, I now
continue the thread of the outline-history of this
world's future.

When the Turks are overthrown, and the land of
Palestine is under the control of Russia, the first stage
of the Jews returning to their own country, by settling
in the land of Edom until the time of the setting-up
of the millennium, will be readily accepted; but they
must be prepared to witness the spirit of prophecy
stiring up the authorities of some of the nations wherein are many Jews dwelling, in order to carry out the
prediction, by causing them to emigrate on the same
principle and measure, as was effected by Russia in
1891, which, by the following quotations from the
press, is verified :-

Western Morning News July 8th 1891. "Special
despatches received here, gives additional particulars
respecting the persecution of the Jews in Russia. In
the Lithuania district, no fewer than 900 Jews had
to emigrate last week, owing to the oppressive conduct
of the local authorities. In the town of Smolensk the
police issued an ultimatum to the effect that all Jews
must either embrace the orthodox Greek faith, or
emigrate at once. The Jews thereupon assembled in
the synagogue, and, after listening to the exhortations

of their leaders, solmnly resolved not to abandon the faith of their fathers. Within two days afterwards, all had sold their houses and left the town."

"Paris, Tuesay Evening. Baron Hirsch, in an interview with Reuter's representative, expressed the belief that the expulsion of Russian Jews would be the means of transporting them to a soil where they would cease to be pariahs and become citizens. The government could not get rid of five millions of Jews without slaughter, unless by the aid of those who took an interest in them."

Jewish Chronicle June 5th 1891. "The misery of the Russian Jews who have lost their houses and their livelihood, and who now arrive daily in innumerable numbers in Berlin, is heartrend- ing. Deprived of all means, they do not know where to direct their weary steps; they want to cross the sea, but they hardly know the place whither they propose wandering. Thus, one set after another of these unfortunate Jews come to Berlin, and Jewish hearts bleed when they see the undeserved misfortune of their poor unhappy ·coreligionists persecuted and exiled only because they are Jews."

Now, we perceive that this expulsion of Jews, was the result of either over-zeal on the part of those who felt the prompting influence of the Spirit in His advisement of the future transfer of these people to their own land, and thereby causing a premature movement, or else it was done in direct disregard to

these promptings, which pointed out the prediction of
this event, to take place at the date we have stated : in
any case, the movement which has now taken place,
has not fulfilled the prediction, and will, therefore, have
to be repeated; but under much more favourable, and
happier, circumstances. The "TIME OF THE END" is
at hand: the 1290 years will have expired at the end of
1927 A.D., when the Tsar of Russia will be able to issue
a decree to the effect of Edom being given to the Jews
as a free settlement, the Jews themselves readily proceeding thither.—"HO, HO, COME FORTH AND
FLEE FROM THE LAND OF THE NORTH,
saith the Lord ..." (Zech. ii. 6.).

Do we require any further evidence in order to
cause the gleam of this truth to settle uppon our perception, and cause us to see the secret influence of
Him upon whose shoulder rests the government, and
fulfilment, of these ordained events ?—"Go and proclaim these words towards the NORTH, and say,
return thou backsliding Israel, saith the Lord (Jere.
iii. 12.).—Behold, the day's come, saith the Lord, that
they shall no more say, the Lord liveth, which brought
up the children of Israel out of the land of Egypt;
but, the Lord liveth, which brought up and which led
the seed of the house of Israel OUT OF THE
NORTH COUNTRY, and they shall dwell in their
own *land " (Jere. xxiii. 7,8.).—This restoration, it is to

---

*Edom, which lies south of Jerusalem, is part of the ordained allot-
ment of land to the children of Israel, and which is Scripturally defined

be understood, is by no means the consummation: but will be the gathering together of the two-tribe Jews, and also, in the guise of Russians, a portion of the ten-lost-tribe Christians who will flock into Palestine on this occasion ; this is to fulfil the many events which are to take place in connection with the antichrist, and the fulfilment of the "feet of the bear" incident (Revl.xiii.2.), herein explained, further on ; together with the purpose of insuring a portion of each of the twelve tribes being at the doors of Jerusalem at the time of Christ's second Advent, that the millennial city "...MAY POSSESS THE REMNANT OF EDOM AND OF ALL THE HEATHEN (portions of each tribe), WHICH ARE CALLED BY MY NAME, SAITH THE LORD" ...(Amos ix.12.). So that, whilst the Jews are to get back to their own country, which, as we have said, extends from the Mediterranean sea to the great river Euphrates, they will not actually inhabit Jerusalem as on former occasions ; that day will, nevertheless, come ! and the great battle on behalf of Judah, and of Israel, in which they are to take part, fought by Christ. But more of this anon !

> Me-thinks I see the calm"still waters,"
> Flowing o'er the Asiatic soil. A.M.

From the time of the fulfilment of these things,

---

as being from sea to sea ; and therefore, embraces the land which is inside the boundary of the Red sea, the Mediterranean sea, and the river Euphrates [see Deut.xi.24 ; Josh.i.4.].

an elapse of, probably, 600 years may be expected. During this period, Russia is to witness the greatest prosperity, and may be expected to rise to the pinnacle of national greatness, and dominant power : until, the wand of pre-eminence being held out to another, she, like all other nations before her, wane, and die.

By this time, viz, the twenty - fifth century, THE "LEOPARD" of "four heads" and "four wings" which, it will be remembered, is the "third beast" of Daniel's prediction, and the prefigurative of a great African empire, will have risen into significance ; and as Russia wanes, will take up a dominant position in the world. She will not have dominion over the "seven mountains" of Palestine, however, because, not being Caliph-governed, will not be one of the mohammedan-beast's heads, and therefore, will not be, strictly speaking, a mohammedan empire ; yet, it must be expected, the greater number of her subjects, will be of that religion.

By the time this Daniel-predicted third nation has grown into a position which may be termed her national pinnacle, another 600 years will have been expended, and she, in her turn, begin to wane : but the downward grade of this nation will be cut short, by an independent and rebllious rise of the kingdom of Egypt (one of the "leopard's heads"—page 23), which, by the increasing power of the   ten-horned-beast king, who, at this time, will come to the throne of Egypt, will usurp this third kingdom, and she herself become the "fourth-beast" nation (Danl.vii.7), and the seventh mohammedan-caliph-head, with a mighty power over the earth ; but only for a short time. But there is a lot more to be said about this, in due course.

THE "SIXTH SEAL" (Revl.vi.). The events of this "seal's" portrayal, may be expected to take place during the latter time of the "third beast's kingdom, or the thirty-first century. Among other occurrences, is an earthquake of a very severe and exceptional nature,—it will not be of the ordinary earth-opening character such as what might be expected from a volcanic explosion ; but rather, is to be a quaking of the earth through a terrible *thunder-bolt, or mighty steam of exploded electricity, which, when striking the earth, is sure to create terror in the hearts of ungodly men. Scripture shows us that it will be defferent to an ordinary earthquake, by the words, which it states, men will express in their terror of this event :—" *The kings of the earth, . . . bondmen, and every free man, hid themselves in the dens and in the rocks of the mountains ; and said to the mountains and rocks, FALL ON US, and hide us from Him that sitteth on the throne : and from the wrath of the Lamb*" (Revl.vi. 15,16.).—Men could not call upon the rocks to hide them, if they were already swallowed up by an ordinary earthquake ! for, alas ! there would be only too many

---

*A thunder-bolt from the near heavens, would cause all things in front of it to be driven against the nearest great planetary body that happened to be in its passage of flight—a Comet for instance, if passing in the path of the exploded stream of electric fluid at the time, would be swept with tremendous force, against any great planetary body.

fallen-rocks upon them! Therefore, by this event
being thus verified, we are justified in expressing the
thunder-bolt theory.—Then this earth, as one of the
great moving bodies of gravitation with attractive influence over each other, by being moved from its pivot
of attraction, would throw out of gear the whole aster-
ism, which would certainly cause two or more of these
bodies to rush together, under the never failing joining-
power of gravity.—"I WILL SHAKE THE HEAVENS,
AND THE EARTH SHALL REMOVE OUT OF HER PLACE,
in the wrath of the Lord of hosts, and in the day of
his fierce anger" (Isa.xiii.13.). And this would cause
the sun's lustre to lessen, and thus be the means of
fulfilling Scripture in darkening this luminary, which
would also give to the moon a reddish hue; for certain
it is, this event will take place immediately after the
quaking of the earth (Joel.ii.10,31; Revl.vi.12.). Full
sway of ungodliness will be the cause of this foreseen
wrath, or figurative "sixth-seal" opening, the principle
feature being debauchery. And this visitation is for
the purpose of giving warning and conviction to the
individual heart, as a final opportunity for anyone to
become converted, previous to the discontinuance for
a time, of the flow of God's Spirit to the earth. The
"seal," in portraying this, speaks of "heaven departing
as a scrowl when it is rolled together;" and thus, men
will be left in their downward grade of excess wickedness. By the spirit's whisperings, the portrayal of the
symbolically-revealed Scripture, prophecy, and type,

I now land on the shores of the "fourth-beast" kingdom : and by the analysis which I derive from these sources, will endeavour to outline this kingdom and its principle events.

THE "SEVENTH SEAL" (Revl.viii.1.). · Subsequent to the wane of the African and third great nation, Egypt, which will have grown into a mighty city by this time, and will have the Mohammed *Caliph.king, will be permitted to come into power in fulfilment of the FOURTH GREAT KINGDOM, which is Scripturally portrayed by the symbol of a "ten horned beast" (Danl.vii.7.). This nation which, hitherto, has only been one of the "four heads" of the "third-beast's" African-empire, by simply proclaiming her independence, and the caliph-monarch, with an easily obtained mohammedan-Military to augment his own army, going forth and overthrowing his hitherto federal master, will be in a position to sign himself Emperor.—This procedure, which brings a subordinate nation into supreme power, will explain why, both the "third," and "fourth," predicted empires, are prefigured under the one and the same emblematic symbol, THE "LEOPARD" (Danl.vii.6 ; Revl.xiii.1,2.).

Having taken hold of the reins of a mighty empire under the jurisdiction of his own city (Egypt) as the Capital, which will have then extended as far north as

*By the "third" kingdom being ruled by the king of Abyssinia, who, therefore, will not be of the mohammedan religion, the Caliphate will have fallen upon Egypt.

Edom, the successive monarchs of this "fourth" nation
will continue in power till three and a half years after
the "ten-horned-beast" king of satanic power has ascended this Egyptian throne; and another, of more
satanic power than him (Revl.xiii.11.), and of whom
we speak presently, is to join him. These two mis-
ruling beings, when in the zenith of their power,
which will last for three and a half years from the
time of the "seventh trumpet-sound," and which is
the last scene of the antichrist drama, will be cut off,
and the dawn of the still morning will hush in the
brighter rule of a Millennial Age.

This "seventh seal" then, which portrays the co-
ercive-rule, and Christian massacring, of a fiend, embraces FOURTEEN EVENTS, their nature being that of
mohammedan retribution. They are classed under
WOES, PLAGUES, and DESTRUCTION: the first seven,
are to be heralded by "seven trumpet-sounds," and
the second seven, by plagues; the last one, or the
fourteenth event, will be the means of opening the
door of the millennium, and is the end of the Gentile
"*time*" (Revl.x.5-7; Luke xxi.24.). Of these fourteen
events, the first four, may be considered as being of
spiritual symbol, they having reference to the disin-
heritance of Satan,—figurative destruction of his third
portion of the universe, supposing him to have once
been a *third person*, but now disinherited and cast down
from heavenly places to the earth. This, the Scriptures verify: for we read of him drawing the third part

of the *stars of heaven : and this signifies that portion
of the heavenly host who, being his followers at the
time of his rebellious movement, fell with him (Revl.
xii.10.). The next three events, viz, the fifth, sixth,
and seventh, are three terrible woes of war and persecution of Christians (Revl.viii.13), the fifth one, having
reference to the Chinese who, it is perceived, will be
allied with the mohammedans, during the "ten-horned
beast's" period of power.—Scripture infers this, by
figuratively portraying a race of people with womens
hair; for we know the Chinese are the only race
of people upon the face of globe, whose malekind
wear their hair long like the women (Revl.ix.7,8.). It
is almost impossible to misunderstand this figure:
moreover, they are represented as coming out of the
bottomless pit (Revl ix.2,3.), the home of Satan or
dragon ; now, the dragon is the Chinese national emblem, and is flown upon their national-standard flag.
Thus, God has used the prefiguration of Satan to bring
to our notice the evil part this idolatrous nation will
play in the world, prior to Christ's second coming.
The "sixth trumpet-sound " is the portrayal of the war
itself, in connection with an immense mohammedan-
Buddha assemblage, in the vicinity of the great river
Euphrates, the camping-ground and battle-field of
Scriptural renown, and which is known by the name
of ARMAGEDDON.—This war is to continue for a

*The word Star is used in many cases of Scripture, to signify Angels.
Christ is called, "the bright and morning Star" [Revl.xxii.16; ix.1.].

period of thirteen months (Revl.ix.15,).—Let us imagine two hundred millions (Revl.ix.16,) of these
mixed fanatics coming into hostile array, against the
Christian "armies of the living God :" it will be like
a tremendous ant-hill-gathering, swarming a few small
flies or a caterpillar family.   The "seventh trumpet-
sound," is, with other events, the termination of this
battle-array, at which Christ is to be a mysterious, and
silent, commander-in-chief, His unlimited power being
displayed in the ethereal-sword of his mouth (Revl.ii.
16.), the bringing in of the righteous age, to follow at
the close of this battle.   All these events, however,
will be more fully dealt with at the time of our giving
the details of the " fourth beast's " kingdom, which will
be brought in as soon as a few arguments have been
adduced, to show that the "ten-horned-beast" does
not refer to the Pope of Rome, which many people
have been led to believe is otherwise :-

Some expositors would have us believe, that it is
the Pope of Rome, who is to be the "ten-horned beast"
and antichrist rule of the future ; but this decision is
erroneous, and does not speak too highly of their spiritual perception : for if a clear insight of Scripture on
the subject is taken, it will plainly be seen that the
power of the Pope, does not coincide with the power
that is attributed to the " ten-horned beast."   We will
prove our statement by the Scriptures :-

1.   It is distinctly set forth that the "little horn,"
(Danl.viii.9.) which I have previouly shown, refers to

Mohammed in the first instances, and then, continuously in his caliphs of whom the "ten-horned beast" will be the seventh, is to sit upon the throne of one of the four resultant-kingdoms of Alexander's empire :- "Four kingdoms shall stand up out of the nation... AND IN THE LATTER TIME OF THEIR KINGDOM... A KING OF FIERCE COUNTENANCE, AND UNDERSTANDING DARK SENTENCES SHALL STAND UP "(Danl. viii. 22, 23): and Egypt is one of these "four kingdoms." Thus it will be seen, that neither Rome, nor the Pope, has anything to do with the matter; but that it rests with either Turkey, Greece, Persia, or Egypt, the four kingdoms in question.—Persia, and Greece, having already held the national sway, can never occupy that position again : and in thirty years time, Turkey will be overthrown; therefore there is but Egypt left to fulfil the prediction. And England, it is visible at the present time, is being mysteriously and wonderfully guided, in planning and marking out for Egypt, a mighty empire. Behold the things that have just taken place !—The English arms had gone to Egypt in 1882, to destroy the *canker-worm ;* and to brush on one side, the lingering remains of the fanatic brigandage of the Arabs : also to sweep away the apathy, superstition, and the long-rusted customs of ancient times, and uncivilization, among the inhabitants of the Soudan. But the time, and circumstances were not quite ripe. On the 26th of January 1885, MAJOR-GENERAL C. G. GORDON, C.B., having been slain at Khartoum, the

spirit of the *lion* was roused, but the ordained hour of
his forward movement was not yet!—God required,
that the work of clearing the area of the future empire
of Egypt at the hands of the English nation, should
be complete: and therefore, it was necessary for all
things to be ready.   Can the word of God return unto
Him void?   Therefore Egypt must become the "ten-
horned-beast's" kingdom, Rome has got nothing at
all to do with it.

2.   The "ten-horned beast" is to "satnd up against
(Christ) the Prince of princes, and destroy the holy
(Christian) people"(Danl.viii.24,25).   Now, the standing up against the Prince, has reference to Christ at
His second coming, when, with the sword of His
mouth (Joel ii.1-11.) to command the death-roll of the
mohammedan army at the battle of Armageddon, mohammedans and "beast," versus the Christians and
Christ, will combat: hence the "beast" standing up
against Him.   We have no reasons to suppose that
the Roman church will be opposed to Christ on this
occasion, any more than they are at the present time:
on the other hand, we do know that the mohammedans are deadly opposed to Christ: and even clamour for the blood of those who honour, and serve in,
His name!   And the enmity, we have grounds for saying, will grow stronger, and stronger, towards the end
of the period to which the prediction refers.   Neither
can we perceive such an event as that of the Pope
"destroying the holy people," which the prediction

states the "ten-horned beast" will do,—he has no kingdom, and therefore, no army : but the mohammedans,
to whom these perpetrations are ascribed, were ever
wont to send their Soldiers to carry out such atrocities
as we have witnessed in Armenia and other places.

3. The antichrist, and "beast's" kingdom, cannot
have reference to the Pope's rule, because, it is predicted (Daniel viii.9.), that the "little-horn" "beast,"
or Mohammed centred in the seventh caliph-head empire, shall wax great in the direction of Judæa, "the
pleasant land," the South, and Eastern parts ; and are
excluded from power in the Western quarter. Now,
these positions the mohammedans fulfil : whereas,
Roman catholicism occupy the western shores, more
than any other part of the globe, and has little or no
footing in the South, Judæa, or in the East. These,
and many other arguments which might be *adduced,
show that, the "ten-horned-beast's" rule, does not
refer to Roman catholicism nor the Pope ; but rather,
to Mohammed's representative, at a previously stated
date of the thirty - third century. Moreover, it has
been shown me that the "ten-horned-beast's" kingdom
will be that of Egypt. [The prophetic Scripture has
been so wisely compiled, that whilst the (spiritually
discerning) righteous shall understand, the ungodly,

---

*As I am writing this work with the assistance of the Holy Spirit,I
trust my readers will not think I am taking sides with Roman catholicism ; I am not of that persuasion. Truth is my aim : and the purpose
of God is to make known the hidden things of the Scripture.

who has nothing but their finite mind to guide them,
cannot understand.—See Danl.xii.10 ; i Cor.ii.12-15.].

Immediately prior to the "seventh trumpet-sound,"
there is to be two great witnesses of truth appear before the mohammedan people of Egypt, to a distance
northward, of mount Calvary (Revl.xi.8.) ; these are
to be the forerunners of the retribution that is about
to take place upon the inhabitants of the "beast's"
Capital City ; exhorting the people to give up their
"worship of devils, and idols of gold, and of silver . . .,
their murders, sorceries, fornication, and thefts," but
this will not bring repentance (Revl.ix.20,21.) : for
both king and people will clamour for the blood of
these men, and they will be killed.   But an earthquake,
which will destroy a large number of the Egptian
buildings and seven thousand men, together with the
fact of these two witnesses coming to life and ascending
to heaven three days afterwards, will have some effect
in bringing the people to repent (Revl.xi.7—13.), yet
not of long duration ; for the gross minds of a people
who have hitherto imbibed Satan, will soon forget the
incident, and, like the Israelites in the case of Elijah's
ascension in the reign of king Jehorams, turn again to
their ungodly ways.   Elijah, and St. John, will be the
two men in question (Mala.iv.5 ; Revl.x.11.) : whether
they will appear in their immortal bodies, or whether
they are to be incarnately re-born, has not been shown
me ; but evident it is, their bodies will be of a destruc-
tible nature, because, they are to undergo death at

at the hands of men. The deduction, therefore, jus- ·
tifies us in the hypothesis of these two men being the
mighty-work of incarnation. Let this not be a stumblingblock to any-one, however; for their is nothing
unscriptural in the matter of two individuals being
born incarnate : may we not count John the Baptist
an incarnate child (Luke i.7—25.)? We do not doubt
the incarnation of our Lord Jesus Christ : therefore,
if God has performed a work in one or more cases,
surely He can be credited with the power of doing so
again, and in the cases in question.

Now let us take a step across the gulf· of time,
counting the "seventh trumpet" as having already
sounded, and come into the immediate presence of
the "ten-horned-beast" who has now ascended the
Egyptian throne (Revl.xiii.1,2.), and follow him along
his Scripturally-portrayed path. First of all, however, let us take a glance at the Egyptian Capital,—
the mohammedan city which Scripture has named,
"BABYLON THE GREAT:-"

Flourishing in all its craft, and wealth, this satanic
realm is permitted to warm the heart of Satan, by
his gloating over the effects of the many allurements
which is set up, at this time, in this city of worldly
magnificence. Numerously spread throughout the various localities, are the domed buildings of blasphemy
and of idolatrous worship, which, looking from an
eminence, gives to the city a nobleness, and grandeur,
far surpassing any other of past ages : and were it

not for the nature of these mosques, the city could
well afford to bost of being an ornament to the earth,
and wonderment to man (Revl.xvii.4,6).   Let us view
the city from yon mountain.—Look at those stately
buildings which are dotted all around, they are the
Theatres.   Behold these grand structures, built of
massive marble blocks, and hundreds of ornamental
pillars bearing up spacious galleries, and vast porticos ;
also the well laid-out gardens ; the interior consists
of magnificently decorated music-halls and saloons,
and private appartments which are furnished in a most
costly manner : these are the palaces of indulgence,
the rendezvous of harlots ; and the whole place per-
vades with sin.   See what magnificent edifices they
build for their baths ! these contain numerous richly-
furnished compartments, each one being fitted with
a bath to suit the lover of luxury, but who care nothing
for those who have not bread to eat : the plunge-bath
of forty yards in length, is provided with every luxury
that the imagination of man can devise.   Come to the
water-fountains which are situate in very nearly every
street-quadrangle, and see their embellishments of
columns and statuary : these fountains, however, will
shortly be turned into blood (Revl.xvi.4).   The streets
of forty yards in width, enables a full view of the fine-
art ingraved stone-work of the dwellings-architecture,
and which seem to blend with the extensively laid-out,
and artistically designed, gardens, lawns and groves,
and open spaces ; the parks we have not seen, they are

however, of grand foliage. Of mankind, they were seen to be none the less fantastical :- decked in purple and scarlet, with gold and precious-stone ornaments to the full extent of the heart's vanity. All these things are Scripturally summed up in the ",GOLDEN CUP OF ABOMINATION AND FILTHINESS OF HER FORNI-CATION" (Revl. xvii.4). So enchanting was this satan-ically-guided city to the sight of St. John, at the time of the angel's prefiguring and showing it to him, that it took him entirely aback, insomuch that he could not refrain from emotion—" AND WHEN I SAW *HER, I WONDERED WITH GREAT ADMIRATION " (Revl. xvii.6).

This Egyptian country, capital of the "ten-horned beast's" mighty empire, is to extend from KHARTOUM to the mountains of LEBANON. The Southern side, has already been marked out, and declared, by the English government, who, in the year 1898 A. D., sent forth British arms to fight, and win, the battles of the Soudan ; and the following extracts, are the statements of the commander of the expedition and others, at a banquet in honour of the conqueror, upon its termination :-

SIR R. COTTON, as the mouthpiece of London, addressing LORD KITCHENER, said :-

"I have first to felicitate you upon the brilliant success so gracefully described by your chroniclers, and by the Commander-in-Chief in the Army Order

---

* " Her," the woman in purple, is figurative for a city of debauched people [Revl. xvii.18.].

in which he conveyed to you the congratulations of her Most Gracious Majesty the Queen upon the conduct of the campaign, which, ending with the action before Khartoum, resulted in the reconquest of the Valley of the Nile. In that order the appearance, bearing, and soldier-like conduct of the British troops under your command is alluded to in deservedly eulogistic terms, and the occasion is taken to refer to the high standard of military efficiency and discipline of the Egyptian troops, not only in the actual fighting, but in the two years of prolonged and most arduous labour in constructing a railroad of 550 miles and doing other pioneer services, without which, the success which has added to the lustre of the British and Egyptian arms could not have been obtained.

I have to greet you, my lord, as the conqueror of Omdurman, the Soudan, and Khartoum."

LORD SALISBURY, the Prime minister of England, also said:-

"The campaign which your gallant guest has won, was a campaign marked by circumstances which have seldom marked a campaign in the history of the world. I suppose such a wonderful combination of all the achievements and descoveries of modern science in support of the infinite gallantry and the well-tried strategy of a British leader, has not been seen in our history before. But the note of this campaign was that the Sirdar not only won the battles which he was set to fight, but he furnished himself with the instruments with which they were wone, or rather I should say, he was the *last and, perhaps by the nature of the circumstances, the most efficient of a list of distinguisned men whose difficult task it has been TO RESCUE THE EGYPTIAN ARMY FROM INEFFICIENCY AND CONTEMPT IN ORDER TO PUT IT UPON THE PINNACLE OF GLORY IT NOW OCCUPIES. . ."

LORD KITCHENER, in reply, said :-

". . . We may say with considerable accuracy that we have spent, two and a half millions as a military special grant.   In this I include the grant that has been recently made for the extension of the railway from the Atbara to Khartoum, the work of which is already in hand. . .   We have, or shall have, 760 miles of railway properly equipped with engines, rolling stock, and a track with bridges in good order. . .   I have freed the vast territories of the Soudan from the most cruel tyranny the world has ever known, AND WE HAVE HOISTED THE EGYPTIAN AND BRITISH FLAGS AT KHARTOUM. . ."

LORD KITCHENER also wrote to the PRESS as follows :-

" Sir,—I trust that it will not be thought that I am trespassing too much upon the goodwill of the British public, or that I am exceeding the duties of a soldier, if I call your attention to an issue of very grave

---

*Sir. Evelyn Wood, Sir. Francis Grenfell, and Sir. H. H. Kitchener, were three British Officers that were sent to Egypt for the purpose of reorganizing the Egyptian army.

importance arising immediately out of the recent campaign in the Soudan. That region now lies in the pathway of our Empire, and a numerous population has become practically dependent upon men of our race. A responsible task is henceforth laid upon us, and those who have conquered are called upon to civilize. In fact, the work interrupted since the death of Gordon must now be resumed.

It is with this conviction that I venture to lay before you a proposal which, if it met with the approval and support of the British public and of the English-speaking race, would prove of inestimable benefit to the Soudan and to Africa. The area of the Soudan comprises a population of upwards of three million persons, of whom it may be said that they are wholly uneducated. The dangers arising from that fact are too obvious, and have been too painfully felt during many years past, for me to dwell upon them. In the course of time, no doubt, an education of some sort, and administered by some hands, will be set on foot. But if Khartoum could be made forthwith the centre of an education supported by British funds and organized from Britain, there would be secured to this country indisputably the first place in Africa as a civilizing Power, and an effect would be created which would be felt for good throughout the central regions of that continent. I accordingly propose that at Khartoum there should be founded and maintained with British money a college bearing the name of the

Gordon Memorial College, to be a pledge that the memory of Gordon is still alive among us, and that his aspirations are at length to be realized.

Certain questions will naturally arise as to whom exactly we should educate, and as to the nature of the education to be given. Our system would need to be gradually built up. We should begin by teaching the sons of the leading men, the heads of villages and the heads of districts. They belong to a race very capable of learning, and ready to learn. The teaching, in its early stages, would be devoted to purely elementary subjects, reading, writing, geography, AND THE ENGLISH *LANGUAGE. Later, and after these preliminary stages had been passed, a more advanced cource would be instituted, including a training in technical subjects, specially adopted to the requirements of those who inhabit the †Valley of the Upper Nile. The principal teachers in the college would be British, and the supervision of the arrangements would be vested in the Governor-General of the Soudan. I need not add that there would be no interference with the religion of the people.

The fund required for the establishment of such a college is £100,000. Of this, £10,000 would be apropriated to the initial outlay, while the remaining £90,000 would be invested, and the revenue thence

---

*The foundation of the "MOUTH OF A LION" which the leopard, [Egypt] it is predicted, will possess.

†Egyptian Suburbs.

derived would go to the maintenance of the college and the support of the staff of teachers. It would be clearly impossible at first to require payment from the pupils, but as the college developed and the standard of its teaching rose it would be fair to demand fees in respect of this higher education, which would thus support itself, and render the college independent of any further call upon the public. It is for the provision of this sum of £100,000 that I now desire to appeal on behalf of a race dependent upon our mercy, in the name of Gordon, and in the cause of that civilization which is the life of the Empire of Britain.

I am authorized to state that her Majesty the Queen has been graciously pleased to become the Patron of the movement. H.R.H. the Prince of wales has graciously consented to become Vice-Patron..."

(Signed) KITCHENER of KHARTOUM.

Now, behold the finger of God in the preliminary of the predicted-fulfilment which states that the mouth of the "ten-horned-beast"(Egypt) will be as the "mouth of a lion" (Revl.xiii.1,2.);—the mouth of Britain, or the English speech. Here we have the English nation, not only deciding and marking-out the Southern boundary of Egypt-proper and the distant-future "beast's" capital, but they are also erecting at Khartoum (south end of the boundary) a College, for the purpose of educating, and TEACHING THE ENGLISH LANGUAGE to, the inhabitants: so that a thousand years hence, the English tongue will be freely, and perhaps wholly, spoken in this land. The following extract from the press, practically verifies this fact:-

CAIRO, Jan.6.

" Lord Cromer yesterday LAID THE FOUNDATION STONE OF THE GORDON COLLEGE AT KHARTOUM. He spoke as follows :-

I feel it a great honour that I am asked by Lord Kitchener to lay the foundation-stone of the Gordon College in the name of the Queen. . ."(of England).

Thus, the prefigured symbol of the " mouth of a lion " was the revelation of God for the purpose of showing the world that, at the time of the " ten-horned beast's " rule, Egypt would speak the English language,—" *And the beast which I saw was like unto a leopard, and his feet were as the *feet of a bear, AND HIS MOUTH AS THE MOUTH OF A LION* . . . (Revl.xiii.2.)—the foundation of which, is now, at our present day, proceeding apace. For "it is the settled policy of the Government of England that the Valley of the Nile is to be Egyptian territory."   These three features of Egypt, viz :" the leopard," " feet of a bear," and " the mouth of a lion," denote the agency of three nationalities :—   Russians, who will have spread themselves over Palestine from the time of the

---

*By the Russian-Jew exody and arrival into Edom, together with other Russians who will settle in Palestine in 1928 A.D., travelling is denoted : for feet is the symbol of travelling ; therefore, Russian emblem being the bear, " the feet of a bear," would mean a number of people travelling from Russia to [Fgypt] the country figured as a " leopard," Palestine eventually becoming annexed to the"leopard"or Egyptian city.

Turkish overthrow together with the Russian-Jews
to the land of Edom, being the "feet of the leopard,"
because these will become the subjects of the "leopard" (Egypt) in the thirty-third century, when Egypt
will have dominion over Palestine ; the English, who,
by establishing their language in the "leopard" land,
produces the "mouth of a lion ;" and the native Egyptians, who are emblematized by the "leopard," this animal being a native of Africa.   These three nationalities, however, are again symbolically set forth, but
under the aspect of "ten horns," which, being interpreted, means the ten-lost-tribes of Israel, as absorbed
in a Gentile community.—But this subject will be
brought on again.

Now let us come, as it were, into the immediate
presence of the "beast," and also portray the anti-
christ:—"I STOOD UPON THE SAND OF THE SEA, AND
SAW A BEAST RISE UP OUT OF THE SEA, HAVING SEVEN
HEADS AND TEN HORNS, AND UPON HIS HORNS, TEN
CROWNS, AND UPON HIS HEADS THE NAME OF BLAS-
PHEMY.   AND THE BEAST WHICH I SAW, WAS LIKE
UNTO A LEOPARD, AND HIS FEET WERE AS THE FEET
OF A BEAR, AND HIS MOUTH AS THE MOUTH OF A
LION : AND THE DRAGON (Satan) GAVE HIM HIS POWER,
AND HIS SEAT, AND GREAT AUTORITY "(Revl.xiii.1,2).
This is the prefigured Sovereign-ruler of Egypt, who
will also be the Caliph of all the mohammedans, at
the future-date of 3,258 A.D.   In him is to be centred
and accredited, the whole of the evil and wickedness

that has been put forth to the world, by the seven heads (which he is portrayed as possessing), or the dynasties which have ruled over the mountains of Palestine.   In fact, he is to be the representative of Mohammed and the combined mischief which the creed of that individual has wrought upon the world, and to the cloging of Christianity.

The name of this Egyptian monarch, it has been shown me, is to be BELTESHAZZAR—"... LET HIM THAT HATH (SPIRITUAL) UNDERSTANDING COUNT THE NUMBER OF THE BEAST : FOR IT IS THE NUMBER OF A MAN; AND HIS NUMBER IS SIX HUNDRED THREE-SCORE AND SIX " (Revl.xiii.18.) :-

Now, the Greek Alphabet has a numerical value : for instance, B, counts 2 ; E, 5 ; L, 30 ; T, 300 ; and so on.   By this arrangement, a number of letters, such as that of a man's name, can be made to set forth a total number, by simply adding up the numer-ical value of each letter.   Now the Scripture states that the number of the name of the " ten-horned-beast," will be 666 (Revl.xiii.18.) : therefore we will give the proof of his name being that of Belteshazzar :-

Name in English :—BELTESHAZZAR
Name in Greek :——Β ε λ τ ε σ η α ζ ζ α ρ
Numerical Value :— 2, 5,30,300,5,200,8,1,7,7,1,100, = 666.

Thus, the name of Belteshazzar numerically spells " six hundred and sixty six."

There is, however, more significance in this name

than what may appear at first, to a casual reader :—
Babylon the lesser, of which Nebuchadnezzar and
Belshazzar were kings, is signified to be the type of
the "ten-horned-beast's" kingdom, by its being Scripturally named "BABYLON THE GREAT :" this being so,
the significant event of coercing the people unto idolatry, and even the putting to death of those who refuse
to worship the graven-image of the "ten-horned
beast," king of GREAT BABYLON which we are told
will be set up (Revl.xiii.11—15.), has surely had its
type portrayed also : for one city could not fulfil the
type of another city, unless it carried with it its principal events.   Let us therefore, take a glance at Nebuchadnezzar's typical kingdom :—Here we see the
national god-idol unto which the Babylonians bowed
down, and that whosoever would not fall down at the
sound of the music and worship it was put to death
(Danl.iii.1—6.), is just what Scripture states, will take
place with regard "to BABYLON THE GREAT !" Moreover, the name of this god-idol being *Belteshazzar
(Danl.iv.8.), the type is complete : for the name of a
type being part of it, the future god-idol which the antichrist will set up, must also have the name of Belteshazzar. Therefore, as these things will be as we have
stated, and the future god-idol of Egyptian-Babylon

---

*Scripture derides this Babylonical god, which was allowed a large
daily supply of food, but which was secretly appropriated by the priest,
by calling him "BEL" [Jere.li.44.].

*Daniel was named Belteshazzar in honour of Nebuchadnezzar's
god-idol [Danl.i.7.].

being a representative of the "ten-horned-beast" caliph-sovereign—for it states, an image will be made to the "beast" (Revl.xiii.14.)—his name must necessarily be that of Belteshazzar also.

This caliph-sovereign, a ruler of Egypt and power of the world, is also represented as having "seven heads" and "ten horns," which, it has been shown, signifies seven mountains of Palestine (Revl.xvii.9.) over which seven mohammedan-dynastic-rulers have had dominion; this figure, however, does not stop at the bare mountain aspect: settlements, or even small kingdoms are to be thereon, and these will form and fulfil the figure of the "ten hornes," except, that there will be three other colonial settlements of Christian religion, the seven being of the mohammedan creed; and it is here that the fulfilment of Daniel vii.24 takes place,—" AND THE TEN HORNS OUT OF THIS KINGDOM ARE TEN KINGS THAT SHALL ARISE : AND ANOTHER (the antichrist) SHALL RISE AFTER THEM ; AND HE SHALL BE DIVERSE FROM THE FIRST (Belteshazzar), AND HE SHALL SUBDUE THREE KINGS "— coerce them into the adoption of the mohammedan religion. By each one of these ten settlements being the progeny of a merged tribe of Israel, who have been secretly guided by the power of God to this end, they represent the "ten lost tribes," and thus give a practical shape to the "beast's ten hornes ;" for they will be under his sovereignty, or, as Scripture has it, "on which the woman sitteth." These may be expected to be the natural growth of that period which will elapse between the Russian exody and the reign of Belteshazzar, king of Egypt; and it will be the policy of this monarch to grant to these settlements at the latter time of his reign their independence on conditions of their remaining stanch allies, a piece of deplomacy calculated to insure their co-operation and zeal, at the time of the great battle of the Lord, his endeavour being to conquer the Christian nations and establish mohmmedism throughout the earth.—"And the ten horns which thou sawest are ten kings, which received no kingdom as yet; but receive power *as kings* one *hour with the beast'" (Revl. xvii. 12, 13.).

The great purpose here gained by portions of each of the merged "ten-tribes" being in Palestine at this time, is that, when Christ has overcome the antichrist along with Belteshazzar and his army, the twelve tribes of Israel will be there ready for the formation of the Millennial city, which is to take place immediately after the battle has been fought. This is the true interpretation of the symbolical "beast" of "seven heads" and "ten horns," and its fulfilment is sure.

Now let us view the antichrist and his career :-

The Jewish people who, having settled and become a city of Edom, will have also become the subjects of Belteshazzar, king of Egypt,—"Rejoice and be glad, O daughter of Edom, that dwelleth in the land of Uz;

---

* "One hour," is figure for shortness of time; therefore this expression means, SHORTLY BEFORE a great event of the "beast's".

the cup (of great Babylon, Revl.xvii.4,5) also shall pass through unto thee : thou shalt be drunken (Revl.xvii.6) and shalt make thyself nacked " (Lamntn.iv.21).—But this will only be for a short time, during which period another man, who is Scripturally called by the names of " beast, false-prophet," (Revl.xiii.11 ; xvi.13 ; xix.20) and others, is to assist Belteshazzar in his reign of darkness ; and is to even exceed him in satanic power and works. This "false-prophet" or ANTICHRIST, is to be the offspring of an Edom Jewess, and will thus come out of the TWO-TRIBE portion of the inhabitants of "BABYLON-THE-GREAT"—"AND I BEHELD ANOTHER BEAST COMING UP OUT OF THE (Jews) °EARTH AND HE HAD TWO HORNS LIKE A LAMB . . ." (Revl.xiii.11.). His "two horns" are attributable, on account of his relationship with the two-tribe Judah-Benjamin Hebrews (i kings xii.21,23.), without which, the Jews cannot count him eligible for their messiah, and which signifies that he is to be permitted to have great power over his two tribal-horn kindred—"for God *did* put in their hearts to fulfil his will, and to agree, and give their kingdom unto the (antichrist) beast, until the words of God shall be fulfilled " (Revl.xvii.17.). By

---

*It will be seen, that while the Belteshazzarn-"beast" comes up out of the SEA [Revl.xiii.1.], that of the antichrist-"beast," comes up out of the EARTH ; this, in both cases, signifies their descending from the Hebrew people [Revl.xvii.15] although each one from a different aspect-community : for, as the sea is larger than the land, so, the Belteshazzarn-"beast," is shown as coming from the larger Hobrew portion—the merged tribes ; and the antichrist-"beast," from that of the smaller, or Judah-Benjamin tribes.

his deceptive skill and miracle-working, together with his assumption in the matter of the Messiahship, of whom the Jews are still looking forward to with expectations, this deluded race, will, by taking this bate, hook themselves to the antichrist; and thus fill up their cup of bitterness, which, through their doctrinal blindness, the vail-remnant upon their hearts has power to induce.—By this heaven-sanctioned delusion, the Jews will actually believe that this man is the true Messiah, and will, with vigour and impetuosity, proclaim him accordingly; and he will have more power over the nation than its king.—"The (Jewish) Egyptions will I give over into the hands of a cruel lord (the antichrist; Revl.xiii.15.), and a fierce king (Belteshazzar) shall rule over them saith the Lord, the Lord of hosts" (Isa.xix.4.)—"even him whose coming is after the workings of Satan with all power and signes and lying wonders" (ii Thess.ii.9.).

[We have reasons to believe that the Jews are only too eager to fall into this trap, and be led by such a man as the antichrist: they did a similar thing in the case of Barcochab, who, at the time of Hadrian (117 A.D.), assumed to be the Messiah, stating that he was that star which was to rise out of Jacob; and so deluded them, that he actually succeeded in the accumulation of a following of about 200,000 men, whilst he himself took the title of king. He, however, was eventually killed by the Romans. These things were portrayed to the Jews, by The Lord, and thus, ample warning has been given :—" For there shall arise FALSE CHRISTS, and FALSE PROPHETS, and shall show great signes and wonders, insomuch that, if it were possible, they shall deceive the very elect "— Matt.xxiv.24.].

There will be a sort of confederacy between the antichrist, and Belteshazzar the king; but in all probability they will be of the rank of Sultan and Prophet; the latter of these, filling the offices of high-priest to the Egyptian-Jews, and counsellor-of-state of the Egyptian Empire. Both these men will possess satanic spirits (Revl.xvi.13.): and the counsells of the antichrist, will be absolute. He will be a man of the serpent-in-lambskin kind—a man full of subtilty and the attributes of Satan, who will assist him in playing the part of high-priest-messiah, and, at the same time, to frame such rites and ceremonies of religion, as will be characteristic of enmity to Christians, worship of Mohammed, and the insuring of an idolatrous satanic-worship; under the guise, however, of the community giving worshiping-allegiance to their king, by proxy of the graven-images which may be expected to be found in every locality of the country. The mohammedans will be none the less eager to obey the antichrist than the Jews: for these people are expecting the fulfilment of the promise of Mohammed, which was, that he would send a messenger to the earth. So that, this man will be doubly accepted, and his task made comparatively easy, yet, as we shall see presently, he will

not stop at any-thing, but carry out his will and prerogative, even to the extent of beheading or some other
form of life-taking, those who refuse to worship the
image of the king.

Having now shook off the coil of mystery, we have
come forth into clear light with two men ; these are the
rulers of the kingdom of Egypt at the date of 3,258
A.D., Belteshazzar, the king, being the name of one of
them, and antichrist is the name by which we shall
know the other.

When Turkey has been overthrown, and the Sultan's rule broken, the Caliphship will devolve upon
some other mohammedan ruler; the monarch of
Barbary may endeavour to gain the exalted position,
and, probably, will succeed ; but this office, must,
eventually, be sealed unto the kingdom of Egypt, by
the distinction coming upon its monarchy.   It is only
a matter of being strong enough to keep it, and this
may not be far distant, for we cannot shut our eyes
to the fact of a greater power than that of nations,
giving its aid unto practical guidance in the matter
of shaping, and lifting-up this kingdom.

Belteshazzar, (by which name we shall henceforth
call the monarch of Egypt) the national-SEVENTH
caliph-head of the "beast," being in full-swing of
monarchial power, will now "tread down and break
into pieces" those nations who are not of the mohammedan religion ;—For the world having "fallen away,
THAT MAN OF SIN, the son of perdition" is revealed.

By his being the Caliph, all mohammedans, who number at the present time about 170 millions, will not
only give him allegiance, but will so flock around his
standard, as to enable him to accomplish his designs
within the limited period that will be allowed him
to carry on with success (Danl.vii.25.), which is for
three and a half years, from the year 3,258, to the
time of the great battle, in the year 3,262 A.D., or 1,335
years (Danl.xii.12.) after the commencement of the
overthrowing of Turkey.—"*In the latter time of their
(Egyptian) kingdom, when the *transgressors are come to
the full, A KING of fierce countenance, and UNDER-
STANDING DARK SENTENCES, shall stand up.
And his power shall be mighty, but not by his own power
(Satan's): and HE SHALL DESTROY wonderfully,
and shall prosper, and practise, and shall destroy the
mighty and holy (Christian) people (Danl.viii.23,24.).
And there was given unto him a mouth speaking great
things and blasphemies; and power was given unto him
to continue forty and two months. And all that dwell
upon the earth shall worship him, whose names are not
written in the book of life (non-Christians) of the Lamb
slain from the foundation of the world" (Revl.xiii.5,8).*

Riches will be one of the alluring instruments in
the hands of Belteshazzar; and this, it may be safely
said, is nine-tenths of all secular power. His wealth,
of untold gold and of precious stones, is to be the gift
of Satan—"...and the dragon gave him his power, and

---

*The Jews, as followers of the antichrist, in the Belteshazzarn reign.

his seat, and great authority (Revl.xiii.2.),"and he has
no greater power to give to man, than untold wealth :
yea, with the exceptions of "*dark sentences*" or lower-
class miracle-working, he has nothing else to give !
and even this, he does not literally give, because, "the
gold and the silver are mine, saith the Lord :" the
most that he can do, therefore, is to point out the spot
where the precious metal, and glittering stones, lie
hidden.   And this he will do—the indwelling satanic-
spirit prompting the king wiht knowledge of the place
of the hidden earthly treasures, which, Scripture has
shown, abounds in the land of which Belteshazzar
will be the sovereign ruler (Gen.ii.11,12.).   This is
what is meant by, "the dragon giving him his power."
The people, however, will not look upon it in this
light ; they will simply see him as a monarch in
pssession of gold, and diamond mines,—those who do
gleam the truth, being ready to shut their eyes to any
confederacy-of-darkness, so long as their pockets become heavier, in which case, the rumours to this effect
will undergo revision, and those things which appeared
to be governed by *darkness*, will be accredited to the
powers of heaven.   The simple fact of Belteshazzar
becoming the owner of valuable mines, ought not
to create suspision of a dark-supernatural kind, but
this does not alter the facts of the case :—if I buy a
piece of land, and I find that it contains a hoard of
wealth, there would not be any-thing supernatural or
mysterious in the matter ; but, on the other hand, if

it was Satan who pointed it out to me as containing the hidden treasures of the earth and a source of great power, then, the transaction would be pertaining to supernatural darkness. These riches, by enabling the king to exercise liberality upon his mohammedan subjects, causing loose and indulgent living, will be of itself a source of enchantment, and power over mens minds : and when he backs this up by supernatural performances, assisted by the antichrist, who, we are told (Revl.xiii.13.), will perform such wonders as that of making fire descend from heaving, all surprise at the words of Scripture which saith,"and they worshipped the beast, saying, who is like unto the beast ?" (Revl.xiii.4.), must vanish, and we, like Job, exclaim, "the earth is given into the hands of the wicked" (Job.ix.24.). And this satanic-being of the hour, will not only circulate his gold freely, but indulgent pleasure unto the gratification of the flesh, will be his key-note to the people of this Babylonical city (Revl.xvii.1—5).

Whilst this Belteshazzarn exaltation is going on, the subtle-minded antichrist will be framing his idolatrous project, he perceiving that these events has produced the necessary impression upon the people, and that this is the favourable moment to set up an idol in the likeness of king Belteshazzar.—A few flattering speeches, such as the portrayal of the glory of mohammedism during the present reign, is all that will be needed to insure, this self-gratification, and the fulfilment of the secret desire of his satanic master, the prince of darkness.

[We have said, the image which the antichrist will set up (Revl. xiii. 14) is to count as being the representative of mohammedism in all its SEVEN dynastic-heads, centred and summed up in Belteshazzar, in whose likeness it will be made; but at the first glance of Revelation xiii. 12., it might seem as if the predict was pointing to an idol-image being set up in the likeness of the Turkish sultan, in consequence of it being his dynastic-head which receives the "deadly-wound" overthrow; it is not, however, portrayed unto this interpretation; because, the sixth-head is represented in Belteshazzar, for is he not portrayed as having the whole of the seven heads upon him? No, it is to the man who heals the mohammedan wound that the image is ascribed: "*which had the wound by the sword and did live,*" speaks of a blow to mohammedism, and the last part of Revelation xiii. 14., simply requires the symbolic-word "beast" to be called mohammedism. The third verse (Revl. xiii.) points this out, and shows that the deadly-wound is not counted as being against any particular person, but rather, is against the mohammedan cause, of which Turkey is one of its dynasties, and which king Belteshazzar is the representative, who is shown to be glorified by the people because of mohammedan ascendency to power, their recovery of Palestine, and in other ways brought into world-wide eminence, through his rule.

The strangely worded IIth verse (Revl. xvii) may also

seem to mystify matters; but it will be quite clear, if the Belteshazzarn reign is perceived to consist of two "beast"- rulers, whilst the official power and authority is invested in only one of them, the king. The words have reference to the "false-prophet-beast" or antichrist, who, having a ruling power in virtue of his influence over both king and people of this seventh-dynasty, is, practically, an eighth ruling-power; but he is not actually an eighth, because he is not a sovereign-ruler: neither is he the seventh, because Belteshazzar fills that office; therefore, he, the antichrist, is nothing more than OF the seventh. The angel that instructed St. John in this matter (Revl.xvii.1.), wished to convey to the minds of men of later periods, that mohammedism will receive a death-blow through Turkey, the sixth dynastic-king, but that there are to be seven kings(mohammedan dynasties) from begining to the end of mohammedism—Revl.xvii.10.].

Coercive measures in matters of religion, is not always acceptable to everybody! The idolatrous taint by the introduction of the Belteshazzarn satanic-idol, will necessitate, such as the following precedent historical facts being promulgated :-

In the reign of the Ptolemy's, Egypt carried out the custom of placing in their temple, statues of men whom they wished to glorify in name.—Ptolemy Philadelphus built a temple in Alexandria to the honour of his father and mother, and placed in it their statues made of ivory and gold, and gave orders that they should be worshipped like the gods and other kings of the country.　Marking of the forehead, which is to be enforced by the antichrist, was also a precedent practice of the Egyptians; Ptolemy Philopator, ordered the Jews of Alexandria to have their bodies *marked with needle-punctures, in the form of an ivy-leaf, in honour of Bacchus; the king himself had an ivy-leaf marked in this manner, upon his †forehead. These things may have been looked upon by the people of those days, as simple acts of reverence towards a deceased person whose name was great : and the people of the Belteshazzarn-period may be also persuaded that the " beast's " image has no other or deeper meaning than this; but the Christian community will know different : for whosoever boweth down to any graven-image, is acting in direct opposition to Biblical history and to the written truth of God's word.　Therefore, this ungodly proceeding being antagonistic to heaven, many Christians will forfeit their heads sooner than become idolaters.　These things of Satan's preparing, are but step-stones calculated to lead up to one vast system of devil-worship; and men's reception of the mark 666, will be none other than the evil-spirit's

---

*The process of tattooing the body, is by gumming a paper-stencil upon the flesh, the stencil-design is then painted with Indian-ink, and then, three needles, which have been tied to the end of a piece of wood and protruding about one-thirtieth of an inch, rapidly applied to the flesh-exposed stencil-design ; the holes thus pricked, sucks in the stain, and leaves an indelible mark of the desired, or stencil shape, pattern.

†Sharps History of Egypt.

seal !—Satan is very subtle : these precedents, as well
as every other of his persuasive methods, are not only
his weapons of strength, but are arguments, enabling
him to speak to the " inner man " of those who receive
the 666 seal ; for we are not to understand that it is
the inanimate idol who will speak (Revl.xiii.15.), but
rather, the satanic-spirit, the seriousness of which
has brought forth a number of Scriptural statements,
which are intended to act as a warning to the people of
that generation, preventing many from coming under
that blinding influence which creates callousness and
the draging down of the attributes of the heart, which
the prince of darkness, in his matured scheme, will
struggle to accomplish in his final attempt of the destruction of souls.   Hence the words of exhortation,
and of condemnation, of the Angel to these people :-
" *If any man worship the beast and his image, and
receive his (666) mark in his forehead, or in his hand,
the same shall drink of the wine of the wrath of God,
which is poured out without mixture into the cup of his
indignation ; and he shall be *tormented with fire and
brimstone in the presence of the holy angels, and in the
presence of the Lamb (Revl.xiv.9,10.).*
Coercion, even unto death, then, is to be the lines
upon which this man antichrist will carry out his idolatrous creed ; for the proclamation will affect and
cause " *all, both small and great, rich and poor, free*

*Cast into the lake of fire and suffer the death of burning. after the
judgment [Revl.xx.15.].

and bond, to receive a mark in their right hand, or in
their forehead: and that no man might buy or sell, save he
that had the mark...(Revl.xiii.16,17.) ...and caused
that as many as would not worship the image of the beast
should be killed" (Revl.xiii.15.). This man, like Belteshazzar, being endowed with the spirit of Satan
(Revl.xvi.13.), may be expected to creep in with
and practise the works of darkness, under the allurements of ritualism : and also to display the works of
real supernatural power (Revl.xiii.13.), deceiving, and
overthrowing the Christian religion, in conjunction
with Belteshazzar, who will make havock among the
smaller Christian-nations. The Scriptures portray
this, as being "plucked up by the roots ;"— if the inhabitants of whole cities are caused to transfer their
promise of eternal life to that of eternal death, through
the worshipping of the "beast's image," this would be
"plucking them up by the roots:" for the figure is
taken from a plucked-up flower, which, is bound to die.

It is comparatively easy for a great nation with an
army of formidable force at their back, to conquer
the world, nation by nation, i.e., whilst one nation is
being dealt with, another nation receives costly gifts
and professed friendship, flattering them, however, only
to strike a more deadly blow at the opportune moment ; thus, these nations may become vanquished.
Or the blow may be struck in virtue of sheer power,
and without any flattery, simply on the grounds of
religion. To do this, however, is one thing, but it is

quite another thing to hold the power thus gained
over a conquered world for any length of time : and
especially when the deeds of the conqueror are of a
satanic, licentious, and creed-revengeful nature, for
the hearts of Christain men will feel the sting of such
monarchical government. And if idol-worship has
been decreed, forbidding Christian-devotion or even
the right of religious freedom, Mohammed's creed
being exclusive, then, such kind of monarchy will
have cause to apprehend trouble at no very great
distance from the time of conquest : for the various
communities are sure to find a way, with God's help,
of deliverance from such national bondage.

Will ye worship the demon, tho' the monarch of earth,
Whose bannor girds the sulphuric-prince of wrath ;—
Pernicious, cruel, the displayer of a despotic sword :
Selling yourselves for nought, to such a god ?
Or will ye have the Being of manifest love,—
The true representative of heaven above,
Whose nature comes within you, for good, down here,
That you might inherit the eternal-realm sphere ?
Choose ye this day, whether Mohammed or Christ ?
Weigh the works of both,—measure each edifice :—
Mohammed's bloody sword, or God's sacrefic'd-Lamb,
Moham's purpose,—self ! Christ's, the redemption of man.
A.M.

Matters having now gone on to such an extent as
to make it intolerable for those nations of firm Christian stamina, who will have perceived in this Egyptian
rule the fulfilment of the antichrist-prediction, the
smouldering emblem of "smoking-flax" will be so
fanned, as to bring them into brilliant flames of devo-
tion towards the true and loving Master. The situation

will now be serious: a confederacy of Christian-nations having been formed, it may be expected that an unanimous decision will be arrived at, and to the effect that they are resolved to resist to the extent of an armed force, the coercive measures which have been decreed, and to renounce allegiance to a Sovereign whose reign and power has been fruitful of nothing else but blasphemy, satanicly-exalted sway, and idolatry. And thus endeavour to rid themselves of the yoke of these fanatic persecutors and Christian antagonists.

Thus, Belteshazzar, in all the glory of his wealth, exaltation, and the city "setting as a queen" upon the world, will find a movement on foot, which, in due cource, will overthrow him. In the meantime, he, Belteshazzar, seeing the national rising of Europe, will "take the bull by the horns" and proclaim a religious war :—a decree of the king and caliph of all the mohammedans throughout the world, will now take the wings of swiftness through the great network of this sphere's electric-system, commanding that all Kings of mohammedan nations with their armies, Governors of provinces with drilled men of special enrolment, and army-reserve-men of all kinds, assemble upon the plane of ARMAGEDDON (Revl.xvi.16) to battle against the armies of the Christian nations of the earth. The Scriptural figure for this decree, is symbolically set forth in three "unclean spirits," which signify the WILL and aspirations of Belteshazzar, the dragon,

and the antichrist;—"AND I SAW THREE UNCLEAN
SPIRITS LIKE FROGS *COME OUT OF THE MOUTH OF
THE DRAGON, AND OUT OF THE MOUTH OF THE
BEAST, AND OUT OF THE MOUTH OF THE FALSE
PROPHET. FOR THEY ARE THE SPIRITS OF DEVILS,
WORKING MIRACLES, WHICH GO FORTH UNTO THE
KINGS OF THE EARTH AND OF THE WHOLE WORLD,
TO GATHER THEM TO THE BATTLE OF
THAT GREAT DAY OF GOD ALMIGHTY"
(Revl.xvi.12—14.). And if the power of deciding
a war rested in numbers, we might give these unbelievers credit for the glee which we feel sure they
will enjoy over the thoughts of now having the sup-
posed opportunity of completely wiping out the followers of Jesus, and for ever crushing the Christian
doctrine. But as the army of the living God does
not always look upon its number of men as being the
power of victory, they can afford to leave these numer-
ically-strong fanatics to chuckle over their delusion,
whilst they praise God and put their trust in Him.
The Chinese, as we have previously mentioned (see
page 131), are to join in this religious-war movement:
the kindred-spirit of idolatry, which is in this nation,
could not resist the opportunity of becoming an ally
in a Christian-extermination cause: why, they hate
the very sound of the name of Christian, at the present
time! The Scriptural prediction, with regard to the
dragon (Revl.xvi.13.) being the emblematic-figure of

*Coming out of the mouth, is figure for speech, or decreeing.

*China, plainly points this out, and portrays under this symbol, the Chinese ruler sending forth to promulgate the edict of king Belteshazzar, through the whole of his Buddha-idolatrous empire. So that, we have in the three "unclean spirits," the portrayed WILL of three evil men, as it were, three clamorous spirits of hell let loose for the purpose of going forth to command the people of all nations and languages which compose the subjects of the caliph, and of China, to muster upon the battle-field of Armageddon.

These perfidious acts, and ungodly times, being foreseen and known of God, provision is made against their being carried out to the extent of utterly ruining the earth's race of people : for, by His coming in the Person of Christ Jesus, and destroying the satanic foe at the open battle, a check will be place upon this mohammedan power, ere it has sapped the vitality of the Cross; for "EXCEPT THOSE DAYS SHOULD BE SHORTENED, THERE SHOULD NO FLESH BE SAVED" (Matt. xxiv. 22).—Once the mohammedans have full power over the earth, woe be unto millions of its people ! But Christ, we have said, is going to prevent this : neverless, these satanicly-guided fanatics will, in a measure, succeed in crushing out the spirit of truth, by the force of evil pleasures which will naturally influence many; as it is written, "BECAUSE INIQUITY SHALL ABOUND, THE LOVE OF MANY SHALL WAX COLD" (Mati. xxiv. 12.). It will be seen, then, that if

*The Chinese national emblem, is the DRAGON : see page 131.

these things were allowed to go on for an indefinite
period, the whole earth would be drawn over to idolatry of heart, as well as in practice, and this would
so bring down the wrath of God, as to consume all
flesh : much in the same manner as was done in the
case of Sodom and Gomorrah, when all righteousness
except that of one man, had been swept away from
the midst of these cities.—These things, I say, if allowed to go on, would place the world in such a
chronic stage of darkness, that all flesh would be inevitably drawn into the net of utter destruction : for,
by the swift wrath of God coming as a consuming
fire upon the whole earth, no flesh, out of perhaps,
three thousand million inhabitants, at this period,
would be saved. On the other hand, by the number
of days of Belteshazzar's mohammedan-rule being
shortened, for he is only to be allowed to have three
and a half years dominion over Palestine and of the
world (Revl.xiii.5.), these things are prevented from
reaching a chronic-stage, and leaves an opportunity
for a goodly number of the population of the East and
Southern parts of the earth being extracted from the
jaws of hell, at the time of Christ's coming to overthrow the mohammedan abomination. And this will
snatch the Jews from the satanic-clutch :—It is a
known fact, that God has always let the Jews go on
in their persistent-will in following of the downward
grade until the extreme point has been reached,
which in nearly all cases has been idolatry, then, at

this point, He has come to their rescue. This eventful period will not be an exception !—When the Jews
have fully surrendered to the antichrist, and they have
become idolaters by the worship of the " beast's " image, then, Christ will descend—(3262 A.D.).

It is at this time, when the mohammedan cup of
iniquity is full, and the eye of Deity beholds the persecution unto martyrdom of Christians, and of the
idolatrously-turned Jews, who are now being marked
with the "beast's" number, 666, that God will send
SIX PLAGUES (Revl. xvi. 2-12), the last of which,
is to dry up the river Euphrates in order to facilitate the journey of the Eastern regular-armies, along
with multitudes of hastily enrolled men, their baggage,
armament, and field equipment, upon camels, mules,
and elephants, to the camping-ground and battlefield
of Armageddon. These plagues are in no ways calculated to cause any abatement in the mohammedan
war-activity; they will act, rather, as a stimulant :
they will certainly have a tendency to bring the enmity
of the heart uppermost, because Satan will prompt
them to believe that these plagues are the result of an
offended belteshazzarn-image god, through Christian-
contempt of him ; greater energy, therefore, may be
expected on the part of these people. And precedents
are not wanting !—in the case of Rome, and during
the reign of Marcus Aurelius, when, because the country had been visited with pestilence, earthquake, famine, inundation, and ravage of devouring locusts, they

not only ascribed these calamities to Christianity, but put a great number of the Christians to death.   These six plagues, although not affecting the war preparations, are sent in justice to the Christians ; and also in retribution to the *Jews and mohammedans of "BABYLON THE GREAT," for all the innocent blood which they have shed at various times and places for ages (Revl.xviii.24.).

The edict, calling upon those in authority to gather together the Buddhists and Mohammedan armies, and a special enrolment of a fanatical host, having gone forth ; and whilst the Christian nations, those of Europe especially, are preparing for a crusade in the full armour of God, two other great and important events are taking place.   One of these events is, that of 144,000 saints rising from their graves ;—the resurrection of those deceased men who have suffered as prophets and servants of God in all times, Disciples and servants of Christ in the earlier part of the Christian era, and all those who have suffered martyrdom in the name of Christ, since : and this includes some of the Turkish massacred (Rev,vi.9—11.), and those who will be killed for refusing to comply with the image-worship decree.   We have already explained that this number (144,000) rested for its completion with the acts of men throughout the march of time, the foreknowledge of God seeing the exact date at

---

¹The Jews, by taking sides with the mohammedans, will be equally imbittered against the Christians.

which this would take place ; this number having been
made up to its total by the deeds of the antichrist,
they now come forth from their various *resting-places*
of the face of the globe, and are appointed to their
individual positions (Revl.xxii.12.), the whole forming
THE CELESTIAL GOVERNMENT OF CHRIST'S KINGDOM
(Revl.xiv.1.).—This first resurrection, is also prophet-
ically portrayed under the figure of a woman in trav-
ail unto delivery, and her child (Isa.lxvi.7 ; Micah.v.3 ;
Revl.xii.1,2,5.); the twelve stars therein mentioned
(Revl.xii.1.), are symbolical of twelve principalities,
which, I have no doubt, will be given to the twelve disciples, each one being at the head of 12,000 of a governmental body (Revl.vii ;Luke xxii.29.).   The"child"
denotes a resurrected portion of the saved-people, or
144,000 of Christ's Church,—144,000 first-fruit, which
stand in the same ratio, with regard to the whole
church, as that of a child is to a woman : hence the
WOMAN-CHURCH is delivered of a CHURCH-FRACTION
CHILD.   This event, of course, will not be visible to
the human sight : it could not be expected that God
would permit the natural man to share the honour of
beholding this glorious resurrection,—*It is by faith we
live, and not by proof such as this would be!*   These
144,000 *immortal men, are to assemble on Mount

---

*We must not overlook the fact of the Gentiles being the ten lost
tribes, because of the modern Gentile-martyrs, who are in accordance
with the Scripture which states that the 144,000 saints were of the tribes
of Israel [Revl.vii.].

Zion (mount Olivet), where Christ is to come in clouds to meet them (Acts.i.9-11 ; Revl.i.7.).

The other great event is, that of THE *SECOND ADVENT OF CHRIST. All things being now ready, listen !—" Behold I come..."

" What for ?"

The answer is nigh unto you, even the word of God :—"... For this purpose the Son of God was manifested, THAT HE MIGHT DESTROY THE WORKS OF THE DEVIL " (i John iii.8.).

The Atonement, God-manifestation, flow of the Holy Spirit, and the destruction of the devil, were all involved in the Sacrificial-offering of the Son of God, but this, did not finally achieve the destruction of the devil's works ; the fruit of the Cross was still hampered with them ; "let them grow up together" seems to be God's plan, but did He mean this to remain so for all time ?—No ! the great battle of the satanic-arms versus the "arms-of-the-living-God " will decide this !—and he, the devil, figuratively chained for a thousand years (Revl.xx.1,2.).

But what position does Satan now occupy? And what are the plans of his destruction ?—

In order to make these things clear, let me point the reader to Revelation xii.7—10., and then let him bring his mind to see the events at the begining of the world :-

At present, there appears to be no barrier of an

*There will be a third Advent, 1,000 years subsequent to the second.

effective character, to keep Satan away from heavenly
places—He having become unholy through rebellion, his presence among the angelic-host must be
repugnant, and a source of annoyance to them.—God
could certainly forbid Satan's presence in the heavenly
realms, but would he obey the command? and to
enforce the order, as Revelation xii implies, would be
to create war between the holy Angels, and the satanic
host; and Jehovah is a God of peace: yet, as we have
said, without this enforced measure, would the author
of disobedience, as portrayed in his words to Eve, comply with decrees of this nature?—Our answer may
be gleamed from the following quotations:- "Joshua
the high priest standing before the Angel of the Lord,
and Satan standing at his right hand to resent him
(adverse prompter). And the Lord said unto Satan,
the Lord rebuke thee, O Satan; even the Lord that
hath chosen Jerusalem rebuke thee..." (Zech·iii.1,2).
But this does not appear to have been a remedy, for
Satan, we read, still *goeth about* "*as a roaring lion
seeking whom he may devour*" (*i Peter v.8.*). So that,
his being forbidden to do evil works, is not a preven-
tive, and, in like manner, his being forbidden to enter
heaven, does not keep him out of it. Therefore, let
us endeavour to ascertain what part, as an instrument,
man has been ordained to play in this most important
matter:— That Satan has got the advantage of us
during our earthly career, is only too true, but, as
soon as an individual accepts Jesus, and becomes the

reipient of the new birth, he gets a Spiritual seed within him (i John iii.9.) which, upon the resurrection, reproduces him in a Spiritually-powerful structurally-formed body, or immortal man ; and as a being of this description, man is Satan's superior.   Now, let us imagine that countles numbers of these Satan-superior individuals have become the eternal inhabitants of the heavenly realms ; would this not have the moral effect of keeping this archfiend and his host away, and thus remedying the evil of their presence any more ?   But what do we mean by " *the moral effect* ?"—

When Satan tempted Eve to disobey Gods commands, he knew what weak creatures mankind was ; he also knew that nothing of a rebellious nature, or impure, would ever be permitted to enter heaven : these two things, together with his not having perceived the reserved plan of redemption, fostered the belief, that he would have nothing more to do than to cause defilement to take root in the human race, in order to gain a great victory over God, and insure the whole family of Adam's progeny being cast at his feet, at the end of time.   But Satan, like everybody else who tries to make God's word void, forgot to count the cost of failure which, by a counterplan of God, is sure to be effectually worked out.   Putting his belief into practice, however, he has succeeded in the gratification of seeing the first man fall; and by his feeding the fire of enmity in the hearts of the offspring has managed to bring them into the downward grade, and by whose instrumentality, as prompted agents, he has had the satisfaction of seeing the very Son of God "*lifted up*," leaving behind a continuous and bitter hatred towards Him from the breasts of both Jew and mohammedan. Satan has accomplished all this: and now, in the 33rd century, and when he has gathered the nations together in arms against each other, thinks to win his final victory in virtue of the number of mohammedans bearing arms. But he has yet to learn that it will be Christ Himself who will safeguard the Christian nations upon the field of battle : and that, the very wounds which he was the secret means of causing to the hands and feet of Jesus, and which will now cause a powerful reaction of Jewish minds, who will accept these wounds as the proof that He who now delivers them from the chains of mohammedan darkness is none other than Him who had been given up to the Cross and who was the true Messiah, recoil upon his own head ;—his own planned works, will have proved a snare to him, and, in place of his scoring a victory over God, will find himself caught into the very lake-of-fire trap (Revl.xix.20) which he had set for God's family. Man will thus become Satan's moral conqueror,—"And I heard a loud voice saying in heaven, Now is come salvation, AND STRENGTH, and the kingdom of our God, AND THE POWER OF HIS CHRIST : FOR THE ACCUSER OF OUR BRETHREN IS CAST DOWN..." (Revl.xii.10.)—the "WHITE HORSE " (Holy Spirit) will have completed His going forth for the purpose of "conquering" for He will then have "conquered" (see Revl.vi.2.). We will, in conclusion of this subject, just glance at the perfect way in which God's counterplan has worked over that of the devil's-trap, and into which, at the great battle, he will have fallen:- Grace, by redemption which is in Christ Jesus, having been practically put into motion by the enmity of the devil towards Jesus ; and the flowing of the Holy Spirit as a resultant power into, and sealing, converted men, who will produce at the resurrection a mighty immortal army (Rom.viii.11 ; Revl.vii.9.), will, by their surrounding the Throne, and filling the "MANY MANSIONS" of the once satanically-occupied realms, so crush Satan and his host at seeing this strength and power of heaven, that in humiliation and shame, they will realize their utter defeat, and will have the moral conviction that it will be impossible for them to ever again attempt to enter these places of such immortal strength.—Do we ever hear tell of a burglar breaking into a Constabulary barracks?

If we perceive, then, in this ungodliness and idolatry of the earthly-powerful satanic-agent mohammedans, Satan still aiming at victory : and then imagine the after-scene of the great battle, when all the Jews will have had their eyes opened to the fact of this war being a ruse of Satan in his final attempt at victory over the human race; we shall understand more of the great mystery of the world, which, with other purposes, centres itself in the fact, that "the Son of

God was manifested, that he might destroy the works of the devil "— he who "had the power of death" (i John.iii.8 ; Heb.ii.14). This testing event, in justice and wisdom, is to settle the question of Satan's power, which, from that date, will be NIL, Christ being, as heretofore, THE ALL POWERFUL: the seed of the woman, then, will not only have bruised the *serpent's* head, but also,—"In that day the Lord with his sore and great strong sword, shall punish *leviathan the piercing serpent, even leviathan that crooked serpent ; AND HE SHALL SLAY THE DRAGON THAT IS IN THE †SEA" (Isa.xxvii.1.).

I would impress upon the reader's mind, that the words of Daniel xii.12.,—"*Blessed is he that waiteth and cometh to the 1,335(year)days*"— does not mean that men of one period, are actually to wait until another peri d in expectation of a blessing: but rather is one of those obscurely-expressed passages which state to the Jews, (who are living at the time of the 1,335 years expiration, which, by adding 1,290 years (Danl.xii) to the epoch-date (637.A.D.), and then adding the 1,335 years to the total, equals the date of 3,262.A.D.) that they will be blessed beyond that of former times, the redemption laying hold of them as well as the out-pouring of the Spirit of God upon them

---

*Another name for devil —see Job xli.

†Sea, or water, in many instances of Scripture, are expressed to represent people [Revl.xiv.2 ; xvii.15 ; xix.6], therefore, "dragon that is in the sea," signifies Satan in the people.

as Christians, and followers of Christ Jesus through a millennial age.

THE GREAT BATTLE :-

To have one's Religion trampled upon, and then to be coerced into idolatry, is, perhaps, the severest sting that Belteshazzar and his antichrist-fiend could have inflicted upon the Christian community: however, it *has put the whole of Europe ablaze !—A wounded "lion" is dangerous !—And a determined "bear" is very difficult to suppress ! Furthermore, to cashier the demoniacal dominion, all are agreed. Arsenals will have been in full swing ; men from every town and village have been flocking into the various garrisons in order to join the Colours ; ships have been placed in commisson ; and now all things are in a state of preparedness. While this has been going on in Europe and in Christian countries of other parts, the satanic foe has been straining every nerve, in order to gather together all available men from out of the vast territory of mohammedan nations—a prodigious death-intent mass.

Armageddon, otherwise known by the names of the plain of Galilee, Esdraelon, and the field of Me-giddon, stretches over the country from Mount Carmel to the sea of Galilee, about thirty miles in length, and twenty in breadth; it is the place where the tents of warriors of every nation under the sun have

*I speak as if the date 3,261 A.D. had arrived.

been pitched ; it was here that the hosts of Sisera was delivered into the hands of Barak (Judges iv. 13—16) ; it was upon this plain that Josiah in disguise, fought against Necho, king of Egypt (ii Chronl. xxxv. 20—22); and it is here that the BATTLE OF THE LORD is now to be fought.   Nevertheless, a war of such magnitude as this one must necessarily be, cannot be expected to carry out the whole of its operations in one place : many fields, and valleys, will be the scene of conflict : the word Armageddon, $A\rho\mu\alpha\gamma\epsilon\delta\omega\nu$, Peter Oliver tells us, signifies "A PLACE OF MEETING ;" therefore every place where an engagement is fought, will come within the meaning of the Scripturally designated Armageddon, although called by other names.   The valley of Jehoshaphat, which is situate between the Mount of Olives and Mount Moriah, and which is also called the VALLEY OF DECISION (Joel. iii. 2—14.), is an instance.   It is here that the final and decisive battle of the Lord will be fought ; JESUS WILL SIT UPON THE MOUNT OF OLIVES, the place of His descension (Acts i. 10—12.), WATCHING, AND WITH HIS SPIRIT-sword, CONDUCT THE BATTLE.   This, I have no doubt, is why it has been called, "the valley of decision,"—"I WILL ALSO GATHER ALL NATIONS, AND WILL BRING THEM DOWN INTO THE VALLEY OF JEHOSH-APHAT, AND WILL PLEAD WITH THEM THERE FOR MY *PEOPLE AND FOR MY HERITAGE ISRAEL . . .

---

*It has been stated that the Jews will take sides with the moham-medans in the war ; hence the figurative pleading of Jesus.

ASSEMBLE YOURSELVES, AND COME, ALL YE HEATHEN, AND GATHER YOURSELVES TOGETHER ROUND ABOUT : THITHER CAUSE THY MIGHTY ONES TO COME DOWN, O LORD. LET THE HEATHEN BE WAKENED, AND COME UP TO THE VALLEY OF JEHOSHAPHAT : FOR THERE WILL I SIT TO JUDGE ALL THE HEATHEN ROUND ABOUT. PUT YE IN THE SICKLE, FOR THE HARVEST IS RIPE ; COME, GET YOU DOWN ; FOR THE PRESS IS FULL, THE FATS OVER-FLOW ; FOR THEIR WICKEDNESS IS GREAT.   MUL-TITUDES, MULTITUDES IN THE VALLEY OF DECISION : FOR THE DAY OF THE LORD IS NEAR IN THE VALLEY OF DECIS-ION " (Joel iii. 2, 11—14.).

The battle-field may now be felt to quiver with the measured steps of the mighty armies which are entering its borders , the re-echo of ancient times. · Here are streams of mohammedan and buddhist military in battle-array, immediately followed by a mixed multitudinous Auxiliary which have been hastily enrolled and drilled for the occasion, headed by kings, commanders, and their staff.   There, in the opposite quarter, are the brilliant armies of the various Christian nations, consisting of the Regulars, Volunteers, men of Conscription, and Naval-brigades ; the whole fully equipped in both armament and provisions.   Both sides are now equally conscious of the gravity of the hour, as they march to the sound of their regimental bands, amid the flying banners and glittering steel of both helmet and bayonet. No precedent of the past ages, which will furnish a parallel to this great event, exists—everything now taking place, surpasses all of its kind that the world has ever known.

On one side of the plain, and amidst a multitudinous foe of destroying-intent, will be seen Belteshazzar and his prophet antichrist in the zenith of their glory, picturing to themselves their achievement of vanquishing every power, whether it be of a natural or supernatural character, which the Christians may have been able to bring in opposition to his formidable mohammedan forces; and thus flushed with the thoughts of victory and triumph over the whole world. For these forces being secretly commanded by the indwelling satanic-spirit of the king, he, (with Satan) now "...Opposeth and exalteth himself above all that is called God, or that is worshipped..."(ii Thes.ii.4. R.v.). His time, however, is but short; his forty-two months (Revl.xiii.5.), or as Daniel puts it (vii.25.), "time and times and the dividing of *time," of exaltation and permitted power, will have expired in the course of 391 †days (Revl.ix.13-16.); yet sufficient for him, with Satan and the antichrist, to test, and decide by this war, the worth of his power; as it is written:-
"...HE SHALL ALSO STAND UP AGAINST THE PRINCE OF PRINCES (Christ); BUT HE SHALL BE BROKEN

---

*Time, signifies one year; times [plural], two years; the dividing of time [half of time], six months.

†Scriptural months, are of thirty days duration.

WITHOUT HANDS " (Danl. viii. 25.).

War having commenced, the hidden enmity ot the Jew and mohammedan towards the Christian, has now risen to the surface : and while the bullets of death are taking their flight, the din of the incessantly fired rifles   vibrating through space, and the air is being rent with the discharge of field-pieces and siege guns, this bitterness of spirit is bubbling over with vehemence.—This hurricane of strife having reached its billow-lashing point, THEN, at this stage, will every Jewish heart present be melted, and every Jewish eye behold, THE ETERNAL MONARCH OF HEAVEN AND OF EARTH, CHRIST JESUS, DESCENDING UPON MOUNT *OLIVET.

How will He come ?—

We require no other authority to enable us to positively settle this question, than that of Acts. i. 10, 11 ; for here we have the statement of two Angels, which, of itself, is an irrevocable decree.   These angels state plainly to the world, that Jesus shall, upon His return, descend upon mount Olivet ; their exact words are : " Ye men of Galilee... THIS SAME JESUS WHICH IS TAKEN UP FROM YOU INTO HEAVEN, SHALL SO COME IN LIKE MANNER AS YE HAVE SEEN HIM GO INTO

---

*Mount of Olives, or Olivet, rises on the east of Jerusalem, stretch-ing about a mile from North to South.   It has three peaks, the ascen-sion having been from the centre peak, which is also the place of His descension, and commands a view of the surrounding country.

HEAVEN." Now, there were eleven of His Disciples present, and these bear witness of the manner in which *He went*; and also *the place, from which He went*; and the details of both these incidents, according to the angels statement, must be repeated upon His returning to the earth. We have settled the question as to the place; now how did He go?—"...He was taken up, and A CLOUD RECEIVED HIM out of their sight," the disciples tesify (Acts i.9.). Therefore, HE WILL CERTAINLY COME WITH A CLOUD.—"*Behold he cometh with clouds*..."(Rvl.i.7). This does not run counter with other passages of Scripture which speak of His coming in great glory: because there are three Advents; and it is the third one, which the eulogical and glorious language is alluding to. Nevertheless, this second Advent will be of great glory, and yet at the same time, will fulfil the Mount Olivet aspect of descension: for the armies of heaven being spiritual Beings, they are not visible to man's finite sight; unless indeed they are specially sent: as in the cases of Abraham, Lot, Jacob, and others, but then, these angelic-messengers would have undergone a preparative change. Neither can the Holy Spirit be seen with the natural eye, other than in appearance of furnace-like brightness, as masses of smoke, or clouds, as shown at mount Sinai (Exod.xiii. 21; xix.18; xxiv.16). Therefore the very cloud which received Christ at His ascension, and which is spoken of in Acts i.9., may have been milliards of angels

encompassing Him, but having the appearance of white
clouds :—"And I looked, and behold a white cloud,
and upon the cloud one sat like unto the Son of
Man,"says St. John in reference to Christ's descension.

Christ's Cabinet, consisting of *144,000 resurrected
saints, being already upon the Mount of Olives, the
heavens will open, and The Lord, upon the figurative
"white horse," and "clothed with a vesture dipped in
blood," will join them there.—"And I saw, and behold, THE LAMB STANDING ON THE MOUNT ZION, AND
WITH HIM A HUNDRED AND FORTY AND FOUR THOU-
SAND, HAVING HIS NAME, AND THE NAME OF HIS FA-
THER, WRITTEN ON THEIR FOREHEADS" (Revl.xiv.i.
R.V.).—And from this place, He will "judge and make
war"(Revl.xix.11—15) ; i.e., having the power to flash
a stream of Ethereal Spirit from out of His mouth, as
if by sharp sword, "THAT WITH IT HE SHOULD SMITE
THE (antichristian) NATIONS" OF "THE BEAST, AND
THE KINGS OF THE EARTH AND THEIR ARMIES, GATH-
ERED TOGETHER TO MAKE WAR AGAINST HIM." Belteshazzar will be seen manœuvring his troops by the
tactical skill of the greatest military Generals,—now
advancing in echelon with occasional volley firing ;
then a sudden Charge with fixed bayonets, forming
into battalion-squares should the enemy's cavalry
attack ; deployments, and the discharge of field-pieces
with Case, and then with Shrapnel ; "throwing out"

---

*Revl.vi.11, portrays them as an incomp.ete number; Revl.vii.1-4, in
re-urrection preparation; and Revl.xii.2,5; xiv.1-3; xx.4-6, resurrected.

skirmishers; whilst another portion of his army is following up with a flank movement. All the arts of modern warfare is carried out, but somehow, they do not seem to gain any advantage over the Christian-arms: the best of generalship, great odds in number, and yet, not a single engagement has been won. Not even the enemy once routed !—Not one victory ! Ah! he sees not that it is The All Powerful who is secretly guiding this war of *decision*! This leader of the satanic gathering of armed forces, is not aware that He who sits on yonder Mount can make the arm which holds the rifle, unsteady : and the eye, so delusive that in judging the enemy's distance, miscalculate, and thus cause them to give an erroneous elevation on the flap-sight, which, results in the bullets either falling short, or passing harmlessly over the enemy's head. Again, and again, do they strive to overcome the opposing arms, and as oftentimes are they repulsed : whilst the battle-field is strewed with the dead of their greatest men. Belteshazzar and his Staff, cannot make it out! It seems a mystey to them ! and especially as things get worse : they hold consultations : but all to no real effect. Even the horses now, seem to disregard their riders ! What could have happened ?—" Thus...saith the Lord, I will smite every horse with astonishment, and his rider with madness : and I will open mine eyes (have compassion) UPON THE HOUSE OF JUDAH, and I will smite every horse of the (Belteshazzarn) people with blindness " (Zech.xii.4.). This may be expected to take place when the battle is at its highest, causing the mohammedans to be utterly confounded : at the same time, the consuming fiery-stream has been going forth from Him with the all searching eye upon Mount Olivet : so that, " by the blast of God they perish, and by the breath of his nostrils are they consumed " (Job iv.9). " Thus,...He shall smite the earth with the rod of his mouth, and with the †breath of his lips, shall He slay the wicked " (Isa.xi.4.). But these men being in a state of frenzy, with sightless horses, and amidst terrible confusion, an indiscriminate slaughter of each other may be expected : for it is God's way of dealing with massed troops of this *character. Whilst Belteshazzar is ignorant of these facts, Satan is only too conscious of them : he knows very well that these things border upon his doom.

Ages upon ages of Scriptural notice has been given to these satanicly-guided offenders, as a warning to them of God's intentions of battling with sin : but they took no heed ; and now, this Spiritual stream like unto a "two-edged sword " has come upon them, in order to rid the earth of at least a portion of its abomination.

But the Spiritual Messenger of death, will not perform this office exclusively : this stream of Spiritual power which has been going forth from Christ Jesus,

†The Spirit of God, which Christ breathes [John xx.22.], may be a messenger of either blissful-love, or of death, at the will of Christ. [see Revl.ii.12,16; xix.15.].
*Judges vii.22; Samuel xiv.20; ii Chronl.xx.23,24.

has also been a messenger of love, and of great joy, to the Jew. Long before the stage which is recorded in the last paragraph is reached, a contingent from each of the ten-tribes, and the house of Judah, will have had their eyes opened ; their perception so drawn towards mount Olivet as to discern Jesus, from whom each individual will received such a thrill of ecstasy by the stream of Spirit then flowing, as to snap every link of the rebellious antichristian-chain which has hitherto held them ; and cause such a reaction in their hearts, as to create firm sentiments, as well as an intense love for this Being whom their forefathers had once bartered for "*thirty pieces of silver,*"in order to put Him to death. "*In that day will I make the governors of Judah (Egyptian authorities) like an hearth of fire among the wood, and like a torch of fire in a sheaf...; (Zech.xii.6.). For God hath put in their hearts to fulfil his will, and to agree, and give their kingdom unto the beast, until the words of God shall be fulfilled (Revl xvii.17).*" These things having been fulfilled, the deliverance has now come :—"*I will pour upon the house of David, and upon the inhabitants of Jerusalem, the spirit of grace and of supplication : and they shall look upon Me whom they have pierced, and they shall mourn for Him, as one morneth for his only son, and shall be in bitterness for Him, as one that is in bitterness for his firstborn "(Zech.xii.10.).*

It is a noteworthy fact that almost everything from which greatness comes, is produced under two

aspects ; the one superseding the other. Adam, for instance, was superseded by Christ ; Cain, by Seth ; Esau
disinherited, Jacob given inheritance ; Manasseh removed from the first-place blessing, and his brother
Ephraim placed in his stead ; and now, the same thing
holds good with regard to the chosen people and
Christ. The Messiah was rejected by the Jews at the
first Advent, but now, at His second coming, is joyfully accepted. This last experience, however, is not
before the Jews have added to their antichrist-vail,
the essence of bitterness, and hatred of Christ, who,
in His great love, has ever watched over them to help
in the hour of need ; also waited till the arrival of this
ordained date to deliver them, for they needed to drink
of tribulation in order to make them true and stanch,
from the time of their conversion. They will now, I
say, joyfully accept Him ; for have they not found the
true Christ ! He who sat upon yonder Mount, has
He not guided this war to their deliverance !—and such
a deliverance ! even from the grasp of the monster
and his mohammedan yoke ! " Now we know why it
is that the last plague did not come upon us—only
upon the Egyptians." "And this is the KING our forefathers would not have to reign over them !" "Oh !
how we Jews have wronged Him !" "But why has He
been so merciful to us now ?" "Ah ! we have not
known the Scriptures, see here what it says ! "—"*The
noise of a multitude in the mountains like as of a great
people ; a tumultuous noise of the kingdoms of nations*

gathered together : the Lord of hosts mustereth the host of the battle. They come from a far country, from the ends of heaven, even the Lord, and the weapons of his indignation, to destroy the whole land. Howl ye ; for the day of the Lord is at hand ; it shall come as a destruction from the Almighty. Therefore shall all hands be faint and every man's heart shall melt : and they shall be afraid : pangs and sorrow shall take hold of them ; they shall be in pain as a woman that travaileth : they shall be amazed one at another ; their faces shall be as flames" (Isa.xiii.4—8.). " *Ye Ethiopeans also, ye shall be slain by my sword"(Zeph.ii.12.*). "*The Lord at thy right hand shall strike through kings, in the day of his wrath. He shall judge among the heathen, He shall fill the places with the dead bodies : He shall wound the heads over many countries"* (Pslm.cx.5,6.). "*. . .So shall the Lord of hosts come down to fight for Mount Zion, and for the hill thereof"(Isa. xxxi.4.).* "*Alas ! for that day is great, so that none is like it : it is even the time of Jacob's trouble ; but he shall be saved out of it. for it shall come to pass in that day, saith the Lord of hosts, that I will break his yoke from off thy neck, and will burst thy bonds. . ."(Jere.xxx.7,8.).* "*And so all Israel shall be saved. . ."(Rom.xi.26.).*—Now listen to His loving words :—"COME OUT OF *HER, MY PEOPLE, THAT YE BE NOT PARTAKERS OF HER SINS, AND THAT YE RECEIVE NOT OF HER PLAGUES" (Revl.xviii.4.).

---

*Egypt,"Babylon-the-great," is figured as a woman [Revl.xvii.1-6.]; hence the words, "come out of HER."

What God required of the Israelites from the very
commencement of the chosen seed was, that they
should be obedient, which, necessarily, must be the
fruit of either love or fear ; or perhaps of both. As
it is written :—"And now Israel, what doth the Lord
thy God require of thee, but to fear the Lord thy God,
to walk in all his ways, and to love him, and to serve
the Lord thy God with all thy heart and with all thy
soul, to keep the commandments of the Lord, and his
statutes, which I command thee this day for thy good"
(Deut.x.12,13.) ?   God tried by every loving and persuasive means towards this free-will people, to bring
this about : He even went to the extent of forgivness
of sins, for the mere acts of the Mosaic law had no
efficacy : but all to no purpose, the free-will failed to
sever itself from the individual-animal-nature.   He
then presented Himself in structural form as a Sacrifice, which, being the door of the Spirit's-habitation
enabled Him to flow to the yielded-up-will person
as a keeping power over the infirmities of the flesh
(self), an act of love unsurpassed in the annals of
time ; but in blind unbelief they rejected even this.—
"He came unto his own, and his own received him
not " (John i.11.).   Nevertheless, with all these apparent failures, God kept in store the means of a great
triumph,—Jehovah had kept until the last, and time
of the pouring out of His Spirit as a re-birth to every
Jew, the final act of melting their hard hearts and
moving them in sorrow by the sight of the nail-prints

which were inflicted for no other reason than that of
His "making Himself the Son of God "(John x.33.);
—a fact beyond dispute, but, as they now perceive, it
was in the sense of The Spirit God taking upon Himself
the structural form—especially as this very same Being
has now delivered them from the iron-yoke of another
Pharaoh, and from an antichrist of satanic-idolatrous
slavery. This, through the spiritual gleam, has melted
the granite heart, and turned the hatred into love ;
making this final act, as He well knew it would, a
complete success. It was necessary, as we have said,
to let the Jews taste of this bitterness and adversity,
and to be deluded by the antichrist in the kingdom of
Belteshazzar (Revl. xvii. 17.), because it was ordained
that they should become zealously energetic Christians, and irrevocable priests of God for the remainder of
time (iPeter ii.9). So that from this date (3262) henceforth, the motto of, " BLESSED IS HE THAT COMETH IN
THE NAME OF THE LORD," will garnish the Israelite's
banderole, whilst the air will ring with their songs of
righteousness.

> " Oh ! my people, if ye'd only obey'd in Canaanite affairs,
> The ' idols,' and the ' thorns-in-your-side ' which grew *apace,
> Would not have engulf'd you with their many sad snares :
> Yet, ye ever held a passport to the throne of grace !"
>   A.M.

"And the SEVENTH ANGEL poured out his
vial into the air ; and there came a great voice out of

---

*Judges ii.2,3.

the temple of heaven, from the throne, saying, IT IS DONE. And there were voices and thunders, and lightnings; AND THERE WAS A GREAT EARTHQUAKE, such as was not since men were upon earth, so mighty an earthquake, and so great. AND THE GREAT CITY WAS DIVIDED INTO THREE PARTS, and the cities of the *nations fell: and GREAT BABYLON came in remembrance before God, to give unto her the cup of the wine of the fierceness of his wrath" (Revl.xvi. 17—19).

This earthquake-visitation, an event adjoining that of the great hailstorm plague at the time of the final engagement of the great war, is to affect Egypt, or BABYLON THE GREAT, by this great city becoming a heap of ruins; and the land upon which it stood, being split open in three places, and thus the city becomeing divided into three [The cavities made by these rents, are strangely suggestive of an opening to admit of each one of this hellish triumvirate, the "beast," the antichrist-"false-prophet," and the satanic "dragon," being cast into separate homes of hell].

The keen observation of Belteshazzar and his confederate having settled in their minds the hopelessness of their cause, their adverse position being accelerated by the Jews deserting from their ranks and going over *en masse* to the enemy, together with the men of their own battalions showing unmistakable signs of madness by their attacking and slaughtering each

*Mohammedan nations.

other, will act upon the principle of discretion being
the better part of valour, and will flee from the scene
of this terrible carnage : but being pursued and ap-
prehended by the Jews when in or near the Egyptian
metropolis, will be conveyed to the nearest *chasm,
which has been made by the volcanic earthquake,
and hurled into this †sulphurous cavity headlong
down to the bowels of the earth, which, being hell, is
stored up with fire (ii Peter iii.7. R. V).—"And the beast
was taken, and with him the false prophet that wrought
miracles before him, with which he deceived them that
had received the mark of the beast, and them that worshipped his image : these both were cast alive into a
lake of fire burning with †brimstone " (Revl.xix. 20.).
The Jews will then set fire to the debris of the fallen city,
and BABYLON-THE-GREAT become utterly destroyed
(Revl.xvii. 16.). By carrying out this drastic measure,
the earth will be weeded of the enviously evil community, and its antichristian trouble, for at least nine
subsequent centuries. And thus, the Christian nations
will be freed from the mohammedan yoke, the mohammedan iniquity being summed up in this city of
Egypt, under the symbol of "BABYLON THE GREAT."—
As it is written, "...She shall be utterly burned with
fire : for strong is the Lord God who judgeth her"

"*In the great earthquake of middle Japan in the year 1891, a rent was
opened in the superficial strata for a length of more than forty miles."

"†The Rev.G.M.Davies, in writing of the earthquake in India, says,
fissures cut the roads in many places, and SULPHURY SMELL fills
the air."—London Times August 10th 1897.

(Revl. xviii. 8; Jere. ch. 50, is both type and future event).

These events will necessarily cause a great change of Jewish locality, notably the assembling of the rightful heirs in the city of Jerusalem ; a second exody may, therefore, be expected.   But the most glorious part of the event, will be that of Christ directing the children of Israel, and handing over to them the city and land of peace.   And the delivering hand upon this occasion will greatly outweigh that of the former exody of Egypt, because, on that occasion, the guiding power of the living God was hidden in the "pillar of cloud," but now, the living God is visible, and present in structural form : so that the voice of Scripture might well ask, "Who is this that cometh from *Edom, with dyed garments from Bozrah ? this that is glorious in his apparel, travelling in the greatness of his strength ? I (*Christ*) that speak in righteousness, mighty to save " (Isa. lxiii. 1.).

Thus we have portrayed the predictions of the great battle, which will leave its numerous dead in "the valley of decision"— Scripture emphasizes the scene, and portrays the justice of this carried-out measure, by the angel crying *with a loud voice, saying to all the fowls that fly in the midst of heaven, come and eat the flesh of both small and great men.*

Oh ! double-link chain, yet cotton threads withal !
Since the Mighty Messiah the bridle-rein took hold,
Who flash'd His ethereal-sword and consum'd leviathan's wall—
The environs, which girth'd the men of His mould.   A.M.

*Christ with the Jewish settlement of Edom, founded A.D. 1928.

CHAPTER III.

Avaunt! desert waste, Jacob's seed shall again take root!
Israel shall blossom, and fill earth's face with his fruit:
"Me-thinks" I see the still calm waters of this blissful age,
Flowing o'er the Asiatic soil, Christ extoll'd by child and page.
                                                    A.M.

THE MILLENNIUM.

Why should the restoration of the Jews be looked
upon as being merely metaphorical, when their wide-
spread dispersion, is a realized fact? Are not both
the dispersion and restoration pronounced in the prophetic Scriptures, as events which are to come to pass?
then why accept one, and doubt the other? If these
two events are given in Scripture, they must both have
their realization! for God's word cannot lie. The
renovation of Palestine by the fertilizing energy, the
ingathering of Judah and Israel, and the building of its
cities, are all ordained events and must have their fulfilment: just as much as the once fruitful country, under its own race of people, has fulfilled the predict of
its becoming a fallen waste, and an empire of Godless
strangers. Sceptics there ever will be! and I therefore
cannot, yea, do not, expect the account herein given, to
be accepted by everyone: nevertheless, the following

statements, which, if God's word is understood in a rightful interpretation, is borne out by the Scriptures. Moreover, having received additional instructions by the whisperings of the Spirit of God, I have been able to write them with assurance; for I know that it is God's will, that the Millennial future, as well as the other parts of this book, should be described as have been herein set forth.

The "ten-tribe" Israelites and the Jews of Edom, who were subjects of the Egyptian nation, and who have been dwelling within the border of the promised land which extends from the wilderness of Lebanon to the Red Sea, and from the Mediterranean Sea to the river Euphrates (Deut.xi.24.), will have virtually had their country restored to them : for Christ having delivered them—"*at that time shall Michael (Christ) stand up, the Great Prince which standeth for the children of thy people :...at that time thy people shall be delivered, everyone that shall be found written in the book*" (*Danl. xii.1.*)—the whole of Palestine is now in their own possession.

"BEHOLD THE DAYS COME, SAITH THE LORD, THAT I WILL MAKE A NEW COVENANT WITH THE HOUSE OF ISRAEL, AND WITH THE HOUSE OF JUDAH (Jere.xxxi. 31.).— BEHOLD I WILL TAKE THE CHILDREN OF IS- RAEL FROM AMONG THE HEATHEN, WHITHER THEY BE GONE, AND WILL GATHER THEM FROM EVERY SIDE, AND BRING THEM INTO THEIR OWN LAND : AND I WILL MAKE THEM ONE NATION ..."

(Ezek. xxxvii. 21, 22; see ver. 16-20).   By these passages
of Scripture, I wish to point out that God's word is
portraying the restoration of the chosen people, of the
date in question ; they cannot possibly have reference
to any other period than that of the Millennium, because, in the first place, it distinctly speaks of both
"houses," Judah and ten-tribe-Israel : but the " house"
of Israel virtually ceased to exist from the time that
they were taken captive and scattered by Shalmaneser
king of Assyria, a hundred years before Jeremiah predicted the above quoted passage ; and they have not
been known or recognised since.   Therefore this event
must be of the future of our time.   But the above passage of Scripture, by Ezekiel, is even of greater proof :
for we know that since Israel (ten tribes) separated
from the house of Judah in the reign of Rehoboam,
a period of near four hundred years before Ezekiel's
time, these two branches of the twelve-tribe family
have not come together ; yet God tells us in the above
quotation, "He will make THEM ONE NATION :" there
is therefore no room to doubt the genuineness of our
statements.   But let us again take up our position at
the date of the scene of millennial events, and resume
the portrayal of that period, and the travelling on of
time unto the end.

    Is it hard for us to perceive that the Jews, who had
witnessed these great events, and who are witness to the
actual presence of the Messiah whom the Cross once
held in its grasp of death , together with the facilities

which present themselves to enable communication by letter, telegraph, and messenger, to all parts of the globe, will take immediate steps to send word to the towns and countries throughout the world, in order to make these things known to their brethren; and thus cause a general conversion unto Christianity of the Hebrew race? Why should we think a general conversion of Jews in this manner difficult to accomplish? Do we not become converted from worldlings to Christianity at the present day, upon exactly the same lines?—Do men wait until they see Jesus before deciding upon this step, or is the decision arrived at by the procedure of hearing the Word? (and this is a written production of the eye-witnesses at the first Advent of Christ Jesus) By the latter way, certainly! Well then, the letters which these men of millennial authority will send, will be of the same character as that of the written testimony of the disciples of Christ: and if the Holy Spirit's influence upon the message suffice to bless in the one case, may we not conclude that the analogous message which will be sent to the outlying Jews, under the same converting power, will suffice to bless also in the other? And thus bring about a change of heart and mind of these people, and their willing acceptance of the truth. So that the very wind will seem to echo the words of Scripture :- " WHO HATH HEARD SUCH A THING? WHO HATH SEEN SUCH THINGS (*before*)? SHALL THE EARTH BE MADE TO BRING FORTH IN ONE DAY? OR SHALL A

NATION BE BORN AT ONCE? FOR AS SOON AS ZION
TRAVAILED SHE BROUGHT FORTH HER CHILDREN.
AND THEY SHALL BRING ALL YOUR BRETHREN FOR
AN OFFERING UNTO THE LORD OUT OF ALL NATIONS
... TO MY HOLY MOUNTAIN JERUSALEM, SAITH THE
LORD. . ."(Isa.lxvi.8,20).   The conversion of the Jews,
then, will not be of a miracle-aspect, as some men
have been pleased to suggest; yet it will be a very
miraculous incident: but of the individual belief and
Gospel-acceptance character.

A portion of the converted Jews of every known
region throughout the world, will now go forth in their
respective streets and villages to preach the Gospel
of Christ,—the European Jew, to the European; Asiatic Jew, to the people of Asia; the Chinese Jew, to the
people of China; Indian Jew, to the Hindoos; African
Jew, to the Africans; and the American Jew, to the
Americans;—as the ordained priests of a risen Saviour.
"Blessed are ye that sow beside all waters, that send
forth the feet of the *ox and the *ass" (Isa.xxxii.20.).
May we not credit the Holy Spirit with the power of
drawing to Palestine as many Jews of the out-lying
districts as God will, and leaving the rest to perform
the office of priests (Isa.lxvi.21) to convert the heathen?
Who gave the power of decision to the six hundred
thousand Hebrews that left their homes in Egypt to
travel through an unknown desert, with only the visible assurance of Moses and Aaron? was it not the

*Denotes travelling to far districts—the Gospel preached everywhere.

never failing prompting-power of the Holy Spirit? then, from this same power will the conversion of the Jews of all parts of the world, be accomplished.—*"In that day shall the Lord of hosts be for a crown of glory, and for a diadem of beauty, unto the residue of His people"(Isa.xxviii.5). "And it shall come to pass in that day, that the Lord shall set His hand again THE SECOND TIME to recover the remnant of His people, which shall be left from Assyria . . . and He shall set up an ensign for the nations, and shall assemble the outcasts OF ISRAEL, and gather together the dispersed OF JUDAH from the four corners of the earth"(Isa.xi.11,12). "For thus saith the Lord; Behold, I, even I, will both search my sheep, and seek them out, . . . and will deliver them out of all places where they have been scattered in the cloudy, and dark day; and I will bring them out from the people, and gather them from the countries, and will bring them to their own land . . ."(Ezekl.xxxiv.11—13).* "Therefore the redeemed of the Lord shall return, and come with singing unto Zion; and everlasting joy shall be upon their heads: they shall obtain gladness and joy; and sorrow and mourning shall *flee away"(Isa.li.11.).

Now let us go in conception to the Millennial City; and I would impress upon the reader's mind the necessity of weighing the evidence which is laid down by the angel in Ezekiel xl—xlviii, for the formation of the

---

*This has reference to the earthly life.—Men, then knowing the truth of the blissful life hereafter, will not mourn over their dead.

City, the Temple and its ordinances.   And by com-
paring the whole of this portrayed event,(Ezekl.xl—
xlviii.) with other Scripturally-recorded accounts of
Jewish affairs of this nature, they will see that this
one, by its being different in many respects, and by
its having some special features attached thereto, is
distinct from the rest ; and therefore, speaks for itself
as being the plans of an. event of some future period,
other than that of the time of the return to Jerusalem
of the Jewish-captives of Babylon.   This being so,
and the Spirit of God having directed me to point out
to the world that these chapters (xl-xlviii) are the plans
of the Millennium, there is no other alternative than
for me to set them forth in there true and proper light.
No matter what took place under Nehemiah in the
reign of Artaxerxes, the Angel is here portraying to
Ezekiel the plans of the City, the Temple and ordinances, and the Allotments of Land, which the twelve
tribes are to receive as their inheritance.—The temple which Solomon built (i Kings vi.) ; also that of
Zerubbabel and *Jeshua (Ezra v.2.) ; and that which
Herod erected during the space of forty-six years(John
ii.20.) ; were all different in size, and architectural
plan, to that of the temple which the angel measured
as a pattern, before Ezekiel (Ezek.xli-ii).   The angel
speaks also of this temple being a place for the throne,

---

*The rebuilding of the city and temple on this occasion [Ezra.i;
iii.8-10], was interrupted and eventually stopped [Ezra.iv.21-24] ; the
work, however, was resumed by Nehemiah in 446 B.C. [Nehemh.i,ii.].

presumadly the place where Christ will dwell whilst upon earth, which, probably, will be for some time, in order to place the new-born Judaic kingdom in going order ; this is evident by the expression, (in reference to Christ dwelling in the temple for a time) "the place of the soles of my feet,"—"THE PLACE OF MY THRONE, AND THE PLACE OF THE SOLES OF MY FEET WHERE I WILL DWELL IN THE MIDST OF THE CHILDREN OF ISRAEL FOR *EVER. . ."(Ezek.xliii.7.). These words have not hitherto been set forth in connection with previously-built temples : and by its defining (soles of His feet) a portion of the Person who is to dwell there, shows that it is alluding to the Structural-God, Christ : and therefore this temple gives proof of its having reference to the erection of a Sacred Building subsequent to the time of God taking upon Himself the form of man. Also by the following words, which are written in Ezekiel xliv.2., it is shown to be a new, and special arrangement of the future :—"Then said the Lord unto me; This gate shall be shut, it shall not be opened, and no man shall enter in by it ; BECAUSE THE LORD, THE GOD OF ISRAEL, HATH ENTERED IN BY IT, therefore it shall be shut." And here is another, and quite a new feature of a priest's office,—"THE PEOPLE OF THE LAND SHALL WORSHIP AT THE DOOR OF THIS GATE

---

*The words " FOR EVER," were expressed in the hebrew language, lebolam ; and was understood by the Hebrews, to signify, AS LONG AS GOD WISHED. This is borne out by the words of Jonah :-"I was in the belly of the fish THREE DAYS AND THREE NIGHTS , ...her bars was about me FOR EVER"-Jonah.i.17; ii.6. For ever,here,meant three days!

BEFORE THE LORD IN THE SABBATHS AND IN THE
NEW MOONS" (Ezek.xlvi.2,3.).   But the greatest proof
of these Chapters (Ezek.xl—xlviii.) being the plans
and guide of the Millennium country, is in the last
one; for the angel, who has marked out the city and
the temple, now points out to the world the allotment
of land which each of the TWELVE tribes will receive:
and I think everyone will agree with me when I say,
that ten of these tribes, having been scattered and lost
sight of since the reign of Shalmaneser, king of Assyria,
have not yet been told off to, nor become possessors
of, these allotted portions of Palestine since the angel
marked them out.   And this is made clearer by the
words of the fourteenth verse of Ezekiel xlvii, which
shows that this arrangement is distinct from that of
the "dividing-of-the-land" times, which was prior to
the scattering of the ten tribes—"*And ye shall inherit
it, one as well as another : concerning the which I lifted
up mine hand to give it unto your fathers : and this land
shall fall unto you for inheritance.*"—By this evidence,
the planning of this city, and the marking out of the
land, would be void of meaning if it were not intended
to be an event subsequent to the regathering of a representative portion of each of the ten-tribes, which,
the Scriptures show, Christ will declare at His second
coming.   Another feature in this angel-drawn plan,
and one which is also new to all former Jewish settlements, is given (Ezek.xlvii.) under the figure of water,
and may be interpreted by the passage of Scripture

in Revelation xvii.15., and which saith, "The water which thou sawest, are peoples, and multitudes, and nations, and tongues." The angel is pointing out to the world, through Ezekiel, what a thickly populated country the outskirts of the millennial city will be :— "A thousand †cubits" distant, and the populous-waters were in proportion to ankle-deep; "two thousand cubits" distant, and the population were, proportionately, knee-deep; "three thousand cubits" distant, and it reached the "loins;" and at "four thousand cubits" distant, the people were so thickly populated that the representative-water is shown as being beyond a man's depth. But this figurative-water is portrayed as flowing from out of the Temple (Ezek.xlvii.1.): well, and quite true, but in a *spiritual sense: for these people of the suburbs of the millennial city, will be largely composed of the Gentile population of the land, and the figure is here portraying the spreading of the Millennial Gospel of Christ, flowing from the Sanctuary in Spiritual-abundance through the instrumental Jewish priests of the Lord Jesus Christ.—" Ye *shall be* unto me a kingdom of priests, and an holy nation " (Exod. xix.6.)—for "the Lord God which gathered the outcast of Israel saith, Yet will I gather OTHERS to him, BESIDES THOSE THAT ARE GATHERED

†There are two measurements of the cubit; the one here referred to is, 21·888 inches.

*Water, in many instances of Scripture, is used as figure to represent the Holy Spirit—Isa.xii.3.; lv.1. Joel.iii.18. Zech.xiv.8. John iv.10,14. Revl.xxi.6.; xxii.1,17.

UNTO HIM " (Isa. lvi. 8). So that the contents of the
Chapters forty to forty-eight of the book of Ezekiel,
are the plans, and is Scriptually proved to be, for the
City and Land of Palestine during the Millennium.

It was very necessary for me to point this out, and
to portray the proofs of this being the ordained plan
of the Millennial age ; because it is this event, in connection with religious worship, which will bring about
as was foreseen, the completion of the ordained "time
of the Gentiles,"—which we will now speak of.

At this dispensation-stage, a sectarian and serious
mistake will be made by the Gentile-Christian community.—The Christian era, is a dispensation of
Grace unto the flowing of the Spirit ; in this, men are
pardoned of their transgressions through the simple
act of their personal acceptance of Jesus, The Saviour ;
this is followed by the gift of the Spirit, who is a keeping power in a counteracting force to that of the weakness of self in the natural flesh under the power of evil
influences. On the other hand, the Israelites received
not the Spirit, for " He was not yet given," and therefore, not having this keeping-power, were brought
into subjection by "many stripes." This, as well as
their being witness of three doctrinally ordained dis-
pensations, together with the knowledge of the ante-
diluvian age which it pleased God's to use as a means
of instruction to mankind upon the wages of sin
which was portrayed in the deluge-death-punishment,
was counted sufficient to work the desired effect upon

them, who, at this period, ought to be strong enough to resist the indulgent-cravings of the five senses; but alas! it will not be so. This taught-by-experience abnegation, will be assisted however, by the strengthening power of the Spirit, which will then be given unto them; together with the fearing of Christ, whom they will have now learned to love, and to give allegiance with an indeavour to make reparation in a true faithfulness of the future.

Although the Jews will become devout Christians from the time of the great battle, several Jewish-rites are ordained to be retained in the Christian Religion of that age: these consist of certain sacrificial ordinances, one of which, probably, will be offered up unto Christ Jesus; and are laid down in the EIGHT CHAPTERS of the book of Ezekiel (xl—xlviii) which portray the Church of the Millennial dispensation.

This new, and practical side of religious worship, however, the Gentile Christians of that date, will not accept: they will turn from these Israelite priests, who, it should be clearly understood, will be the only Spirit-blessed ministers and servants of God during the thousand years,—refusing to listen to them, much in the same manner as the Jews, up to our present time, refuse to listen to the Gentile minister.

"But why bring in sacrificial ordinances," cry out the good Christian?

Simply, for the following reasons :-

a.—To sacrifice unto Christ Jesus, who is God

structurally formed ;—The Son.

b.—The "OLD MAN" OF ADAM, can never be literally, and actually changed :—whilst the flesh remain,
he will, under all circumstances, and every condition
of dispensation, be the same earthly being.—This
being so, nature will assert itself during the millennial
age, just the same as it has done at all other times : and
the acts which pertain to progeneration, will go on
as heretofore.—Men, however, take for granted, or
rather, arrive at a conclusive decision, that this thing is
permissible : but, for the want of a little individual
scrutiny of the matter, they have never perceived how
indulgence of this kind must act upon holiness. I do
not deny that these acts have been ordained : but,
nevertheless, be it understood, that what was essential
in the matter of fruitfulness unto the replenishment of
the earth at all other periods of time, will not be so
pressing at this date, when the whole earth has become
populous. Therefore, these acts at the time of the
millennium, being no longer of an essential character,
they are expected to fall into a state of chronic-ebb.
Now, although the "old-man" has been pronounced
in the creation-sense as being good, it does not follow
that his acts are pure! This being so,—if these acts
are impure deeds—a certain amount of uncleanness
must exist ; and, if this be the case, the inhabitance of
the millennial country who are ordained to be a holy
people,. will be placing HOLINESS AND UNCLEANNESS
SIDE BY SIDE, two things that can never be expected

to agree. Therefore, a sort of compromise is ordained to step in,—the unclean must take part in a cleansing-symbol—blood and sacrifice must atone for this permissible defilement : in a disciplinarian point of view, an offering to Christ as an act of confession of individual uncleanness, is to be enacted ; not as a real atonement, for the Blood of Christ only, stands good unto all time for this purpose : nevertheless, a *bona fide* act which will keep the flesh from self-righteousness, and self-justification, which it is prone to assume, even to the extent of self-exaltation. The wisdom of this rite is obvious : for God cannot wink at uncleanness ; to do so, would be giving men authority to count permissible acts as being outbalanced by the designative, " holy-people ;" whereas, uncleanness will remain the same under all circumstances, and of whatever aspect :—the Mosaic law did not enable men to mount up to the pinnacle of righteousness, but rather, was given to the Israelites to show them that the natural man, was unrighteous : "For, by the law is the knowledge of sin." "Moreover, the law entered that the offence might abound,"—and, "There is none righteous, no, not one." Whether we believe or not, in the necessity of these Jewish-rites, matters very little at this period ; suffice it to say, the Jews will believe in them ; and they will not again fall into the error of looking upon themselves as being perfectly holy in the face of the existence of natural uncleanness, a state of things, and a stumbling-block of the former

·times, which led them to rely upon the *name* of holiness more than that of its actual fulfilment : and all because God had said, "Thou art a holy people." But it is easy to see, that the calling of a man holy, does not make him so : any more than the calling of Judas Iscariot to the discipleship of Christ, did not make him a disciple :—an adherent to his Master's doctrine. The fact of God having repeated the message, by His saying to the people by the mouth of the prophht,— "Be ye holy even as I am holy," goes to prove that holiness is a matter of being free from uncleanness. Yet, as we have shown by the "old man" still existing, it is not ordained that tnis is to be the absolute rule : the means, therefore, to overcome the difficulties of the case, is to be established in a Judaic cleansing-rite, which God has laid down through the pen of Ezekiel.

As we have already said, the Millennial doctrine will be a stumbling-block to the Christian Gentiles of that age ; and for no other reasons than that of the dogmatic sway which has always created in man a prejudice to any other form of doctrine than that which is then being taught, and carried out by them. But why should it be so, when God has said, "My DOCTRINE SHALL DROP AS THE RAIN?" Why do men think that the handed-down form of worship is continuous, and their present principle of doctrinal ordinance is the standard religion, and must hold good along the future ages?—This fact, however, ought never to be lost sight of :—whilst the earth remain, in Jesus only, is Redmption to be found—from Jesus only, is Salvation given—through Jesus only, by the workings of His Spirit, is Conversion accomplished— and in Jesus only, by an indwelling " new birth " of *His Spirit, is Eternal Life a reality.   But the method whereby the human creature is taught to see that he is nothing of himself, that obedience unto God is re- quired of him, and that he is very prone before the " new birth," even after conversion, to follow the dic- tates of (self) the flesh, has been varied in every dis- pensation since the world began.

And has not this dogma been made by men them- selves, a stumbling-block throughout the ages ?   Are we not aware of the terrible mistake the Jews made in this direction ?—Did they not say, in meaning and effect, We will not have this man Jesus, nor his doc- trine, because we have already got hold of the true worship,—the law of God by Moses, which was given to our forefathers at mount Sinai, and therefore, our doctrine must be the true one for all time ?

Do we not say the Jews were very foolish in this ? that they ought to have known the Scriptures suffic- iently to have seen that the coming of the Messiah must necessarily change the form of their religion, which was the Will of God ? yet, upon exactly the same lines, the same thing will be done by the Gentile Christians, at the second Advent !   Can it not be seen that these Judaic rites, will not in any way interfere

---

*Christ's Spirit, and The Holy Spirit—God, are one and the same.

with the Gospel; any more than the acts, and the teaching of Christ when upon earth, did not interfere with the law: for He saith, "I am not come to destroy the law." The Scriptures show that any Judaic-rite may be performed, SO LONG AS THERE IS TRUE BELIEF IN THE LORD JESUS CHRIST; "Do we then make void the law through faith? God forbid: yea, we establish the law" (Rom. iii. 3i). What Paul sets forth is, THAT THERE IS NO SALVATION IN THE LAW: nevertheless, he entered into some of its Judaic rites (Acts. xviii. 18-21; XXI. 26, 27.). "But there rose up certain of the sect of the Pharesees WHO BELIEVED, saying, It is needful to circumcise them, and to charge them to keep the law of Moses. And the apostles and the elders were gathered together to consider of this matter "(Acts xv. 5, 6. R. V.). Now, this apostolic-council, after St. Paul and others had given their evidence, agreed to put certain restrictions upon the Gentiles only (Acts xv. 29.); this, it will be seen, by there being no record in Scripture as to any doctrinal measure being put upon the Jews, shows, that these believers in Christ Jesus who were now under the religious care of the disciples, had permission to carry on with any of the Judaic rites; as it is written,—"Thou seest brother, how many thousands of Jews there are WHICH BELIEVE; AND THEY ARE ALL ZEALOUS OF THE LAW" (see Acts xxi. 15-24). And again: Jesus took part in these rites; He not only read the lessons in the synagogue on the sabbath-day, but also, entered into THE FEAST OF THE

PASSOVER (Luke.xxii.7-16).—I know, it was necessary for Him to fulfil His office as the realization of the typically-portrayed paschal-lamb, whose blood was sprinkled upon the door posts of the Jewish habita-tions of Egypt, but this does not alter the fact of His recognition of the rite.   And we must not lose sight of the fact, that the millennium will be a recognised Hebrew age.   By these things, we have no right to be dissatisfied with the method of religious-worship of the millennium, and especially when it has been seen what decision the early disciples arrived at ; for, these men being led by the Spirit, they could not have sanctioned these things, had they been wrong acts.

Why, then, should not the Gentile-Christians join in with the Jews, at the time of the Millennium ?—Will the following quotation of Scripture—"*If any man shall add unto these things, God shall add unto him the plagues that are written in the book : and if any man shall take away from the words of the book of this prophecy, God shall take away his part out of the book of life...*"*(Revl. xxii.18,19.)*—be a stumbling-block ? if so, it is a sign of great blindness ! for any unbiased mind that pos-sesses the knowledge of the way in which God's word grew into it's present size, can see that this passage of Scripture does not refer to the whole of the present Book, or Bible ; but rather, that it is simply referring to St. John's book of prophecy, or the Apocalypse. Let me point this out clearly :—

There are sixty-six books in the bound Volume,

called the Bible : these books, with few exceptions,
were written at different periods, and were, in many
cases, separate epistles. Thirty-nine of these books,
were written before the birth of Christ : the other
twenty-seven were the writings of inspired Christian-
men at various times, and places, during the first
century ; the whole being collected and formed into
one great manuscript-volume, about the end of the
third, or the begining of the fourth, century. By
these facts, it will be seen that, when John wrote his
Apocalypse which contain the words in question, he
could not have known of its becoming attached to
sixty-five other books and epistles, the existence of
some of which, he had no knowledge of. Now, half an
eye can see that, when he penned the words, "*If any
man shall add unto these things...,"or"...take away from
the words of the book of this prophecy,*" that he referred
to the book—the Apocalypse—he was then writing.
Therefore, this passage of Scripture (Revl.xxii.18,19.)
has got nothing whatever to do with the other sixty-
five book-parts of God's word. But I may here state,
the Millennial Doctrine will not "add to," nor "take
away from," the already-written word of God.

Nevertheless, it should be perceived by the future
generation, that a new dispensation must necessarily
bring in a different form of religious worship. This
is seen to have been the case all through the lapse of
time : and I have no doubt, the form of worship that
was carried on previous to the calling of the Hebrews,

although, perhaps, not of the strictest character, was acceptable to God ; for He judges according to the light which men have received. The first law that was put upon man outside of Eden, was, "Whoso sheddeth man's blood, by man shall his blood be shed" ...(Gen.ix.6.) : this was dated from the time of Noah, and when sin was not imputed (Rom.iv.15; v.13.) ; i.e., there was no sin in doing that which had not been forbidden : the shedding of man's blood, then, was the only law at this time. When the Mosaic law was brought in, however, a new aspect of things appeared, and all acts not of a righteous character, were prohibited : which things were qualified and regulated by the written law. Then, after about fifteen centuries, Christ came and established the Christian era, which brought in a Spiritual dispensation ; i.e., the ages in which all things needed for Salvation and Eternal-life, are procurable to "Whosoever shall call upon the name of the Lord" (Rom.x.13), as a gift of Grace. This brought in the Gentiles, for whom St.Paul was ordained to be a teacher ;—"That a hardening in part hath befallen Israel, UNTIL THE FULNESS OF THE GENTILES BE COME IN" (Rom.xi.25.), when, as we have been pointing out, a new and final dispensation will be established, and at which, the rites in question are to be carried out ; "For verily I say unto you, Till heaven and earth pass, one jot or one tittle shall in no wise pass from the law, till all be fulfilled"(Matt. v.18.). This thing is also shown in Christ's message

to the *Thyatirans (Revl.ii.25) in which He says,"That
which ye have already hold fast till I come ;" signifying
that it only stands good in it's present form, until He
does come.   In fact, His words, " I will put upon YOU
none other burdens " (Revl.ii.24.), shows us that the
proper consummate worship is not in use at present,
and proves that other doctrinal-burdens ARE to be put
upon men, at that time.

Moreover, has not God portrayed a possible limit
to the Gentile-ingrafting? yea, it can be seen looming
in the distant future !—"*If some of the branches be broken off and thou, being a wild olive tree, wast grafted in
among them, and with them partakest of the root and
fatness of the olive tree; boast not against the root, but
the root thee.   Thou wilt say then, the branches were
broken off, that I might be grafted in.   Well; because
of unbelief they were broken off, and thou standest by
faith.   Be not high-minded, but fear.   Behold therefore
the goodness and severity of God : on them which fell,
severity; but towards thee goodness, if thou continue in
his goodness : otherwise thou also shalt be cut off "(Rom.
xi.17—22.).*   St. Paul here shows his perception of
the stumbling-block, and points out to the Gentiles
their position, which is that of the ten-absorbed-tribes
as wild olives, being placed upon the Judaic olive-tree,
until, their " boasting against," or the rejection of, the
doctrinal-olive-tree root.   For, alas ! it was foreseen

---

*Tho inhabitants of "a city of lesser Asia, on the frontiers of Lydia ;
now called Akishar " [Peter Oliver's Lexicon].

that this "boasting" event would come to pass, and would bring upon them their predicted end ; as it is written,"...UNTIL THE TIMES OF THE GENTILES BE FULFILLED " (Luke.xxi.24.).

The incidents which we have just related, will be the means of giving fervency and impetuosity to the Jews in their capacity of preachers to the outside world, which, otherwise, they would not attain : of course, the atoning redemption of Calvary's Sacrifice, will be as efficacious to all who accept Christ through the teachings of these Hebrew priests as Millennium-"vessels," as it is at the present time (Isa.lx.3,5; Amos ix.12.), the only difference being, that in this new dispensation, abnegation, righteous-dealings, implicit obedience to God, and sobriety in the fullest sense of the word in all matters, will be practically carried out. A lot of mystery will vanish from Scripture, because Self will not continue in his misinterpreting ; dogma, social position, and other circumstances, will not then rule unto bias : for outside of prophecy, self is the root of Scriptural mystery.

It is misleading to indulge in the imagination of Christ Jesus being "meek and lowly" upon this occasion, for the Scriptures do not portray Him as such (Isa.xlii.13,14.) ; there is a limit even to mercy : and this event will witness Him in power, and for conquering purposes ;—the Jews thought at the time of the destruction of their city by the Romans, that God's mercy would still be held out to them, and thus

they clung to the hope of being delivered: so sang-
uine were they, that it gave them courage to misera-
bly hold out during the burning of their temple whilst
a tremendous large number where within, and who
perished in the flames. These Jews were blind to the
fact, that God was punishing them for their rejection of
Jesus and His doctrine, and the committal of the cruel
act of putting Him to death;—He submitted then, but
now, at this second Advent, He comes to war against
those who still reject Him. This, however, must not
be looked upon by the mohammedans with an entirely hopeless eye, for there will still remain the mercy
of Christ: even after they will have received the fatal
blow of the great battle by an immence number of
them being killed, and when the few which escaped
will have told their tale of how they felt that some
supernatural power was overruling them at the time
of the conflict, together with the mysteriously-sudden
change of sides of the Jews by their going over and
allying themselves to the Christian ranks, at the very
time when victory seemed to be within the reach
of the mohammedan arms. But, alas! though these
things will have been indelibly written upon the
minds of the mohammedan people, subduing them
and crippling their cause, and being the instrument
that will carry out the fulfilment of the thousand years
which is figuratively portrayed as "an angel coming
down from heaven having the key of the bottomless
pit and a great chain in his hand, and laying hold of

the dragon, that old serpent, which is the devil, and satan, and binding him a thousand years" (Revl.xx. 1,2.), yet the spirit of Satan will still be in them!— And, by the crushing of Belteshazzar and his hoards, the predicted words of the Scripture will be fulfilled in the Jewish exclamations :—"...*How hath the oppressor (Belteshazzar) ceased! the golden city(Egypt—Babylon the great) ceased! The Lord hath broken the staff of the wicked, the sceptre of the rulers; that smote the people in wrath with a continual stroke, that ruled the nations in anger, with a persecution that none restrained. The whole earth is at rest, and is quiet: they break forth into singing. Yea, the fir trees rejoice at thee, and the cedars of Lebanon, saying, Since thou (Belteshazzar) art laid down, no feller has come up against us. Hell from beneath is moved for thee to meet thee at thy coming: it stirreth up the dead for thee, even all the chief ones of the earth; it hath raised up from their thrones all the kings of the nations. All they shall answer and say unto thee, Art thou also become weak as we? art thou become like unto us? Thy pomp is brought down to hell, and the noise of thy viols: the worm is spread under thee, and worms cover thee. How art thou fallen from heaven O day star, son of the morning! how art thou cut down to the gound, which didst lay low the nations! And thou saidst in thine heart, I will ascend into heaven, I will exalt my throne above the stars of God; and I will sit upon the mount of congregations, in the uttermost parts of the north: I will ascend above the heights of the* *clouds; I will be like the most high.   Yet thou shalt be brought down to hell, to the uttermost parts of the pit. They that see thee shall narrowly look upon thee, they shall consider thee, saying, Is this the man that made the earth to tremble, that did shake kingdoms; that made the world as a wilderness, and overthrew the cities thereof; that let not loose his prisoners to their home?   All the kings of the nations, all of them, sleep in glory, every one in his own house.   But thou art cast forth away from thy *sepulchre like an abominable branch, clothed with the slain, that are thrust through with the sword, that go down to the stones of the pit; as a carcase trodden under foot (†Isa. xiv. 4—19. R. V.),*

Having proceeded to the blisful home which Christ has been preparing (John. xiv. 2.), Christ's Cabinet of 144,000, will now sit at His table for a thousand years (Luke. xxii. 30; Revl. xx. 4-6.).   This will probably· be the instruction-period, in order that this Government may learn their duties and be prepared to receive the harvest which is to be a multitude that no man can number, in the eternal realms (Revl. vii. 9.).

And now, at this time, by the exceedingly abundant flow of the Spirit upon the inhabitants who are within the boundary of the Millennial city, which includes those of the Gentile races who accept and carry out their Christianity in the orthodox manner of that

---

* See Revelation xix. 20.

†This paragraph, whilst appearing to have reference to the ancient Babylon, is the prefigure of Belteshazzar, king of Egypt, [Babylon the great] at the time of his destruction and the millennial dawn.

era, will be fulfilled the predicted words of the prophets which saith, "Behold a king shall reign in righteousness, and princes shall rule in judgment; for I will pour water (Spirit) upon him that is thirsty, and floods upon the dry ground : I will pour my Spirit upon thy seed, and my blessing upon thine offspring" (Isa. xxxii. 1); "...for I have poured out my Spirit upon the house of Israel, saith the Lord God" (Ezek. xxxix. 29).   It does not follow, however, that everyone who avails himself of the Millennial form of worship, will have to live within the boundary of that city, or even in Palestine : the Scriptures show us that the people of those cities and countries which are near, however, will be expected to take steps to be present upon the occasions of the ingathering of Jews at the monthly NEW MOONS ; AND ALSO ANNUALLY, from sunset on the evening of the ninth, to sunset on the evening of the tenth of *Tisri, the seventh month, which is called a "sabbath of rest" (Levi. xxiii. 32; Ezek. xlv. 17, xlvi. 3; Zech. xiv. 16.) : and those nations who refuse to †come to this city on these occasions, are to be plagued with drought (Zech. xiv. 17—19.).   This will pave the way for the outside world ; and be the means of overcoming a lot of prejudice.   Locomotion through the air, may be an accomplished fact at this date, and thus facilitate the travelling upon these occasions : I do not say that it will be so.

*From the middle of September, to the middle of October.
†This, probably, will be carried ont by distant cities, by delegation.

Of course, Christ will have gone along with His Cabinet: erroneous it is to suppose that He remains upon this earth during the Millennium :—the flesh is not able to bear such an ordeal !—Men are too weak now ! but if they had the opportunity of seeing Christ continually, as assuredly they would if He remained upon the earth, their weakness would be increased to such an extent, as to make men unable to contain themselves, and they would become prostrate with overwhelming feelings at the sight and presence of the Lord. This has already been tested : Ezekiel fell upon his face when beholding a certain vision ; Daniel became prostrate at the sight and presence of immortal beings ; but in the presence of the Immortal Lord, as soon as the finite sight beheld, as in the case of St. John, man became, as it were, dead (Revl.i.13-17). Earthly occupation too would suffer, and business in a general sence, become paralyzed. No : mortals, and The Immortal, are far too wide apart in nature's-path ! "Touch me not," said Christ to Mary Magdalene. . . But why should we expect such a thing? cannot Christ, who has the government of this earth "upon His shoulder" (Isa.ix.6.), rule the things of this city from a far-off distance, just as well as if His Structural Person was actually present ?—Distance is no impediment to The Omniscient Spirit : in fact, The Spirit cannot be other than present, for "do I not fill all space, saith the Lord ?" This earth's suifaᴄe has been prepared for mortals, and is not suitable for immortal habitations, and especially that of God in Structural Form. Night, for instance, with its slumbering hush, would have no meaning but be a useless blank to the immortal, if dwellers of this earth, for they sleep not. But it might be said, are not such beings just the very ones to guard us, and watch over our city by night? Those who are of this way of thinking, however, have very little spiritual perception, and know little or nothing of God's power; for it is absolutely impossible for an enemy to lift a single finger against any of His children, once He has willed otherwise; as in the case of the Millennial city, which, it has been ordained, shall remain in peace until the loosing of Satan, which means a literal invasion of Gog and his army of whom we will speak presently. No: God's power of protection of a city is of a different character than that of literally posting night sentinels therein.

The Israelites, to say the least of it, have great prospects and a blissful future, from the time of the overthrow of Belteshazzar and the antichrist, and their conversion to Christianity. God's messages to them are very assuring: they provide mercy, bountiful goodness, and even such glory as, "Arise, shine; for thy light is come, and the glory of the Lord is risen upon thee. The sons also of them that afflicted thee shall come bending unto thee; and all they that despised thee shall bow themselves down at the soles of thy feet; and they shall call thee, the city of the Lord, the Zion of the Holy One of Israel"(Isa.lx.1,14).

Speaking as though these events had really come
to pass,—that we were actually living in the Millennial
era, let us take a glance at this once heathen-trodden,
and desolate land :—

Marvellous are the accomplishments of man when
led by the Spirit!—Here, this once-forsaken land,
with its scattered buildings of inelegance located near
the fertile patches and tracts which were spared from
the wrath of God, now abounds, and are still fast
growing, with habitation-buildings and stately structures of institution, and of business character, of the
newest designs of architecture. This long slumbering
spot, has awakened to both godliness and activity.
A wonperful peace has taken hold of men of this land :
—their minds are no longer disturbed by the study of
the quickest way to fill up a bank-book : nor the an-
xiety of finding out the best class of rifle, the most
powerful gun, and the handiest pattern of sword and
spear, for all these things are forged into " plowshares
and pruning hooks." And what has become of selfish-
ness, and bitterness of breast ? behold " the wolf with
the lamb, and the leopard lying down with the kid :
and the calf, and the young lion " being led by the
little child. "For thus saith the Lord, behold I will
extend peace to her like a river " (Isa.lxvi. 12.).

The pools of Bethesda are again endowed with
miraculous virtue, and the well of Jacob is rejoicing
in its bubbling abundance : and the land is now showing forth " THE GARDEN OF THE LORD."

This is the most prolific of all the Jubilee seasons : and is yielding the hundred-fold production, as in the days of Isaac ; when "the dew of heaven, and the fatness of the earth, and plenty of corn and wine" filled the souls of men with gladness.

Here, those once craggy parts, which, for ages have been struggling to bring forth its natural folage, but has only been able to produce thorns and thistles in clusters upon the land, is now spread over with rich grass ; and the once withered-looking boughs of the few gasping trees which have annually disappointed mankind in their production of dwarf, and sour fruit, no longer pine in despair for the want of a little moisture to their parched roots, for they are now supplied with "brooks of water, of fountains and depths, springing forth from valleys and hills "(Deut.viii.7.R.V.).

There, for many miles beyond the range of the eye, the once hot and dazzling sands of Peræa, which for ever seemed to be drifting hither and thither as if moved by the hand of a soul of unrest , spreading terror in the hearts of men, especially those who found themselves within its travelling area, lest these simoom sand-pillars in mysterious swiftness would swallow up and consume them, are now changed as if by magic wand, into "a land of wheat and barley and vines and fig-trees, and pomegranates..."(Deut.viii.8). The cedars of Lebanon are made merry by the increase of its family,—"Behold, I WILL PLANT IN THE WILDERNESS the cedar, the acacia (chittah) tree, the

myrtle, and the oil tree; I WILL SET IN THE DESERT
the fir tree, and the pine, and the box tree together"
(Isa. xli. 19,).

See yonder territory, which has lain waste for the
past ages in consequence of the ignis-fatuus fire which
has been continually passing and repassing over its
surface, blighting all vegetation within its area in fulfilment of God's wrathful prediction; it has now been
permitted to burst forth into prolification and is again
clothed with beauteous verdure, as "fields which the
Lord hath blessed" unto the "flowing with milk and
honey." Look at this hill; from barrenness, it now
brings forth rich olives abundantly; and yon mountain, with its healthful almond, palm, balsom, and the
joy-inspiring rosy-cheek fruit, the apricot and peach,
trees of the Millennium production, at which the
people huzza!

Among the many changes which this consummate
era has wrought, is this vale with its attached fields:
this once gloomy and solemn grave-like dell, with its
few scattered briers as if mourners for the dead, has
now a soft velvet-sheet appearance, intermingled with
lilies and other flowers of perfection; and the fields,
behold, that which was once without tree or shrub, is
now the vineyard! and is not only sufficient to export
rich delicious grapes, but also, to supply the nations
with choice raisins, and a superior wine. Also the
once barren mountain-hills adjoining, have become so
fertile, as to enable the exportation of millet, linseed,

and other grain, which now, these hills are the product source.

The oaks of Carmel too, are now majestically
spreading their arms of foliage ; and Lebanon, as we
have said, is again rejoicing in its cedar production,
the ancient plantation having dwindled down to seven
in number; but the Lord foresaw this contingency, and
predicted that, "The wilderness and the solitary places
shall be glad ; and the desert shall rejoice, and blossom
as the rose.   It shall blossom abundantly, and rejoice
even with joy and singing ; the glory of Lebanon shall
be given unto it, the excellency of Carmel and Sharon;
they shall see the glory of the Lord, and the excellency
of our God " (Isa. xxxv. 1,2. R. V.).

Oh ! plains of Ramah, Esdraelon, and Zebulum,
how hast thou become so marvellously changed ? the
bramble, and the underwood, has hitherto been the
limit of thy glory ; but now thou art clothed in the
most brilliant of robes !   Thy beds of enchantment,—
the sweet array of botanic nature, filling the soul
with reflection as the eye scans thy lovely bloom in all
its various hues ; whilst thy fragrance gives delight by
the olfactory nerve drinking in the emitted perfume
which revives the languid and the sorrowful of heart,
amid the scene of tulip, dahlia, fuchsia, jasmine, rose,
and many others, upon which the gaze is drawn.   And
none the less productive has the land been of things
pertaining to business :- over that vast expanse with
the mystic looking surface,—having an appearance of a

woolly-white carpet thickly intermixed with irregular ebon-spots; this is the cotton plant, the pods having burst with ripeness, as much as to say, we are now ready for the spinner, and for the supply of the weaver.

Palestine, in fact, having received of the Creator's will, has produced vegetation indigenously : and various are its fruit, as if the different climatic-influences of all the earth had been brought to bear upon the soil of this country, for the purpose of re-producing in the millennium the garden of Eden, for which," God hath given it of the dew of heaven." Everyone bursts forth into "singing," and their song is fertility, fertility ! for behold, " Her wilderness like Eden, and her desert like the garden of the Lord "—" Then shall the lame man leap as an hart, and the tongue of the dumb sing : for in the wilderness shall water break out, and streams in the desert " (Isa. li. 3; xxxv. 6.).

> "The glowing sand shall become a pool,
> And the thirsty soil, bubbling springs."   [Isa.]

Palestine being in a central position of the world, will obviously flourish in its manufacturing industry. By the Jews of the past ages having been located in every country throughout the world, and by their sons having learned the many trades and sciences, they will have sufficient knowledge to enable them to become the great manufacturing country of the earth. Instructed as apprentices and otherwise, they will have become proficient in the industrial crafts of every nation,—the

French Jew will introduce into Palestine, silk-weaving;
Greek Jews, the art of sculpture; the Persian Jew,
spinning; England (Manchester), will have instructed
her Jewish sons in the manufacture of cotton fabrics,
whilst other English and Scotch towns, that of cloth
material; the Birmingham and Sheffield Jew, will be
able to manufacture all sorts of cutlery and the like,
also certain machinery. America, and Germany, will
in no way be behindhand in the production of Jewish
artisans, America taking the lead in the Jew-supply
of cabinet makers and all the necessaries of the furni-
ture branch. Russia, and Africa, may also, at a future
date, be expected to cultivate the Jew-mechanic; and
all countries will have taught him the art of agriculture.
So that we may come to the conclusion that, the Millennium will not only produce its own skilful artisans,
but that they will prosper to the extent of supplying
the people of the earth. In fact, by the great store
of minerals which are now laying dormant under the
surface of the land of this country, and also the fact,
that a thousand years hence the mineral-product of
other countries will have become exhausted, will give
new and energetic life to the people of the country;
for the Jews will feel under these circumstances, what
an importance the great city of the last ages, will be to
the rest of the world. And especially when they realize the fact of these possessions, and hidden riches,
which it had pleased The Almighty to lay up in the
earth's-store of the holy land, and thus keep for them

until the Millennium, in order to make their city the
centre of attraction in both material things of men's
requirements, and that of Spiritual matters.   The
Israelites will therefore, succeed to wealthy possessions,—"A LAND WHOSE *STONES ARE IRON, AND OUT
OF WHOSE HILLS THOU MAYEST DIG BRASS" (copper
and zinc); and where there are "TREASURE HIDDEN IN
THE SAND" (Deut. viii. 9; xxxiii. 19).—The sands, which
we have shown are too terrible for man to attempt
the discovery of its treasure before the time , are no
longer the simoom-terror to man at the Millennium,
when the Hebrew-dower and consummation-treasury
will be fouud to be of gold, and of precious stones
(Gen. ii. 11, 12.).

As the natural things of this earth are not, nor
never were, perfect in a true sense, everything being
of a decaying nature, so will the enmity of Satan in
the breast of the mohammedan, be kindled, in the
course of the millennial ages, and will burst forth into
rebellious flames.   Satan is to be loosed ! (Revl. xx. 3)
And his fanatic-host, under the leadership of Gog and
Magog, are to be permitted to rush upon their own
doom.   They have seen the protecting mercy of God
to the Hebrews, and His power over their land to
make them prosperous and happy, and yet, in the
face of these things, they will say, "*I will go up to the*

---

*Iron, as found in the earth, is absorbed in stone ; hence the saying,
"stones are iron."— The smelters extract the iron, by bringing the
whole substance into a molten liquid state.

land of unwalled villages; I will go to them that are at rest, that dwell safely, all of them dwelling without walls, and having neither bars nor gates; to take a spoil, and to take a prey; to turn thine hand upon the desolate places that are now inhabited, and upon the people that are gathered out of the nations, which have gotten cattle, and goods. Thou shalt ascend and come like a storm thou shalt be like a cloud to cover the land, thou, and all thy bands, and many people with thee" (Ezek.xxxviii 11,12,9). Before we proceed, however, with the Gog and Magog invasion, let us see who these two men, and their forces are :—

The Scriptures speak of four men,—Gog, Magog, Meshech, and Tubal (Ezek.xxxviii.), these were the sons of Japhet. Now, MAGOG, was the father of the Scythians, or Tartars, who, through the overrunning of Tartary, produced the Turks, a multitudinous mohammedan race. Scripture also tells us, that the (offspring) people of Meshech and Tubal, Gog, and Magog, will invade the city and villages of Palestine, in the last days (Ezek.xxxviii; Revl.xx.8). Gog, in the Greek language, means, "a roof of a house :" now, in building a house, the roof is the last operation ; thus Gog, signifies the last operation of the mohammedan house. And Magog, which means, "covering," points to the same thing as roofing, or, the finishing part of mohammed's dynastic-house. The mystery of that passage of Scripture (Ezek.xlvii.11) which states, "THE MIRY PLACES THEREOF AND THE MARSHES THEREOF

SHALL NOT BE HEALED, THEY SHALL BE GIVEN TO
SALT," is therefore, now made plain : for the MIRY
AND MARSHY .places, is a figurative portrayal of the
mohammedan villages and towns, whose inabitants,
it was foreseen, would retain a smouldering enmity
from the time of the great "battle of the Lord," and
therefore, the people of these places were not to be ex-
horted to accept Christ, but were, in the words of the
allegory, to "be given to salt." So that, Gog, Magog,
Meshech, and Tubal, together with Persia, Ethiopia,
Libya, Gomer, and Togarmah (Ezek. xxxviii. 5, 6.),
which, virtually, means the whole of the mohammedan
races, are here portrayed as comprising the army of
invasion at the date below stated ; Gog being the chief
nation, is to be led by its prince, and who will, probably, be in command of the invading forces.

Well then, at the date 4,262, Satan will be permitted to go forth to prompt the hearts and minds of the
people who are outside the consummate-area, even
"to decieve the nations which are in the four quarters
of the earth, Gog and Magog, to gather them together
to battle : the number of whom is as the sand of the
sea " (Revl.xx.8.).   This, however, will not be a legit-
imate assemblage of troops, as in the case of an up-
right war : but rather, will be might to overcome
right, and which will have been actuated by enmity
towards the Christians, as the spite of a once beaten
foe ; and the plundering instinct of an evil and crafty
people, venting itself in the sense of greed, and gain of

spoil. This invasion will, of course, terrify the people of Palestine, much in the same manner as the Hebrews were terrified upon the occasion of the persuit of Pharaoh and his six hundred chariots and horsemen with the rest of his army, and who came within sight of them in their rear, whilst the waters of the Red sea at Pi-hahiroth glared at them with the look of death, in their front; and also, when the Philistines came against Israel at Socoh, in Ephes-dammin, when a mere stripling saved them with the aid of a sling-stone guided by the hand of God. Therefore at this time, when there is great trembling and "shaking in the land of Israel," and apparent destruction through Gog and his moving mass being within measurable distance of them,—when thou,"...O Gog, the chief prince of Meshech and Tubal" have "come like a storm, and like a cloud to cover the land," then, as in the other cases, will the jealously of God bring the fury into His face; and in His wrath, He will "RAIN FIRE AND BRIMSTONE" FROM HEAVEN UPON THEM; as it is written, "*And they went up on the breadth of the carth, and compassed the camp of the saints about, and the beloved city: and fire came down from God out of heaven, and devoured them (Revl.xx.9).* The immense number of men that will comprise this hostile force, and who think to carry all before them, because they do not possess any spiritual discernment, or light beyond that of the finite sight and mind, and therefore do not credit anyone with the power of helping these

God-fearing and peaceful Hebrew races of Christ's
family, may be estimated, by the time it will take the
inhabitants of this city, who will themselves be millions in number, to collect from the environs of Jerusalem and deposit in a valley, the charred remains of the
dead bodies whom the fire-visitation will have cut off
in their mad attempt to invade the City of the living
God,—a presumption in itself of terrible offence : and
we are told it will take the Israelites seven months to
cast these dead bodies into a place which will then
be called the valley of Hamon-gog (Ezek. xxxix. 12—
15.).   And a further light may be gleamed as to what
an elaborate undertaking this invasion will be, when
we consider that the *axe-handles, carbine-buts, lance
or spear, hand-staves, and other wood-attached war-
implements and weapons of destruction, will supply
with firewood the whole of the Israelite inhabitants
of the city of Palestine, for a period of SEVEN YEARS
(Ezek. xxxix. 9, 10.).

Although the ages in question will be called the
Millennium, and which means a thousand years, it
must be understood that the nations of the earth
will remain for some time beyond that period.   The
Scriptures stop giving a portrayal of future events from
the time of the end of the Millennium, except, that of
an all-men perfectly-holy period, when the Spirit of

---

*The Scripture sets forth those weapons of war which were in use in
the days of Ezekiel ; but of course, the weapons that will actually be
used upon this occasion, will be those in use at the date of the invasion.

God will fill every soul upon earth, who, by the terrible
event of the fire-visitation upon Gog and his multitudinous hoard, will now be seized with fear and trembling in conviction of their error, and will perceive His
power towards those who reject Him and His love
and mercy to whosoever will ; thus, literally fulfilling
the statement of Christ which saith, "EVERY KNEE
SHALL BOW, AND EVERY TONGUE SHALL CONFESS ;"for
"I WILL SET MY GLORY AMONG THE HEATHEN, AND
ALL THE HEATHEN SHALL SEE MY JUDGMENT THAT
I HAVE EXECUTED, AND MY HAND THAT I HAVE LAID
UPON THEM" (Ezek.xxxix.21.). And also the third
coming of Our Lord ; the final judgment of mankind ;
the great harvest of this earth's creation ; and the
"lake of fire," which the Scriptures show us is to be
this earth.

Why did the heathen rage, and the people imagine a vain thing?
And the kings of the earth, with rulers, take counsel together,
Against the Lord God, and against His anointed, saying :–
Let us cast the cords from us, and break their bands asunder.
He that sitteth in the heavens, laugh'd at them in derision :
Then He spake to them in His wrath, and in His displeasure,–
"I will declare a decree," and sit my King upon Mount Zion ;
That the heathen shall be His inheritance, and for ever.
They tried to gain spoil, but the heavens rain'd fire devouring,–
Broken as a potter's vessel ; The Spirit-wisdom seized the rest !
And in fear they serv'd the Lord with rejoicing and trembling :
They have kissed the Son ! and the whole earth is *now bless'd.
A.M.

The duration of this holy period ,however, has not
been shown me ; nevertheless, in answer to my asking
for information upon this subject, I have been shown

*At the date 4,262 A.D. [Paraphrased ii. Psalm].

the figures *8888 ; now, assuming these numbers to mean the whole period from the creation of Adam, to the date of the "lake of fire," it will add 364 years to that of the allotted period of time, which is 8,524 years (see page 240).   But it should be clearly understood that this period of 364 years, does not add to TIME :—when the whole of the events heralded by the trumpet of the "seventh angel" (Revl.x.6,7; xi.15; xvi. 17.) which carry us down to the end of the Millennium, are finished, the last half of time (that period which is known as ANNO DOMINI, or the Christian era)will have been fulfilled ; and the world virtually ended.   For when we speak of this earth's TIME, we mean the period that the world has possessed a propagating population, and who have access to Grace ; or, as the Scripture puts it, "space for repentance ; and both these time-features will have discontinued at this date, the 364 years being applied, probably, to the resurrection, and judgment purposes.

Every human creature upon earth, then, is to become a holy child of God.   By this wise provision and blessed end, the living harvest will be fit to ascend to the immortal home beyond the skies when Jesus shall utter that loving and ecstatic call,—"...COME YE BLESSED OF MY FATHER, INHERIT THE KINGDOM PREPARED FOR YOU FROM THE FOUNDATION OF THE WORLD " (Matt.xxv.34), which, as Paul puts it, is being

---

*The incident in connection with this sign, will be fully related in my biography,—The life of a modern seer.

"caught up with them (the resurrected Christians) in the clouds, to meet the Lord in the air." By this, I wish to point out that from the time just prior to the holy host unto Salvation ascending from off this earth, all propagation will have ceased : for there will be holiness on the one hand, and the out-of-Christ risen castaway on the other, the latter left on earth. Thus, there will be no children to witness the judgment.— And it has been shown me that deceased children will be raised up in a similar body to that which the child would have attained, had premature death not taken place, viz, an adult ; and Christ will have decided the question as to who were old enough at death to be held responsible for their act of rejection, or at least their non-acceptance, of Him ; those who die when children, therefore, will rise as adults.

At the end-of-time and closing of the Millennium period, that all things might be fulfilled, for a few years the worship of the whole earth will not require pressing ; for, as we have said, it being a stage when absolute consummation has laid hold of every mind by the indwelling individual new-birth Spirit (which is the means of changing their personal body's, Rom.viii.11.), every being will accept, and rejoice in, abnegation. This will make this portion of the subjects of the kingdom of God, keen for the ordained worship on every sabbath, and upon the dates of every new moon.—"FROM ONE NEW MOON TO ANOTHER, AND FROM ONE SABBATH TO ANOTHER, SHALL ALL FLESH

COME TO WORSHIP BEFORE ME, SAITH THE LORD.
AND THEY SHALL GO FORTH, AND LOOK UPON THE
CARCASES OF THE MEN THAT HAVE TRANSGRESSED
AGAINST ME : FOR THEIR WORM SHALL NOT DIE, NE-
ITHER SHALL THEIR FIRE BE QUENCHED ; AND THEY
SHALL BE AN ABHORRING UNTO ALL FLESH." (Isa.
lxvi.23,24.)—For they will see in this mass of dead
bodies, the Gog-transgressors.

By the above passage of Scripture which state
that, "their worm shall not die, neither shall their fire
be quenched," many influential men have made a mistake in supposing that this event had reference to the
final castaway, resulting from the judgment. In the
first place, the Scripture states that flesh, or men,
whilst on their road to the place of worship, will look
upon the carcases of men that have transgressed :
now, this proves two things, viz : that there were still
mortal Christians upon earth, and that these carcases
were deposited in some place, such as a deep valley ;
otherwise they could not very well be looked upon
as described. This, if it was meant for the portrayal
of hell, would paint that place in a very insignificant
colour, and would seal the judgment-day as an event
which does not end the existence of mortal beings ! I
need hardly say that both these accounts are erroneous. But let us go to the Scriptures and see what is
there said upon the subject of judgment and hell :—
The final castaway, it tells us, are to go "INTO EVER-
LASTING FIRE, PREPARED FOR THE DEVIL AND HIS

ANGELS" (Matt.xxv.); the SAVED,—both those alive
and of the resurrection—are to be "CAUGHT UP" AND
"EVER BE WITH THE LORD" (i Thess.iv.13-17): and,
"WE SHALL ALL BE CHANGED...,—MORTALS must
put on IMMORTALITY" (i Cor.xv.13—17.).   This
entirely upsets the idea of there being MORTAL Christians remaining after the judgment : and it shows that
HELL will be a far different event than that of a place
for men to "go forth and look upon!"   Moreover; *if*
the scene in question had reference to the castaway-
aspect of eternity (Isa.lxvi.23,24.), where, let me ask,
are the NEW MOONS coming from which decide the
dates of these looking-upon-the-dead visits? for bear
in mind "*the Scriptures cannot lie,*" and it is distinctly
written ;—That in the "new earth" (eternity) "there
shall be no night," consequently no moons : yea, there
cannot be any moons because there will not be any
sun-light, it being well known that the moon derives
her light from the sun ; and the Scripture states that
neither the sun nor the moon, but the glory of God
only, is needed.   But we will shortly show by the
written Word, that this earth subsequent to the judgment bar of Christ, will become one mass of fire ;
making any such scene as that which is spoken of
in Isaiah.lxvi.24., then impossible.   This evidence is
so complete, that it is only left for us to briefly lay before the reader the true aspect and interpretation of
the Scriptural passage in question :—

The carcases of the invading army of Gog, having

been collected and thrown into the valley then called
"Hamon-gog"which, as we have already shown will
take the Israelite inhabitants of Palestine a period of
seven months, will form such an immense mass of
flesh, that the food for the maggot-WORM will be
inexhaustible, and therefore, "SHALL NOT DIE." And
with regard to THEIR fire being unquenchable, common sense tells us that this great mass of dead bodies
must cause a FIRE OF CORRUPTION : and a fire of this
nature, is unquenchable.   Mark the wording of this
passage :—" Neither shall THEIR fire be quenched ;"
it is not a fire of conflagration, but rather, a fire of
putrid matter.   Job portrays the thing in an individual sense; he says:—"I have said to CORRUPTION, thou
art my father : to the WORM, thou art my mother and
my sister " (Job.xvii.14).   He, anticipating death, is
alluding to himself as a putrid-corpse, and covered
with the maggot worm.

The scene which the Gentiles go forth to look upon, has also its wise purpose :—the mass referred to,
having been the instrument which brought about the
conversion of the residue of mankind, will now act as
a devout-stimulant, not only to those who look upon
this awful scene of God's visitation, but also to the
others, who will have had their minds impressed by
the terrible story which the delegates have had to
tell ; and thus tend to keep the whole in the fear and
love of God.

It will be seen then, that these connecting links of

the chain which gives rise to the predict-passage of
Scripture, as written in Isaiah lxvi.23,24., has nothing
whatever to do with the result of the judgment of the
ungodly.   This, the last event of a thousand years
of this world's history, which will date from the year
3,262 A. D., as shown on the following page which is
the remaining part of the Scripture-Chronology on
page ninety-three, will close the Millennial ages ; and
the chosen people, including a percentage of those
who are absorbed and called Gentiles, will have peopled and possessed the allotted portion of the land as
laid down by the Mosaic law, and which is known by
the name of the promised land,—"*For the Lord will
have mercy on Jacob, and will yet choose Israel, and
set them in their own land : and the strangers shall be
joined with them, and they shall cleave to the house of
Jacob*" *(Isa.xiv.1.)*—"And the name of the city from
that day shall be, THE LORD IS THERE " (Ezek.
xlviii.35), or JEHOVAH-SHAMMAH, in the Hebrew
tongue.   And this period of the world's time, will be
productive of the greater portion of the living harvest :
whilst the few years of " HOLINESS UNTO THE LORD "
which is to be permitted beyond it —a short period
of all the earth's people "in spirit and in truth "
giving worship unto God, will be the final time of
ripening.

CHRONOLOGY CONTINUED.
(SEE PAGE 93)

Period of the world prior to the Anno Domini epoch (typical half).   4262 years

Date of the abomination setting up(Matt.xxiv.15), and EPOCH.   637 A.D.

Daniel's first predicted-period of 1290 year-days (Danl.xii.11) to be added to the epoch-date, when the overthrow of the Turkish Empire(1927A.D),or the beast's deadly wound(Revl.xiii.3),will take place.   1290 y'rs

From the date 1927 A.D. to the end of the desolation, a period of 1335 years and Daniel's second predicted-period (ch.xii.12), when Christ will come, overthrow the "beast,"and set up the Millennium.   1335 y'rs

The Millennial dispensation,—   1000 y'rs

The total Christian-era period.   4262 y'rs

After the Anno Domini epoch,   4262 years

Total length of world's TIME.   8524 years

About four years of entire holiness, the resurrection, and then 360 years of the process of judgment.   364 years

From Adam to the end, when the earth will become a lake of fire.   8888 years

It is contrary to the balance of Scriptural evidence to say that this earth is to become the eternal home of mankind. There is some evidence in its favour, I grant.: but the weightier side, by far, is that of the immortal family dwelling in a home prepared above. Let us, however, produce some proofs, by adducing a few of the many arguments that could be brought forward in support of this question ; and thus show, that our immortal home is to be, not upon this earth, but of a more glorious latitude, even that of " heavenly places :—"

In the first place, we have God's written word for the fact, that He has cursed this earth :—" Unto Adam He said : because thou hast ... eaten of the tree ... CURSED IS THE GROUND FOR THY SAKE " (Gen.iii.17). Now, is it likely that God, who is the possessor of boundless space, and has the power to create worlds at will, would make a land He had cursed the eternal home of His choicest creatures ? to do so, would be the portrayal of a limit to His power, which, when we remember that He spake this world into existence, is utterly impossible.—By one single thought, He could make this earth completely vanish, and out of the nothingness, form another world. And to believe that He is going to patch up this earth like unto painting and renovating an old house, for the eternal dwelling-place of His children, is not consistent with what our reasoning power ought to perceive in an Almighty God.

Secondly. Satan, with his angels, is the acknowledged prince of this present world—"Now shall the prince of this world be cast out" (John xii.31.), "of heavenly places:" "into the earth" (Revl,xii.9.). If the angels rejoiced at Satan and his host being cast out of heaven into this earth : surely, God will not make it man's immortal home !—It is Satan's dwelling place !

Thirdly. When Christ was upon this earth He made several statements, all of which, go to prove the fallacy of immortal men dwelling upon earth for eternity; He told Peter, for instance; in answer to his question of "Lord, whither goest thou?"—"Whither I go, thou canst not follow me now; but THOU SHALT FOLLOW ME AFTERWARDS" (John xiii.36). This expression of Christ, must have reference to some place other than this earth, because they were then both upon it, but He who said, "thou shalt follow me," has gone off the earth to another place !

Fourthly. Jesus said :" I GO TO PREPARE A PLACE for you" (John xiv.2.)—the SAVED : now there is no getting away from this passage of Scripture, because, about forty days afterwards, He who uttered these words, left the earth from Mount Olivet : He is therefore, preparing a place for mankind, elsewhere.—Moreover; when asked a question by Pilate, Jesus said :"...MY KINGDOM IS NOT OF THIS WORLD...." (John xviii.33—36.).

Fifthly. In the Revelation xxi.16., it is written :—

"And the city lieth FOURSQUARE, and the length thereof is as great as the breadth : and he measured the city with the reed, twelve thousand *furlongs : THE LENGTH and THE BREADTH and THE HEIGHT thereof ARE EQUAL." This is a portrayed profile of the City and dwelling-place of the redeemed of the earth, in their immortal state. By the length, breadth, and height, being equal, this celestial city forms the shape of a cube of 12,000 furlongs from wall to wall, and the same distance from the base to the top. Now, by the law of gravity, which exerts a drawing-power of all bodies towards the centre of the earth, a four-parallel-wall structure of this height, cannot be placed upon this earth !—It would collapse. All buildings upon this earth, needs to be erected in a vertical plane ;—four vertical walls 12,000 furlongs apart, erected upon this globe of about 8,000 miles diameter, must, necessarily, form the shape of the four-sided-top of a coffee-grinding mill.—If a wall of this height (facing south), is built in Scotland, and another wall (facing north) built in London, were looked upon with a bird's-eye view, it would be seen that they formed the shape of the letter V : for the base would measure 12,000 furlongs, whilst that of the top would measure more than 16,000 furlongs. Therefore, it will be seen, to place such a city as this Scripturally described one upon this earth, AND TO HAVE ITS WALLS PARALLEL, or, as St. John portrays it, the length, and

*A Scriptural furlong equals 243·2 yards.

the breadth, foursquare, is impossible. This shows us clearly, and without any doubt whatever, that this city, the habitation of eternity, does not allude to this present earth.—No : the city in question must either stand upon a globe wherein there is no gravitation, or it will form part of the globular construction of some world ; and the latter is the most probable.

But some may say, "what about Abraham being promised the land of Canaan ?"

I know that God promised to give Abraham and his seed for ever, the large territory of Palestine : but, as we have shown, the words, *for ever*, as used in the Scriptures, does not, necessarily, mean for eternity (*ii Kings v.27.) ; and the possession of this land by the Hebrew race, having taken place twice during the lapse of time, i.e., at the driving out of the Canaanites (Num.xxxiii.51-56), and at the Millennium, the promise will have been fulfilled. But if we spiritually read the language of Scripture, we shall see that God was alluding to some other earth, when He made the promise : this, Abraham, and all the servants of God, fully understood :—" By faith, Abraham . . . looked for a city which hath foundations, whose builder and maker is God (Heb.xi.8,10).—For here we have no continuing city, but we seek one to come (Heb.xiii.14) . . . a better country, that is, an heavenly : wherefore God is not ashamed to be called their God : for He

---

*As there will not be any leprosy after this life, this passage of Scripture proves that a limit may be placed upon the word " ever. "

hath prepared for them a city "(Heb.xi.16). Let us examine this particular-city clause :—

There are two planet-candidates for our considera-tion, Mercury and Venus ; and both of these are favour-able in a fulfilment-of-Scripture sense. I would like also to point out, and ask the reader to examine, the Scriptural figure which, by being of no mean order, will be of great importance in helping us to arrive at a true decision in this planetary question :—

In the Revelation xii. 1., a symbolical figure is por-trayed, which, if perceived in its true light, will convey to man's mind the celestial planet where, in all prob-ability, he will spend his eternity (see page 170). This symbol, which is that of a woman, and which repre-sents the whole Church of Christ in their home of bliss, is shown to occupy a position in the universe be-tween the sun and the moon—"*clothed with the sun, and the moon under her feet* ;" thus corresponding with both Mercury and Venus, which also move in its orbit round the sun, in between the sun and the moon. But as Venus answers more correctly to the predict of John, than that of Mercury,—" I JOHN SAW THE HOLY CITY, NEW JERUSALEM, COMING DOWN FROM GOD OUT OF HEAVEN, PREPARED AS A BRIDE ADORNED FOR HER HUSBAND"(Revl.xxi.2.)—inasmuch as the planet Venus travels a periodical distance also of 136 millions of miles towards this earth : we perceive in this planet a complete fulfilment of the symbol. By this planet moving in the direction described, and by its extreme brilliancy, two things which would, naturally, actuate St. John in his framing the words of the figure, we come to the conclusion, and believe, that this planet, Venus, is the "new Jerusalem which John has figuratively pointed out ; and is the blissful home of the immortal fruit of the earth, which CHRIST HAS GONE TO PREPARE. This hypothesis, for I have not received any special information upon the subject, is greatly strengthened by the many sacred writers who occasionally allude to this supremely brilliant planet, as the "son of the morning," "the day star," and "the bright and morning star," which, whilst being emblematic of the light of Christ, has, also, reference to the home He is preparing for Himself and His redeemed family. "THE LORD HATH PREPARED HIS THRONE IN THE HEAVENS..."(Psalm ciii. 19). These arguments, I think, will lead us to perceive a home of the celestial order.— Any intelligent mind, with the least spiritual perception, must come to the conclusion that, "...THE NEW EARTH, which I will make..., saith the Lord" (Isa. lxvi. 22.), means what it says, "a *new* earth,"— another one.

Caught up to the realms from among children of men,
Thou, of many mansions, wont to prepare a home for them.
A.M.

THE THIRD ADVENT, AND JUDGMENT :-

The third Advent—the begining of the last scene in the life-drama of this earth, which is the opening-day of "THE JUDGMENT SEAT OF CHRIST" (Rom. xiv. 10.)—will be heralded amid scenes of great joy: but alas! the scene will be changed to that of one of howlings and terror.—Joy on the part of the saved, and terror on the part of the castaway. Two aspects then, will be witnessed at this great event: 1st, will be that of the people rushing out of their houses in ecstasy to meet the Lord ;—If I had a brother, say, in the Navy, and I saw him coming down the street after his having been away upon a long voyage, I should be apt to run to meet him, and should wel-come him with fond greetings, why? because there is kith and kin in the heart,—love must energetically flow. The saved, in like manner, having the indwel-ling Spirit, will, in an heavenly sense, be related to Christ. The other aspect is, that of the risen ungodly in anguish and dread upon their beholding Christ ; giving them a terrible eagerness to vanish, as they rush into every vacant hole and cupboard in their endeavour to hide themselves,—they are not of the kith and kin of Christ :—The dark-minded at-large criminal, on beholding the constable of peace, soon recedes, and endeavours to be lost to view.

The third Advent, we say, will be heralded in glo-rious sounds, and brightness, giving the ready-to-be-changed redeemed-saints a thrill of transporting joy,

as they gaze upon the glorious scene of the descent of
"THE GREAT WHITE THRONE" in countless numbers
of the holy host of heaven which were made by the
breath of the Spirit-God (Psalm xxxiii.6.), together
with the governmental body of 144,000 structural
saints who will have been dwelling with Christ in the
blissful realms for the past 1,000 years, bearing Christ
to the earth for the purpose of the making up of His
"jewels."—A triumphant-glory far surpassing the conception of a finite mind.

What rapturous joy bursts forth of the soul,
As he views Christ, and His Cabinet of control.
A.M.

"THE LORD HIMSELF SHALL DESCEND FROM
HEAVEN WITH A SHOUT, WITH THE VOICE OF THE
ARCHANGEL, AND WITH THE TRUMP OF GOD"(i Thess.
iv.16), in fulfilment of that passage of Scripture which
saith, "The Son of man shall come in his glory, and
all the holy angels with him, then shall He sit upon
the throne of his glory"(Matt.xxv.31.)—"THE GREAT
WHITE THRONE," which, by its brilliant purity, and
magnitude, will abase every other thing which appears
in its presence (Revl.xx.11.).

The "books" which are spoken of (Revl.xx.12,15),
and which will consist of one containing, probably,
the righteous deeds, and another containing both the
thoughts and deeds of the unsaved (Revl.xx.12), of the
whole earth's creation throughout the lapse of time,

will be produced in evidence ; there is also a third,
" the book of life :"—the book wherein are written the
names of all the Saved human-beings for the whole
period of 8,524 years.   This book, of course, will
include the names of those who are living at the time.

"THE DEAD IN CHRIST SHALL RISE FIRST"(iThes
iv.16.) !   " But some one will say, How are the dead
raised ? and with what manner of body do they
come ? "   Do we not understand the word seed to
mean, that which will reproduce ?   Well then, animate
things are reproduced by their seed !—If I pick a seed
trom off a withered, or even dead plant, and place it
in the ground, in due season this seed will reproduce
a similar plant.   The same thing will apply (but subject to the will of God) to all deceased men, *their seed*
being within, with this difference :—In cases of the
reproduction of deceased mankind, the seed is of a
natural-spirit character,—being nature's-essence-spirit
called the Mind, or faculty of man.   But this seed of
man, will not reproduce a Glorified-body in the likeness
ot Christ : to do this—to be raised up in His likeness
(iJohn iii.2) and become an eternal subject of the kingdom ot heaven, it is necessary to possess the Spirit-
seed which emanate from God as a gift of grace to believers.   If thus " born of the Spirit " (John iii.5), this
seed is retained for ever ;"WHOSOEVER IS BORN OF God
...HIS SEED REMAINETH IN HIM..."(John xiv.16; iJohn
iii.9); and this seed will so co-operate with the natural
spirit-seed, as to produce persons distinctly-different

to the castaway, at the time of the dead being raised
by Christ (John vi.44.) as portrayed in Lazarus. For,
"if the Spirit of Him that raised up Jesus from the
dead dwell in you, He that raised up Christ Jesus
from the dead, shall also quicken (raise up) your mortal
BODIES, BY HIS SPIRIT THAT DWELLETH IN YOU"
(Rom.viii.11).   It will be seen that the castaway, or
rejecter of Jesus, do not possess this new-birth Spirit-
seed : hence the figure of the "sheep" and the "goats."

Well then, the dead at this time having been
raised, and the whole of the living-mortals having
undergone a change "in the twinkling of an eye"
as Paul puts it, their only remains the rewards of
position &c to be dealt with ; when this joyful proceeding among the worthy has been accomplished,
then, the whole of this glorified family will be "caught
up in the air."   Of course, it will be Our Lord who
will issue the rewards :—" BEHOLD I COME QUICKLY ;
AND MY REWARD IS WITH ME, TO GIVE TO EVERY MAN
ACCORDING AS HIS WORK SHALL BE" (Revl.xxii.12).
It should be understood, however, that everyone will
not receive a literal crown, i.e., a kingship : for if such
was the case, there would be no subjects to form the
kingdom with,—all would be kings !   What St. Paul
says upon the subject, is this : " Henceforth there is
laid up for me a crown of righteousness..."(Tim.iv.8) :
this sort of crown All may receive, as well as degrees
of position in the government circle of the heavenly
realms.

It will now be the moment for Christ to say to His children the sweetest words He could possibly express to a redeemed family of the loving God :— "...COME, YE BLESSED OF MY FATHER, INHERIT THE KINGDOM PREPARED FOR YOU..."(Matt.xxv.34). And they shall "ever be with The Lord." Thus, will the allegorical "dividing of the sheep from the goats " be fulfilled.

There are many passages of Scripture which speak of the coming judgment-day, and, to a casual-reader, may seem conflicting : but upon a little reasoning, and closer study of the word of God, it will be seen that all is planned out to a burning-up end (Malachi iv.i.). The passage of Scripture in which it says : " ON SUCH THE SECOND DEATH HATH NO POWER"(Revl.xx.6.), is, deciuedly, a proof that before unsaved mankind can reach eternity, they must undergo TWO DEATHS : first the natural death, which, as we must all die—fall into death's sleep, requires no explanation : and second, the destroying death of resurrected creatures, in a lake-ot-fire ; as it is written," DEATH AND HADES WERE CAST INTO THE LAKE OF FIRE. THIS IS THE SECOND DEATH " (Revl.xx.14). So that, to use plain language, God tells us their shall be two deaths attached to every individual human creature, but that, under certain conditions, male or iemale may escape the second one. But in wisdom, the *details* of the judgment has been kept back from man, and therefore no detailed account of it is to be iound upon Scripture-record.

The prophets of olden times, and the apostles of
Jesus Christ, received information of the Spirit ; and
they had the previously written Scripture, together
with the teachings of Christ : but these things did not
produce a detailed record of the events of the very
last days.   What these holy men have given us, has
been the result of God's doctrinal showers; no wonder
then, that the statements recorded in the Scriptures
are various ! yet, whilst one sums up the judgment
event in a few words, and another dwells longer upon
the subject, the whole, supplies us with a complete
evidence, and enables us to arrive at a satisfactory,
and truthful account.

St. Paul states : " We must all appear before the
judgment seat of Christ :" and he also portrays the
joyful-side of the resurrection ; but the key-note to the
whole of the judgment-side event, is to be found in the
Gospel of Matthew xix. 28. : for it there portrays the
opening process of the whole business as an immense
assizes of a twelve-fold character, the Apostles being
the twelve judges upon thrones, and each one giving
justic in an individual trial of a tribe of Israel.—Men
will have to give an account of their deeds done in the
body, or the things which are found written of them
in the second book.   This will insure a fair and impartial trial, for God is just ; and they will see that, by
their rejection of Christ, who could have blotted out
their deeds and given them the Spirit-seed, it is now
absolutely impossible for them to become heavenly

subjects, because, as we have said, their bodies were indivldually-void of the component of the soul, or seed of the glorified body ; and thus, their resurrected bodies are of different material to those of the Saved. In this matter then, there will be no opening for any dispute as to the right of inheritance ; for each individual will now see that they have missed their passport of the heavenly realms, through their rejection, or at least the non-acceptance which is the same thing, of Him who had the prerogative to give to whosoever will the eternal-*Spirit life which maketh "sons." But even should there be disputants among them, the Lord will have witnesses there in readiness to give evidence : thus St. Paul (and many others)will testify as to his administration of the Gospel to the Jews at Jerusalem and Rome, and of their rejection of it (Acts xxiii. 11; i Cor. vi. 2).

The ungodly, now at this time left upon earth with the rejecters doom, will, probably, remain for some years : for the judgment of the whole, can hardly be expected to be gone through in a short time :—to carry on an individual examination of almost countless numbers, which the Chinese as idolaters (Revl. xxi. 8.) alone will supply, will, in all reasonable calculation occupy a long period of time : and especially so, when we consider that God's ways are perfectly just, and

---

*Children of whom it is seen will die prematurely, are sure to receive the new-birth-spirit, without seeking Christ: for God holds no human creature responsible beyond their capability.

that He has never shown signs of being in a hurry:
it is not hard therefore, to perceive the immensity of
this event, and the time it is likely to occupy. So
that, the judgment will be an event of greater magnitude than what men are willing to give credit for:
and the period between the end of time—4,262 A.D.,
and that of the final end, we may conclude, will be
fully taken up in this manner. These assizes of the
castaway, in all probability, will move from country
to country, as they keep completing, until the whole
world has been judged; when this has been done,
and the whole event has been completed in fulfilment
of the Scriptures, then, there will remain but one
more act of justice in the way of a firm expression
of Christ, but in words as deeply awful, as that of
the command to the glorified sons was blissful; for
His words to those of the earth will now be:—
"DEPART FROM ME YE CURSED, INTO
EVERLASTING FIRE..."(Matt.xxv.41).—"There
shall be weeping" and "wailing and gnashing of teeth"
(Matt.viii.12; xiii.42.): "...And His enemies shall lick
the dust" (Psalm.lxxii.9.).

It is necessary to notice, that when Christ utters
the final and fatal words to the castaway, He does not
tell them to go to any particular place:—He does not
even hint at there being any other place for them to go
to besides this earth: and yet, mark you, He finishes
his sentence with the words, "INTO EVERLASTING
FIRE!" they are thus sent into everlasting fire, but not

off this earth. This indicates, plainly, that the FIRE is to be of this earth, and whilst they are yet upon it : making it clear to our perception, that this earth is to become the "everlasting fire." This shows us at a glance, and without the other evidence which I am about to produce, where the Scripturally-ordained "lake-of-fire" will really be ; but we will proceed with the proof :—

In order to draw the atheist to a sense of conviction, I will, in the first instance, adduce some evidence of a scientific character, and which is outside of the Scriptures ; this evidence, however, will be closely followed with the indisputable proofs which God has provided in His Word.

THE LAKE OF FIRE :-

If we were to take, say, one hundred men, and place them at an equal distance from each other in a line from the summit to the base of a high mountain , and each man, having a thermometer of special sensitiveness in his possession, was to mark at a given moment the registered temperature , it would be found that the heat increased at every stage downwards; or, the nearer the base, the greater the heat. Also, upon the same principle, if men were stationed from the top to the bottom of a deep mining-shaft, it would be found that the heat increased, the lower they were situated. So that, the lower one goes towards the centre of the earth, the greater will the heat be found. On this principle, the most learned men of science have come to the conclusion that, were it possible for man to descend into the bowels of the earth, he would find that it became so increasingly hot the farther he went down, as to melt, at a certain distance, everything into a fluid;—that all matter of whatever material, must be in a molten liquid state through the intensity of heat which exists a few miles below the surface of the earth. The exact distance down at which the fusing point commences, is, to a certain extent, a matter of conjecture: and various statements have been made with regard to the question : but the conclusion which has been arrived at, and which fairly meets with all calculating minds, is, that the distance towards the centre of the earth at which fusion takes place, is from ten to twenty miles from the surface. This decision, so far as I am aware of, is not disputed by those competent men, who, were there grounds for doubting the truth of the above statement, I feel sure, would have done so.

In order to be within the limit of every event or contingent, we will take the fusing point of every class of material which the earth may contain, to be at the greater distance of the two, viz, that of TWENTY MILES FROM THE SURFACE.

Now, the circumference of the earth being 24,860 miles, if the crust of twenty miles thick was extracted from the surface, it would leave an exposed interior of a huge globulous mass of molten liquid—like unto a sea of fluid material boiling with intensity of heat, which, in circumference, would measure more than 24,000 miles. It would be like peeling the rind from an orange, and then finding that the orange was of boiling liquid. This, then, is the present state of the interior of the earth, arrived at by science. And this furnace, or molten-sphere lake, is analogous, by its answering to the Scripturally portrayed "lake-of-fire."

But now let us go to the Scriptures, and learn from that wonderful book, the hitherto-neglected precepts which prove, without a doubt, that this earth, under certain surface-conditions, will become an immense burning lake, from the time of the final end.

In the first place, the Scriptures tell us that, THIS EARTH IS STORED UP WITH FIRE: Peter says, in his ii Epistle.iii.7 :—

(Authorized Version-1611) "But the heavens and the EARTH, WHICH ARE NOW, by the same word are kept in store, reserved UNTO FIRE againat the DAY OF JUDGMENT AND PERDITION OF UNGODLY MEN."

(Revised Version-1885) "But the heavens that now are, AND THE EARTH, by the same word have been STORED UP FOR (or with) FIRE, being reserved against the DAY OF JUDGMENT AND DESTRUC-TION OF UNGODLY MEN."

If the reader will look at the margin of the Revised Version of the Scriptures, they will see the words :— or, "*stored with fire.*" So that either, "*stored up for fire,*" or, "*stored with fire,*" are correct: therefore, if we bring in this marginal word "*with,*" the resultant truth will read thus :— THE EARTH HAS BEEN

STORED UP WITH FIRE, being reserved against the day of judgment AND DESTRUCTION OF UNGODLY MEN. This, it will be seen, coincides with the decision arrived at by the men of science; and is a verification of the interior of this earth being at the present time and for ever, the ordained "lake-of-fire," but now held in check, by a twenty-mile crust of solid matter.

But this does not conclude our evidence!

If we turn to Isaiah xxxiv. 1, 9, 10,—the intermediate verses, 2—8, with the remainder of the chapter, being of a symbolic character—we shall read as follows :— "COME NEAR, YE NATIONS, TO HEAR ; AND HEARKEN, YE PEOPLE : LET THE EARTH HERE, AND ALL THAT IS THEREIN; THE WORLD, AND ALL THINGS THAT COME FORTH OF IT "(verse I). This first verse, un-doubtedly, is speaking of a matter concerning the whole world. And the 9th verse, in following up these words, goes on to say; "AND THE STREAMS THEREOF SHALL BE TURNED INTO PITCH, AND THE DUST THEREOF INTO BRIMSTONE, AND THE LAND THEREOF SHALL BECOME BURNING PITCH." Now water, and dust, being the materials which compose the earth's surface, or crust, "the streams" and "the dust," cannot mean anything else than the surface of the earth : therefore, it is impossible to misunderstand this revealed truth, and to see that it refers to the previously explained twenty-mile-thick crust of the earth, which, now sheltering the human race from its molten-lake interior, will, at the time appointed, change into pitch and brimstone. Now, pitch being a material of a very inflammable nature, whilst brimstone is that which accelerates heat, can it not be seen that, by the water and the land of even a portion of the earth's crust becoming changed into these two inflammable materials, the intense heat of the present interior will immediately ignite them, and the earth burst forth into unquenchable flames?—And this, as the 10th verse goes on to say, "SHALL NOT BE QUENCHED NIGHT NOR DAY ; THE SMOKE THEREOF SHALL GO UP FOR EVER..." [It should be understood, that the old Idumea, being the great centre of mohammedism, that verses 5—7 (Isa.xxxiv), having reference to these people, is speaking of a great slaughter with the SWORD : whereas, the event which is spoken of in verses 9,10, is a matter of fire and brimstone at the last days : showing two separate events. In both cases, however, the hammer is striking the nail of mohammedism, as an ungodly community]. Here we have then, the "lake of fire" as it will take place at the ordained date ; but at present, as the Scriptures and science have shown, is stored within the surface-crust, ready for the changing process at a subsequent date to that of the handing over to the invisible jailer the out-of-Christ castaway to undergo the inevitable sentence ; and when, the sea having given up its dead, and the dead which were in *hades also delivered up ,

---

*In Greek language, the grave ; see Revl.xx.14., Revised Version 1885.

and they having been judged every man according to his works (Revl. xxi. 8), were cast into the lake of fire.   (See Revl. xx. 13, 14; Psalm ix. 17.).

Moreover, the Scriptures further state by Peter, that, "... THE EARTH AND THE WORKS THAT ARE THEREIN SHALL BE BURNED UP" (ii Peter iii. 10.).

[The words, "cast into," do not signify that it is essential to use manual labour to carry out its fulfilment; for it is easy to see that, by the earth bursting forth into flames, these castawsys must be, inevitably, swallowed up].

Can greater evidence than this, in regard to the locality of hell, be desired ?—Has there not been sufficient proof put forth to convince the most sceptical ? Very few of the Scriptural matters are so strongly verified as this one of hell's locality !—Why the evidence is overwhelming !—It is as plain as language, and test, can make it.   There are many more points of evidence if needed, however, both in and out of the Scriptures : the 41st verse of Matthew xxv, which states that the everlasting fire is "prepared for the devil and his angels," for instance : for, if a GREAT PLACE OF FIRE IS PREPARED FOR THE DEVIL, who, the Scriptures tell us, has been cast down to this earth, does it not follow, THAT THIS PREPARED FIRE MUST ALSO BE OF THIS EARTH ?   "The great dragon, was cast out, that old serpent, called the devil, and Satan, which deceiveth the whole world : HE WAS

CAST OUT INTO THE EARTH..." (Revl.xii.9.).

Revelation xx.10., indicate the same thing : for we cannot do anything else than apprehend that the compiler of the Bible has caused the various discourses therein to be written in wisdom, both unto our common understanding, and in figure. And the incident of casting Satan into the lake of fire being in connection with the Gog-invasion, makes it clear to our understanding that the whole thing is an event of this earth. If then, God says, *"The devil that deceived them was cast into the lake of fire and brimstone,"* which is pure literal language, He means it to be understood as being indicative of a place in our midst ; it follows, therefore, that it is of the interior of this earth that He is speaking : but there can be no doubt as to its alluding to the same place as that which is portrayed in our last argument (Matt.xxv.), because, here is portrayed the actual carrying out of the casting of Satan into the very place—"THE EVERLASTING FIRE" —which Matthew tells us, has been prepared for him !

In conclusion, the final top-stone of the set-forth truth of a molton lake, or stored up hell-fire within the earth, may be actually seen in the form of a natural chimney at any time, both at Mount Etna, and at Mount Vesuvius.—The latter of these two boiling-lake chimneys, on the 24th of August 79 A.D., so asserted itself as being the outlet of pent-hell, as to throw hot ashes, or lava, over the surrounding country of more than a hundred miles distant; and upon this occasion, many towns, including *Herculaneum and *Pompeia, were completely buried.

Thus, we have adduced, Scripturally, Scientifically, and practically, overwhelming evidence in support of the truth of our earth being at the present time, internally, a molten-liquid lake; and which, at the time appointed, the external part turning into combustible matter, will become the ordained "LAKE OF FIRE."— Evidence, which is more than sufficient to convince the most sceptical.

The changing into pitch and brimstone process, will, probably, take place in stages; patch by patch, here and there throughout the world, and eventually, becoming joined, until the whole earth is in one mass of flames. This, as the earth of inhabited localities become the consuming foe, will cause these doomed castaway-inhabitants to flee from one spot to another thinking to procure a place of safety, but, to their grief, only to find that this portion of the land has but mocked them, and it, in a very short time also turns into combustibility, sending forth its flames with all the intensity of a horrifying scene. The doomed will thus be driven from place to place until, in the course of time, the last free-from-fire portion of the earth is reached ;—Something after the same manner as that which took place during the destruction of the ante-

---

*These towns were buried in lava, and thus lost to the world until A.D.1713., when Herculaneum was discovered about 24 feet below the surface ; and Pompeia, 40 years after, 12 feet underground.

diluvian world : when men, having refused to listen to Noah, were visited with the flood, and from which they climbed up higher, and higher, as the deadly ocean crept after them , until, reaching the highest point of land, and their last hope, the element of death arose, and rose till it reached the vital point, when all unsaved flesh were compelled to succumb to the just penalty of death. But the suspense, in the case of the "lake of fire," will be far more terrible than that of climbing up from the death-grip of the waters! for, as soon as the death-sentence, "Depart from · me ye cursed into everlasting fire," has been spoken by Christ, which will seal all remaining matters unto a fiery end, the doomed will have before their mind's eye the horrifying picture of immence flames sending forth its fangs. And those who are the earlier judged, will have to undergo a longer suspense than the latter-judged ones : but all of them tremblingly watching for any sign which may appear to indicate that the combustible change is taking place ;—the least portion of smoke, under whatever circumstances, or anything burning upon the ground, will have the effect of sending a thrill of horror through their individual frame, and a cry from the lips of a tortured mind ; for of such will be the symptoms of the opening of hell, and their final doom. (See Matt.xiii.40—42; ii Peter.iii.7.).

What a contrast !—Behold "THE BLESSED OF MY FATHER,"who, long ere this, have reached the place of bliss :—Hark ! those streams of melody are flowing from the joyful in the realms of heaven : it is the ring of the "new song," from the voices of the redeemed-of-the-earth structural family in stupendous glory, (they are enveloped like as we are enveloped in the air we breathe, as a breath unto food in the pure Ethereal Omnipotent Spirit of God, Who occupy the whole expanse of the universe) amid the splendour of the holy host, with CHRIST UPON THE THRONE.

Say not in thine heart, God is cruel in the end ;
'Tis not He who casts men to this fiery fiend !
But man himself, who rejects The Fire-Escape
Whereby God calls all men to flee, ere 'tis too late :
If Christ, "The Escape," is a passport to The Home,
Can men blame God, their staying to the fire-doom ?
Virtually, they choose thus on earth to remain,
Tho' residue-works 'twill burn, as He didst ordain ;
In refusing The Life then, surely, this doom men deserve !
Therefore brother, "Choose you this day whom Ye will serve."
There's room in abundance for the SONS of The King,
But not those who remain in the fatherhood of sin,-
Rejectors of mercy altho' scores of times ask'd,
Missing the "birth," alas ! void, till the harvest had past.
A.M.

"DESPISE NOT PROPHESYINGS."
[i THESS.V.20]

THE END.

BENEDICTION.

THIS WORK I COMMEND WITH EARNESTNESS,
TO THE FAITHFUL CARE OF THE SPIRIT, TO BLESS.

www.ingramcontent.com/pod-product-compliance
Lightning Source LLC
Chambersburg PA
CBHW030627030726
47497CB00006B/1667